DANGEROUS MEN

Some of the men were hulking, with the brute power of heavy bones and thick sinews. Others had the lean hard look, all spare flesh hacked away, that comes with relentless endurance combined with great strength. Each in his own way had an animal energy, the feral alertness of body and reflexes tuned to ultimate pitch.

One of them, passing a padded dummy, whirled and unleashed a kick to the balls that buckled the canvas man and sounded like a rifle shot in the cavernous gym.

"You missed," said another in a high falsetto.

A few laughed, but there was something frightening about the sudden violence. Behind it there was a personal savagery of which anyone in this group appeared capable.

These were the men selected to hijack the *Ludendorff*.

THE LUDENDORFF PIRATES

Al Ramrus and John Shaner

A DELL BOOK

Published by
DELL PUBLISHING CO., INC.
1 Dag Hammarskjold Plaza
New York, N.Y. 10017

Dell ® TM 681510, Dell Publishing Co., Inc.

ISBN: 0-440-15260-7

Reprinted by arrangement with
Doubleday & Company Inc.
Printed in the United States of America
First Dell printing—May 1979

To *Alleen* and *Madeleine*

CHAPTER 1

The ax-like bow of the British destroyer *Connaught* smashed through the Atlantic, its collision alarm howling like an angry animal.

Two hundred yards to starboard, the German U-boat *117*, bridge hatch pouring smoke, diving mechanism damaged, tried to escape on the surface, its diesel engines straining to dodge and twist at nearly twenty knots, its commander desperately seeking refuge in a nearby fogbank.

The bowels of the destroyer shuddered as an engine reversed, clawing the warship around to intercept the U-boat's tighter turning circle.

The injured U-boat churned for the shifting gray fog as the destroyer leaped forward again, charging through the sub's foaming wake, cutting the distance to a hundred yards, seventy yards, forty yards . . .

The U-boat sliced into the fog bank, but the destroyer's bow rammed it at an angle with the stopping power of two thousand tons, tearing away the stern. The impact drove *U-117* down and the destroyer's momentum carried it directly over the sub.

The sub's shattered body was keelhauled along the full length of the destroyer's bottom with the sickening, water-muffled shriek of metal on metal, its panicked crew slammed against the smashed bulkheads, the sea thundering in on them as the pressure hull and ballast tanks cracked open with a roar. Then *U-117* ground free of the destroyer's keel and nose down sank toward the bottom, gasping out its air supply in trails of rising, spinning bubbles. Schools of cod and flounder darted out of its descending path, terrified by the death throes of the steel monster.

The *Connaught* waited, poised, motionless on the sea. In duffle coats, oilskins and flak helmets, officers and crew at battle stations trained eyes on the choppy water. With dusk falling, the blue-white beams of the destroyer's great searchlights lanced into the sea, trained on the rollers stained with oil from the sunken sub.

Suddenly, a vague, shimmering mass rose from the deep and burst to the surface. It was a corpse, and for a second its momentum thrust head and chest out of the water as though the whole body were going to rise from the sea and attack its executioner, but then it sank back and floated limply, the face blackened with oil and slime. As if in a grotesque water ballet another body rose, its head turned away from the ship till a wave slowly spun it around and sightless eyes stared up accusingly at the British on the destroyer. It was joined by a third body, a fourth. Small clusters of corpses appeared now, formed by wave and current into a grim geometry of death.

The destroyer's davits creaked, lowering three long-boats, each with four men, one armed with an Enfield rifle. They rowed to the field of corpses, and working efficiently hauled the bodies in with grappling hooks. Sometimes the hooks caught a jacket or a belt, sometimes speared a bare arm or an exposed neck. It didn't matter. The dead were indifferent.

Suddenly, just as the sailor hooked it, a shadow below the surface took shape and darted at one of the bodies. The body convulsed crazily as the shark attacked, coming in straight, then making a quarter twist clockwise to tear the body from the hook. The sailor held on, the hook alive in his hands. The Enfield cracked as the rifleman emptied his clip into the sea. The blood of the shark mingled in the water with the blood of the man before the shark thrashed away, releasing the body to the human predators.

Twenty dripping corpses lay on the upper deck in neat rows of five as the *Connaught*, beneath a swollen moon, raced back at flank speed to Portsmouth. Hunched against the cold, machine gunners watched uneasily from ack-ack mounts as under the moonlight, two lieutenants bundled in duffle coats moved along the rows, scavenging the bodies for personal possessions. These were placed in little burlap sacks, which were tied, tagged and then put in a steel strongbox. A rotund petty officer followed the lieutenants, inspecting the items first and making precise notations in a ledger.

"Soldbuch and *erkennungsmarke,"* he said nasally, studying a paybook and set of ID tags. He tried to peel open the pages of the paybook, which had been soaked together. A couple of pages shredded and the petty officer as well as the lieutenants shot an uneasy glance up at the wing of the bridge from which an officer had been intently watching them.

Except for the slash of moonlight that fell across his mouth and jaw, the officer's face was concealed in the shadow formed by the visor of his cap and the high collar of his sheepskin coat. They had no idea who he was, except that he was not ship's company, did not eat with the other officers and pulled no duty. Highly irregular in submarine patrol, where almost every man was on constant alert.

Under the unknown officer's scrutiny, the rattled petty officer peeled open the first two pages of the paybook and copied out the name: Zimmelbacher, Erich, First Engineer.

The three men moved to the next body, mutilated with shark gouges the size of large hunks of steak on shoulder and stomach, the right leg severed at the knee. White bone gleamed in the moonlight.

"Von Brennerman, Viktor. Kapitänleutnant. *Soldbuch, erkennungsmarke*, Knight's Cross Second Class. One letter, postmarked Berlin." The petty officer handed it to the lieutenant who, uncomfortably aware that his every move was being observed by the unknown officer on the bridge, carefully opened the soaked envelope.

"*Mein Lieber Sohn, Ich bin heute* . . ." he read with difficulty. The rest was indecipherable, streaks of running ink which he quickly shook off his hand as if it were the German's blood.

The younger lieutenant shuddered. "I hate to ask this late in the game, but any idea what this is all about?"

"Admiralty's orders," the older lieutenant shrugged, flicking a glance at the bridge where the officer never moved, where the cap and sheepskin collar still con-

10

cealed the face except for the slash of moonlight that now revealed only the eyes.

"What the hell could he be up to, robbing graves?"—

"God knows," the other shrugged.

"I don't think He'd want to," the young lieutenant muttered.

CHAPTER 2

The steel strongbox holding the identification papers and possessions of the crew of *U-117* rested in the back seat of an Austin naval staff car as it swung down the Mall past St. James's Park in London. Beside it, one strong hand gripping it protectively, sat the officer who'd stood in the shadows of the destroyer's bridge.

In the pale morning light, dressed in the smartly tailored uniform of a lieutenant commander, he no longer looked especially mysterious, but there was still something distinctive about him. In his mid-thirties, with the chiseled good looks that come in aristocratic families that consent to breed only with the finest genes of other aristocratic families, Vyvvyan Beatty had the unmistakable bearing of one of those Englishmen who've attended the best schools, paid dues at the most exclusive clubs and traveled in the most distinguished circles. But there was also a coiled electric quality about him that suggested restlessness, a potential for action.

Beatty wound down his window to let in the clean summer air sweeping through London after a week of rain. The air and sun were new, but the barrage balloons floating gross and bloated at the end of their cables, scarring the sky, the buildings with their sides ripped away by bombs, revealing crazily twisted plumbing, fire-blistered paint and, sometimes, furniture untouched and still in its place as if on a stage, waiting for the actors to appear . . . all these seemed very old by now. Hard to believe, in early June of 1941, that the war started only two years ago, that Hitler had overrun most of Europe, that England found herself fighting alone.

Beatty stretched his long legs in the cramped Austin, but instinctively maintained body contact with the strongbox whenever it shifted. He was not a man given to melodramatic flights of imagination, but he knew how important the contents of that box could be in terms of lives lost or saved, battles lost or won. Also, how important to himself. But he buried this personal thought because it should have no bearing on his duties, and he wanted to be ruthlessly objective about that. His judgment as an officer could not, must not, be swayed by any personal motivation.

Vyvvyan Beatty was born to a family that traced its lineage back to King Henry II, and in England, a country of distinct stratas of wealth . . . in trade, in the professions, in merchant banking . . . the Beattys were land-rich; the richest of all, with holdings in London and vast estates in Buckinghamshire and Kent. Because Eton was so famous, and considered rather vulgar, young Beatty was sent to exclusive Winchester and then to Cambridge where he received somewhat better than gentleman's grades, which astonished his father, and numerous large cups as a tireless sculler and slashing polo player, which also astonished his father. From childhood on, his education was supplemented every summer and during vacations by trips to the Continent, where Sir Reginald Beatty was British ambassador to Berlin. Sir Reginald insisted that the entire family become fluent in German, and though Beatty resisted, he was eventually grateful because the German which his father hoped would enable the boy to glory in the cadences of Heine ultimately enabled him to seduce and glory in the flesh of Bavarian servant girls.

Upon graduation from Cambridge, Beatty settled into the role for which he'd been groomed . . . the right clothes from Savile Row, the right hunting guns from Holland & Holland, fishing tackle from Hardy's, a membership in White's, dinners at the Berkeley. But if he was rich, he wasn't idle. He began to take over, very capably, the management of the family's estates and had two or three serious love affairs. One, with Lady Evelyn Owen-Childs, led to marriage, and several years later to a discreet divorce. All in all, a typical, well-ordered life for a member of his class.

When the war started, Beatty volunteered for active duty, but because of his background was assigned, under tightest security, to Special Operations Executive (S.O.E.), which planned subversion and sabotage on the Continent, in Churchill's grandiose directive when it was formed, "to set Europe ablaze."

From the safety of their desks, which somehow emboldened their already overheated imaginations, Beatty and his associates tried to outdo one another in planning hazardous raids, though in the privacy of his own mind, each man secretly congratulated himself on pulling good duty in a dangerous war.

The strongbox shifted again on the seat and Beatty looked up as the staff car swung right at Nelson's Col-

14

umn and turned into Whitehall Street, a corridor of government buildings that, in the midst of war, seemed reassuringly massive and permanent.

Precisely six minutes later, in Room 38, whose high ceiling looked as if it hadn't been painted since the Crimean War, Beatty placed an Iron Cross, a German ID tag and a paybook from the strongbox on the tooled-leather desk of the Director of Naval Intelligence.

Admiral Thomas Redmond, G.C.B., K.C.V.O., D.S.O., stared at them for a moment, then looked up at Beatty through thick white eyebrows that always bristled like barbed wire.

"These, sir," Beatty began, "are from . . ."

"I already know where they're from," Redmond cut in, his tone implying that as Director of Intelligence he was at least one step ahead of everyone in the naval department.

"Of course, sir," Beatty agreed. "As for their purpose . . . I said in my request for this meeting, I've come up with an idea that is slightly unorthodox."

Redmond consulted a memorandum. "You said it was highly unorthodox."

"Yes, sir," Beatty agreed again.

He had prepared a detailed explanation as clear and logical as a mathematical equation, leading to the essence of his plan. But he could see that the admiral, who was known to suffer from a painful case of hemorrhoids that made sitting for long periods an agony, had shifted the soft pillow under his seat and was in no mood for prologues. Better to hit him with it straightaway. Beatty made sure that his hands remained perfectly still and his voice level.

"The plan is to hijack a German battleship," he said.

"Hijack a battleship?" Redmond snapped, as if he

15

hadn't heard it right the first time and thought Beatty had proposed an evening of child molestation.

"Yes, sir," Beatty replied calmly. He knew that Redmond, a tough old sea dog, prided himself on being open to innovation, even though he really wasn't. Somewhere between Redmond's view of himself and the reality, Beatty would have to slip in by being as cool and matter-of-fact as possible.

"Which battleship, may I ask?" Redmond asked dryly.

"The *Ludendorff*," Beatty replied.

Redmond tossed a *soldbuch* back onto the desk with a snort. "Now look, Beatty. Your section has come up with some very valuable ideas. But this . . ." Shaking his head, he turned to another officer seated off to the side. "Crawford?"

Captain Ian Crawford gazed out of the window which looked out on 10 Downing Street as if weighing the idea very carefully. His sharp, hooked nose and dark complexion made him resemble a furious eagle, very untypical of the British officer class. Crawford was approximately Beatty's age, but with the weather-lined skin and squint-etched eyes of a front-line naval officer. His chest blazed with ribbons, in marked contrast to Beatty, who had none. Crawford was aware of Beatty's planning work at S.O.E., like the reconnaissance of enemy defenses between Cap d'Alprech and the Pointe de Hautbanc, a moderately successful operation, if one overlooked that when the men straggled back to England in their small, unidentified craft, they looked so disreputable and suspicious that the military police arrested them as deserters. Perhaps there was a place in war for such escapades. He knew that Churchill had a weakness for the flamboyant, but Crawford regarded them as sideshows, on a par with freaks and midgets, and too trivial to be worthy of his consideration.

After a moment, Crawford turned from the window.

"We know you like to think big, Commander, and I respect you for it," he said, even though he really didn't. "But this isn't blowing up some shacks in Norway. The *Ludendorff*'s the largest ship in the German Navy. When fully loaded, forty-eight thousand tons displacement."

"Fifty," Beatty said.

Crawford tried to hide his irritation. He'd been trained in terms of squadrons, fleets, vast naval actions. He'd been taught to respect the awesome power of capital ships. And while God knows he had no personal affection for a German battleship, he resented the idea that some deskbound officer like Beatty had the sheer brass to think you could just go out and hijack one.

"It's easy for Commander Beatty to come up with these wild schemes," he said, "as long as other men float home on the wreckage. . . . If they're lucky."

Beatty forced himself to ignore the lash in Crawford's words.

"If I may, Admiral," he said, moving to a wall map of Europe and pointing to the Baltic Sea. "For weeks we've known that the *Ludendorff* is having its boilers retubed here, at the Deutschewerke in Königsberg."

Crawford shifted impatiently, but Admiral Redmond gestured for him to sit still, allowing Beatty to continue.

"In four days the *Ludendorff* will give those boilers a test run," Beatty went on. "Now then. Suppose fifteen men were set down in the Baltic, in a raft, looking like shipwrecked German sailors. With these authentic papers and all. And they're rescued here, say at 55 lati-

17

tude, 19 longitude, by the *Ludendorff*. Why couldn't they take it over?"

"Against two thousand men?" Crawford grimaced.

"There won't be two thousand," Beatty replied. "The *Ludendorff*'s rejoining Naval Group East at Kiel to pick up its full complement. It's sailing with a trial crew."

"They wouldn't dare," Crawford growled.

"With all due respect, sir, they already have." He handed them copies of two reports from the Secret Intelligence Service (S.I.S.), the intelligence arm of S.O.E.

"In the first half of January 1940, and in February of this year, the battle cruisers *Scharnhorst* and *Gneisenau* were tested in the Baltic. They were out there. We didn't stop them. The arrogant bastards have turned the Baltic into a German lake and now the *Ludendorff* will have barely three hundred and fifty unsuspecting men testing those boilers. If we can catch them with their shoelaces untied, and I'm sure we can with a rather neat plan we've been working on, we can take the *Ludendorff!*"

In the astonished silence that followed, Admiral Redmond shot Crawford a look.

"Even if you could capture it, which you can't," Crawford exploded, "nobody can sail a battleship with only fifteen men."

"Why not?" Beatty leaned in, expecting this, prepared for it.

"Because as any cadet knows you need at least a hundred men."

"Look, Captain. Suppose you're in a fight. Everybody's dead. What's the barest minimum number of men you'd need to get the hell out of there?"

"Well," Crawford thought for a moment. "Even if

you used only two of the four engines, you have to have three men in each engine room, two in each fire room, an electrician, three on the bridge, another thirty for . . ."

"Don't read me the King's Regulations," Beatty interrupted. "Everybody's dead. *How many?*"

"This is all chalk-talk," Crawford growled. "What would you know about sailing a battleship in a combat situation, *Viscount* Beatty? The only thing that floats in your section is your desk."

"Now, now. Answer the question, Captain," Admiral Redmond said firmly. "How many men do you need to sail a battleship?"

"Well, if the bloody thing's already moving," Crawford began seething, "one at the helm. One at the forward engine. Another at the second throttle board. One in each fire room."

"That's five," Beatty said softly.

Crawford shot him a look that could have sunk the *Ludendorff*, then stared at the paint-flaked ceiling as if searching for another man or two up there. Beatty didn't say another word, letting Crawford thrash in his own swamp.

"Hmm . . . in the last war," the admiral mused, "the *Dorset* got back from Scapa Flow with a handful of men, in fact my brother-in-law was one of them. I suppose that kind of thing could be done again. If you had the right men."

"We do, sir!" Beatty said sounding confident, though he knew he was still far from port.

He rose and in a far corner flicked out the lights, plunging Room 38 into mid-morning darkness; then he turned on a motion picture projector he'd requested in advance from Property, where a quartermaster had suspected Beatty requisitioned it to show a Portuguese stag film that was making the rounds of the officers' clubs.

A grainy black-and-white 8-mm image, obviously shot hand-held, flickered on the wall, revealing in a secluded wooded area a heavily guarded barbed-wire fence surrounding a series of barracks.

"Our Combined Training Center," Beatty explained. "On the Hog's Back near Guildford in Surrey. They have an excellent German language pool."

"Thank you for telling me," Redmond said coldly. "I set it up."

Beatty cursed himself. With all the research he'd done, that was one point he missed.

The silent film cut from the S.O.E. barracks to a handful of men climbing a ladder to a platform towering above a large swimming pool, then moved in close on one of them, in his mid-twenties, slim, blond hair, determination lending strength to a sensitive face.

"Albert Perth, pianist," Beatty said.

"Pianist?" Crawford wondered.

"S.O.E.'s word for radio operator," Beatty explained. "Born in Hamburg to a German mother and an English father. Lived in Germany until he was seventeen, then went to Oxford."

"His mother still lives in Germany," Crawford said, using a slash of sunlight coming through the closed drapes to eye Perth's service records, which Beatty had placed in front of them. "He's a security risk."

On the wall, an instructor flipped a wooden match into the gasoline-covered pool, which exploded into flame. Some of the men on the high platform hesitated, but Perth immediately turtled his head into his collar, leaped into the pool and swam under the liquid inferno to the other side. As he swiftly pulled himself out, some burning gasoline clung to the jacket, and for a terrifying moment he looked as if he'd become a human torch. With the help of some others he beat out the flames and tore off his clothes. Stripped to his underwear, smoke still curling from his scorched hair, Perth rose slowly from the ground and without a word rejoined the line, risking the jump again.

"Security risk? I don't think so," Beatty said. "Perth volunteered for this duty to prove he's loyal to England."

The film cut to an ox of a man, whose head looked like a massive, scarred rock covered with a mat of red Brillo-like hair. In hand-to-hand combat, he wielded the butt of a Sten submachine gun to stand off four attackers wearing wire masks, chest protectors, arm padding. It was a grueling but an even contest.

"Henry Hammond. Coal miner and labor organizer. Born in Bolton," Beatty narrated. "Learned his German working as a boy in the mines in German East Africa. The best engineer we've ever seen."

"Former member of the IWW, arrested four times for fighting with the bobbies during strikes," the admiral read sourly from Hammond's records. "Arrested once for threatening a mine foreman with a pick handle, with the pick head still attached."

"Ran for Bolton town council, 1938, and lost," Crawford added. "The man's probably a Bolshevik. Wants to win a medal for votes after the war, no doubt."

"The stronger his motivation, the better," Beatty said, as Hammond, with a savage butt thrust, laid out the last of his four opponents. Breathing hard, he waved them on for another go.

The film jumped to a drizzle-soaked field where a

sergeant pulled the pin from a grenade. Five yards off stood a lean, tense teen-ager, whose face was too young-looking for his body. The sergeant tossed the live grenade to the boy, who in one movement caught it in the air, threw it over a hill and hit the ground as it exploded.

"Ronald Tanner," Beatty narrated, hoping that the other two men were as impressed as he was with the boy's cool courage. "Tanner's an orphan. Raised by his grandparents who spoke only German at home. He ran off and enlisted under age because they constantly beat him . . ."

". . . which probably developed a resentful and violent nature lurking behind that angelic face," Redmond added.

"He's only nineteen but one of the best gunner's mates in the North Sea Command," Beatty noted. "He's something of a prodigy."

"Prodigy indeed," Redmond sniffed. "Three times recommended for talks with the chaplain for excessive masturbation."

The film cut from Tanner to a long shot of a lone figure leaping over a high hurdle, climbing a sheer wall, dashing across a swaying toggle-rope bridge. He was panther-quick and wiry, but when he passed directly in front of the camera, it could be seen that his hair was completely white.

"Byron Shanks. Served in the Great War, then as navigator in various merchant marines for nearly twenty years. Knows every inch of the Baltic," said Beatty.

"How old is that man?" Crawford asked.

"Sixty. But he's in remarkable shape. It's something of an obsession with him. Hunza diets, figs, nuts, fast-

22

ing, cross-country runs. When he volunteered the Navy waived regulations to take him back."

"Why'd the old bone volunteer?"

"I suspect to prove he can still get it up." Beatty diplomatically averted his eyes as Redmond, jowly and sixtyish himself, squirmed a bit and adjusted the pillow under his bottom.

Tiring over the muscle-killing course, Shanks stumbled in a barbed-wire maze, but quickly looked around to see if anyone had noticed, then vaulted over and pushed on with nothing injured except his pride.

"Cesar Falco, gunner's mate. Free French," Beatty continued as the film switched to a swarthy man of twenty-six with long anthropoid arms, A Sten gun slung over his heavy shoulders, going hand-over-hand across a rope suspended fifty feet over a ravine. He looked as if he were enjoying it. "Falco was decorated for bravery at Metz. Learned his German working in a brothel owned by his father in Alsace-Lorraine."

Out of respect for Admiral Redmond's Victorian background, Beatty declined to mention that one of Falco's brothel duties was to stage wrestling matches in the mud between two nude girls while he refereed, sometimes also in the nude.

In the film, Falco released the rope with one hand, unslung his Sten gun, and dangling in the air, sprayed a burst at silhouette targets on the ground.

"He's a tough Frenchie and he doesn't like Germans," Beatty said. "It's a personal thing."

"A man with a private war. Very dangerous," Admiral Redmond said flatly. "I think we've seen enough, Beatty."

With the lights back on, Beatty was uncomfortably aware of Crawford's I-told-you-so look to the admiral.

"Not exactly the Coldstream Guards are they, Beatty?" Redmond said, tapping a pencil, which Beatty knew was the prelude to dismissal.

"Sir, consider what we need. Elite commando training. Know how to run a battleship. Speak fluent German. Given that shopping list, they're the best men we have."

"Perhaps you should try a cruiser first for practice," the admiral suggested wryly.

With Redmond's pencil tapping more impatiently now, Beatty leaned in again and said, "Admiral, with that kind of muscle in the middle of the Baltic, think what we could do. . . . We could blast any port we wanted."

The pencil stopped tapping. "What port?"

"This one," Beatty said, pointing on the map to the northeastern tip of the Jutland Peninsula. "Skagen, Denmark." He gave Crawford and Redmond time to exchange a wondering look before driving on. "Sir, for months you've wanted Skagen destroyed because its U-boats help control the North Atlantic. So far, planes haven't been worth a damn against their concrete pens and anti-aircraft protection. But if we can ram the *Ludendorff*'s 15-inch guns down its throat, we'll rip Skagen apart!"

"Not bloody likely," Crawford jumped in. "You might sail a battleship with a few men, but to be operational in combat, hell, each gun turret takes eighty men."

"Tear your mind loose, Captain," Beatty shot back. "Forget about safety procedures. You know everything is automatic anyway. Shift over from fire control to local control in the turret and two men can fire those rifles."

24

"But how do you aim? What about elevation, azimuth, trajectory?"

"At point-blank range, all you have to do is point!"

A long silence in Room 38. Admiral Redmond dropped his pencil, drummed his fingers on his desk. He hesitated to gamble fifteen lives on such a reckless long shot. He knew that nothing a few men could do, not even destroying a major U-boat base, would win the war . . . that was the stuff of storybooks. But they could loosen the U-boat noose and give England another couple of weeks, another couple of months of life. It could also be an electrifying boost to national morale, which in its own way was more important than destroying U-boats. For that, fifteen men was a reasonable price to risk, a reasonable price even to pay. And though Redmond was somewhat ashamed of his next thought, he recognized it as only human. If the mission succeeded, it'd make the newspapers for weeks, and he and Naval Intelligence would receive the credit. If it failed, since it was secret anyway, the records would be quietly locked away in a steel basement file as just another gamble that failed. It was one of the dubious advantages of intelligence and sabotage operations over the poor buggers who had to fight huge naval or land campaigns with everybody—M.P.'s, cabinet ministers, nosy war correspondents—breathing down their necks and, when things went bad, eager to pin the blame on the military. At least he wouldn't have that to worry about, he thought, with a sense of relief mixed with a feeling that the war and his job were turning him into a Machiavellian old son-of-a-bitch.

"All right, Beatty," he said abruptly. "You've made a sale."

Beatty, who'd been unaware of the tension in his

neck and shoulders, let out a deep breath and felt the knotted muscles start to relax.

"Thank you, sir." He rose. "I'll brief the men at once. We'll be on our way to the Baltic in under forty-eight hours."

"We?"

"Yes, sir," Beatty said carefully, realizing he was not through yet. "You see, Commander Wakely, who was to have led the mission, broke a shoulder in training. I'm taking his place."

"You?" Redmond automatically reached for his pencil again without even realizing it.

"Yes, sir."

It was Crawford's turn to lean in. "What are you trying to prove, Beatty? That you're as good as the men you've been sending out to die?"

A muscle in Beatty's jaw tightened again.

"Now, now, Captain," Redmond cautioned, suddenly wishing these two would leave so he could have the exquisite pleasure of scratching his tormenting ass.

"With all respect, sir," Crawford insisted. "Feeling guilty about sitting out the war in an office. That hardly qualifies a man to lead this kind of mission."

Beatty knew he had no reason to feel guilty over sending volunteers on missions of known maximum risk. But the casualties on some of the raids he'd planned were fearful. At times barely half, sometimes none of these men with the cavalier courage of youth ever returned. And then Beatty and the others at Baker Street would avert their eyes, avoid each other as much as possible until the pressure of the next problem, the next target, somehow pushed the memory of the previous one and its toll in lives from their minds. But something ineradicable remained. Maybe the sense of failure. Perhaps the scar of guilt. Whatever it was, Beatty had had enough of it. He turned to Admiral Redmond.

"There's no one else who knows this mission and I do," he said truthfully. "That's what qualifies me."

"But you're not a combat officer, Beatty," the admiral said. "Train somebody!"

"No time for that, sir," Beatty said. "The *Ludendorff* sails in three days."

CHAPTER 3

Moonlight lanced through the high windows, and picked out the parallel bars, mats, rings and ropes in the huge deserted gymnasium at the Combined Training Center on the Hog's Back in Surrey. Suddenly, the double doors banged open and the overhead lights protected by wire grilles blazed on. A pair of beefy army corporals with sidearms stationed themselves at the entrance. Then, in twos and threes, fourteen men in fatigues filed in past racks of weights, barbells and dumbbells in graduated sizes.

Some of the men were hulking, with the brute power of heavy bones and thick sinews. Others had the lean hard look, all spare flesh hacked away, that comes with relentless endurance combined with great strength. Each in his own way had an animal energy, the feral alertness of body and reflexes tuned to ultimate pitch.

One of them, passing a padded dummy, whirled and unleashed a kick to the balls that buckled the canvas man and sounded like a rifle shot in the cavernous gym.

"You missed," said another in a high falsetto.

A few laughed, but there was something frightening about the sudden violence. It didn't come from pride in having mastered hand-to-hand combat, or from high-spirited exhibitionism, the priority of youth. Behind it there was a personal savagery of which anyone in this group appeared capable, for unlike most men who try to avoid violence, these felt a special kinship with it. Violence was as much a part of them as their fingerprints. They weren't criminal types, but they were dangerous men who had to keep this primal element in their nature in some dark corner. Except in wartime.

These were the men selected to hijack the *Ludendorff*.

As they headed for a row of folding chairs facing a scarred desk at the north end of the gym, Ronald Tanner, the teen-age gunner's mate, turned to a dark, squat man, and almost in a whisper said, "Training with one officer, then going out with another bloke . . . I don't know."

"Ah . . . as long as he has the desire to kill Germans," Cesar Falco said loudly.

With an antagonism bred by generations of conflict, the Frenchman shot a hostile glance at the blond German-born radioman, just to make sure he heard it. Perth did, but kept his eyes straight ahead, trying to ignore the Frenchman. He wasn't afraid of Falco, but feared a clash might get himself scrubbed from this mission, whatever it was. There would be time enough to prove who had the greater desire and ability to kill Germans.

Taking a seat, Byron Shanks, looking twenty years younger, brushed back his hair, now jet-black. "What do you think?" he asked Jeremy Ayles.

"Aye, you did a better job than they do on my girl," grinned Ayles, a sturdy, good-natured Scotsman.

"How is the arm?" Falco asked Shanks.

"The stiffness is gone," Shanks said, adding with a slyly raised eyebrow. "It's traveled elsewhere."

"*Oui,* but has it traveled to the right place?" Falco leered.

"God, I hope so," Shanks chuckled.

"Ten-tion!"

The command from the guard brought the men to their feet as Beatty entered. Striding to the desk, he was acutely conscious of the men fixing him with a steady, hooded appraisal. He shrugged to himself. He had expected that look, but under their gaze it still came as a slight shock to find the act of walking incredibly complicated.

He motioned the men to sit. Then there was an angry grunt, the sound of scuffling at the door, and a figure Beatty instantly recognized as Hammond, the radical labor leader, was led in, gripped firmly by one of the guards.

"All right, all right, leggo," Hammond whispered hoarsely. "Yer scraping the bark."

"Fuck your bark and the tree it came from," the guard grated. "Sorry, sir," he said to Beatty as he jostled Hammond toward a seat.

"That's quite all right," Beatty replied. Ignoring Hammond, he opened an attaché case and began to spread out some papers.

Hammond stood there, glaring at him. The burly engineer, a pint bottle badly concealed in his back pocket, bleary but trying to act sober, turned to Ernest Jenkins, a former international soccer player. Sporting a mashed nose and a magnificent set of obviously false teeth, Jenkins before the war had earned a good living playing soccer in Germany for a professional team which needed his running power but whose owners insisted he play under the Teutonic name of Ernst Janack for the sake of nationalistic German fans.

"Say, I know that 'umper," Hammond whispered to Jenkins, drunkenly exaggerating his Lancashire accent. " 'E's Viscount Bloody Beatty."

"How do you know?"

"From 'is bleedin' pictures in the paper, that's 'ow," Hammond sneered, his voice rising. "Giving silk hankies to ladies at Ascot. What's 'e doing 'ere?"

"I don't want to tell you 'cause you'd shit in a bucket," Jenkins whispered.

Hammond thought a moment, then looked around in disbelief.

"You're joking," he said, a bit louder this time. "The 'ardest fight 'e's ever 'ad is opening a tin of anchovies."

"Yeah, and the anchovies won," came another low growl.

Everyone in the room heard the exchange. The men tensed, enjoying this, waiting for Beatty's move. Slowly the lieutenant commander looked up. He knew his control over these men hung in the balance and hoped the words would come out cool and level.

"Step this way, will you, Hammond?" he said, heading to a door leading to a side room. Hammond swaggered after him, playing to an appreciative crowd.

As soon as the two men disappeared behind the door, the others jumped up and silently rushed over to listen, jousting for position with a vicious flurry of knees and elbows.

On the other side of the door, at a distance of two paces in a windowless storeroom, Beatty studied Hammond and Hammond studied Beatty. Like all S.O.E. officers, even the ones from Baker Street, Beatty had gone through hand-to-hand combat training, but unlike the others had kept at it. He figured that he could handle a tipsy Hammond without too much damage on either side . . . if he was careful.

"Hand over the bottle," Beatty commanded.

"I've no bottle," Hammond sneered, belching wetly in Beatty's face.

Beatty backhanded him hard. Hammond charged, clutching Beatty by the throat with two huge paws. The attack almost lifted Beatty off his feet and he could feel his breath choked off, Hammond's thumbs digging into his jugular. Beatty tried to throw him with a judo hold, but he was off-balance, and Hammond was too heavy, too strong and only tightened his grip. Afraid of blacking out, Beatty smashed two cupped hands against Hammond's ears. Momentarily deafened, his head exploding with pain, Hammond loosened his grip. Beatty shifted a foot behind Hammond's, this time gaining perfect position, and spun him around, slamming him against the wall. The pint in Hammond's back pocket smashed.

An ass full of glass and aching eardrums that made the floor and ceiling spin crazily took some of the fight out of Hammond. They also sobered him enough to realize the danger of attacking an officer, even one who hit him first.

Beatty saw Hammond hesitate and quickly gave him an easy out.

"All right, I believe you. You have no bottle. Now let's get back in there."

Outside, the men scrambled back to their seats, badly playacting that they'd been there all the time as Beatty held open the door for Hammond. Beatty returned to the desk, but Hammond, like a surly bear, stood there with a wet patch at the back of his pants, stalling rather than sitting down again.

"Have a seat, Hammond," Beatty suggested smoothly.

"I prefer standing, sir." Hammond grumbled.

"Have a seat anyway."

Unwilling to own up to a butt full of broken bottle, Hammond sat as gingerly as he could, but the crunch of glass was unmistakable.

"That's what comes of being a hard ass," Ayles whispered.

"Not hard enough," Shanks smiled.

He and the others turned back to look at Beatty now in a new way. They weren't yet prepared to accept him as one of their own, an elite at swift, lethal destruction. House-training Hammond was one thing, leading a raid against German guns was another. But they were willing to wait and see.

"All right, gentlemen," Beatty said, knowing just how far he'd come with these men and just how far he'd have to go. "Let's get into it. You've been trained to take over a ship. Now you're getting your chance. A big one. We're going after the *Ludendorff*."

At the word *Ludendorff*, a current, a higher pitch of emotion seemed to leap like an electric arc across the gymnasium and the dead silence was pierced only by a long, low whistle from Falco. The men looked at each other. They'd been trained, combat-hardened to expect the unexpected and take it in stride, so there were no other exclamations of astonishment. It would've been bad form. Beatty waited for Falco's whistle to echo away against the bare white walls. Then, next to a map of the Baltic he pulled down a detailed diagram of the

33

Ludendorff. In the glare of the gymnasium's naked lights, even the diagram, barely five feet across, looked menacing, a deadly mosaic of engines, armor, magazines, barbettes, turrets, guns.

"Holy shit!" Tanner muttered.

CHAPTER 4

The mission began badly.

Under tightest security, Beatty and his men boarded a navy patrol boat at an isolated, rotting pier on the River Yare at Great Yarmouth on the North Sea, an hour after dark. A rain that had begun lightly early in the evening now lashed them in a downpour whipped by high winds.

The launch and its captain, both veterans of the Great War and more recently Dunkirk, had seen better days, and the engine sputtered and died and sputtered feebly again before choking out.

"She always does that. Nothing to worry about," the captain said, resigned, sucking on a cold pipe, as if he could think of better ways to spend an ugly night than taking his relic into the choppy waters of the North Sea.

Beatty heard a chuckle behind him in the stern. "Back-to-Baker-Street-in-the-morning," a voice sing-songed.

He knew it was Hammond but decided to let it pass. Hammond was at least sober and the others had paid no attention anyway. They had the tense quiet that comes over men about to leave shores they knew for dangers they don't.

The engine caught at last, the four-man crew slipped the lines and the fragile wooden hull nosed down the Yare, following the marker buoys into the sea. Almost immediately Beatty could feel the air change. There was a snap and salt to it that swept away some of the oily stench of the patrol boat, although not enough. He turned to look back. The shore, in wartime blackout, had already vanished. Ahead, the moon struck silver off the water.

Beatty took a seat on the bare deck near the stern and felt the engine surging below him. Its roar was too loud for much talk, so the men sat in two rows facing each other silently.

Beatty studied them, Shanks sitting ramrod straight as if afraid at his age to relax the fight against gravity for a second, Falco methodically munching a chocolate sandwich, Perth with eyes closed and trying to store up as much rest as he could while he had the chance, Tanner, his teen-aged face marked with acne, staring out to sea. Next to Tanner sat Hammond, watching Beatty, trying to stare him down. Then, silhouetted side by side like twin mountain crags, Lester, a former factory worker and the only one of the men who had a home, wife and children, and Jenkins, who hated the Germans and this war mainly because they were robbing him of his best years as a world-class soccer player.

They had all proved themselves in combat and Beatty wondered whether he had the same qualities, whatever they were, that enabled such men to do what they had to do. He'd find out soon enough.

The engine's roar died to a coughing throb, then cut

out. The silent launch rose and fell with the choppy waves, rain drumming on the cabin roof, streaking down the windows.

Time passed to the rhythm of rain beating against the rolling, creaking hull.

Shifting uncomfortably on the wet deck, Beatty peered into the cold inky blackness that engulfed the boat and glanced at the luminous hands of his watch. The submarine was late. What if something had happened to it and it didn't show up? Secretly, he knew that a part of him wished it wouldn't, because then he could feel that at least he had tried and it wasn't his fault if the mission died stillborn. But he immediately felt a flush of shame over this and strained for some sight of the submarine, as Captain Crawford's words kept invading his thoughts.

Guilt. Beatty *did* feel guilty about sitting out the war in Baker Street, but that alone, he knew, wasn't enough to push him into this kind of mission any more than it had pushed thousands of other armchair officers who were secretly grateful that fate had given them a chance to serve their country respectably and patriotically, but far from the scream of shells. His guilt was mixed with a feeling that gnawed even deeper. Throughout his life, in intelligence and position and wealth, Beatty had been one of the chosen. Nothing had ever come hard to him, and he had never sought anything beyond his reach. He never had to. But now, at thirty-six, with half his life gone, he had realized that he'd never taken full measure of himself as a man. He'd never know how much he could do or endure or overcome unless he accepted some ultimate challenge. And if he didn't accept this one, the *Ludendorff*, he knew he'd never be able to face another one again.

Then Beatty saw it rising from the sea. In the dark, it looked like the sea itself rising, a wave moving in the opposite direction from the other waves. Now the conning tower broke free and the submarine, looking blurred and phantom-like through the rain-streaked windows, loomed to port.

The launch swung alongside the *Barracuda* and Beatty and his men scrambled aboard without a word and ducked down the hatch into the submarine. The bridge hatch slammed shut. Beatty felt the bow dip.

They were on their way to the Baltic.

"Commander Beatty?" Beatty turned. "Commander Poole. Welcome aboard."

They shook hands. With a wisp of beard and taut pink skin, Poole looked startlingly young even for a submarine commander, which was a young man's game. Beatty guessed he couldn't be over twenty-three or twenty-four. His eyes showed none of the nervous exhaustion of most submarine commanders, but he must have had a lot under his belt or the Navy wouldn't have given him anything this important. At least Beatty hoped not.

Poole led Beatty to the captain's cabin amidships, a cramped cubicle with narrow bunk, one chair and a paint-chipped writing desk, one small reading lamp.

"It should take us just under two days," Poole said, sitting on the bunk and motioning Beatty to the chair, "and I suggest for security your men and mine have as little contact as possible. Separate meals, separate quarters. My men have some idea what you're up to, of course, but the less they know or talk about when they return to base, the better."

"Agreed," Beatty nodded. He had planned to recommend the same orders. Poole obviously knew his business.

"I've been briefed on the general idea myself," Poole added, "but the same rule applies. I'd appreciate not knowing any more," Poole said. He adjusted a piece of paper on his desk, then looked up. "You're all rather mad, you know."

Beatty glanced at the surrounding bulkheads that separated them from a hundred thousand tons of water on all sides. "I could say the same of you," he said.

"Quite so," Poole admitted flatly. He turned and opened a locker. It was filled with pullovers, gray-green overalls, sea boots, leather pants, oilskins. Standard captured gear from *U-117*, with a typically heavy, dank smell. "We've never cleaned this stuff, but I'd think you and your men would want to get into it as soon as possible. Just to absorb some more atmosphere."

A sharp rap on the door interrupted Poole.

"If I might see you, sir," Shanks said, sticking his head in.

"In a moment," Beatty answered.

"Yes, sir," Shanks mumbled. He hesitated but after a second closed the door behind him.

"See him now," Poole said.

"That's all right. He'll wait," Beatty replied.

"I think you had better see to him now," Poole said evenly, more an order than a suggestion.

Beatty opened the door again. Shanks stood in the narrow passageway, his lips white, edged with purple, breathing rapidly. He looked like a sick clown. Beatty swiftly led him to the deserted torpedo room.

"What's wrong, Shanks?"

"This," Shanks said. "Being down here." He gestured with a shaking hand. His chest heaved while he looked

39

around at the bulkheads as if they were closing in on him. "I have to get air."

"There's plenty of air," Beatty said, trying to calm him.

"I need to get in the open, sir. Please," Shanks said, his voice low, trying to keep a grip on himself. "I can't help it."

"God man, why didn't you say something about this before?"

"Didn't know. Never been in one of these before," Shanks gasped. On the edge of panic, he looked as if he'd just awakened to find himself buried in a coffin. Poole appeared behind them.

"Surface for a few minutes, Commander," Beatty said.

"It's getting light. Too risky I'm afraid," Poole answered, a glint of iron showing through the easy charm.

"We've got over six hundred miles to go. You'll have to surface anyway, at least seven, eight times to recharge batteries."

"We were jumped by a Stuka near here. I don't want to push our luck again."

The tense voices had brought an audience—Tanner, Lester and Falco, who listened grimly. Beatty feared that Shanks's panic, if it mounted, would shatter not only Shanks—the sight of the old man screaming and clawing at a hatch would shake all the men and crush their confidence before they even reached the Baltic.

Beatty signaled Poole to step back into the captain's cabin and shut the door firmly.

"Surface now," Beatty said.

"Sorry."

"It's my mission."

"It's my ship."

Poole had him there. They held identical rank, but even if Beatty had outranked him, it *was* Poole's ship and Poole had the final authority. If Beatty, however, had learned anything from his father, who'd spent a lifetime as an ambassador and politician, it was how to get others to do things that training, common sense and self-interest told them not to do.

"Surface immediately," Beatty said, "or I scrub this whole thing and we turn back."

"Very well. We turn back," Poole replied evenly.

"We'll both face a Board of Inquiry," Beatty warned.

"I'll risk that," Poole said. "It was my judgment over yours."

Beatty turned for the door as if giving up, then stopped and almost as an afterthought said, "You know, you're blowing a chance, perhaps your only chance in this war, to help capture a German battleship."

"So?"

"That's up to you," Beatty shrugged.

The diesels whined through the cabin bulkheads as a long moment passed. The twenty-three-year-old buccaneer looked up. "I'm afraid my ego shows rather badly," he said.

Beatty couldn't help smiling. "Yes, rather."

Within minutes, the *Barracuda* broke the surface of the North Sea at dawn and a second after the bridge hatch opened, Shanks bolted through like a drowning man coming up for air. Beatty came right behind him. Had the years taken too much of a toll on the old man? Had he made a mistake in taking Shanks?

"Feel better already, sir. Really," Shanks said over the wind sweeping the bridge, as if sensing Beatty's doubts. He was breathing deeply again and the panic seemed to be leaving his eyes.

Beatty nodded and clipped both of them to the harnesses on the bridge.

A great wall of water lifted the *Barracuda* like a candy wrapper and for a second at the crest they saw the rising sun, a cold metallic disk. The sub plunged bow first, as if down a waterfall, into the trough between the first wave and a second which hit her amidships and she heeled over, the tower almost level with the sea before snapping back again. Beatty watched with almost hypnotic fascination as the whole sea seemed to rise higher than the conning tower and higher still, moving silently toward him, gathering weight and malevolent force, foaming angrily at its crest, blotting out the sky and crashing down as if to smash the sub to the ocean bottom. It wallowed in another trough for a moment, then rode up a wave as Shanks wiped the spray from his eyes. The air, and the smack of frigid water, had restored some of the color to his ashen face.

"I'm all right now, sir," Shanks said.

Beatty coughed up a lungful of sea.

"It won't happen again . . ." Shanks began, embarrassed.

"Forget it, it wasn't your fault," Beatty said, trying to keep his eyes off the rolling sea, which made his stomach queasy.

"Yes sir, but I'll make it up to you. I promise," Shanks said. He peered at Beatty closely. "You don't look so good, sir. Perhaps we should get below," the old man observed, taking Beatty's arm as they headed down the hatch.

The submarine dove, cutting from the North Sea into the Skagerrak, then swung southward through the Kattegat, the two straits that led to the narrow sound that separated Denmark and Sweden and spilled into the Baltic.

The *Barracuda* surfaced again at the northern tip of the sound, and in the dark, rocked gently in the calm water. Beatty and Poole climbed through the bridge hatch. To starboard, on the Danish side, framed beneath the starred sky, loomed the silhouette of a castle with octagonal towers, its battlements bristling with ancient guns, as if still defending the sound from ghost ships under sail. Beatty had never been here before, but somehow it looked familiar.

"Elsinore," Poole whispered. "A bit melodramatic," he added dryly, "but when you're Shakespeare you can get away with anything."

Beatty smiled politely, but briefly. Even in the dark, he didn't like being exposed on the surface so near to German-held territory.

Across the water, the wind carried voices. The words, the language were indistinguishable but as his eyes adjusted to the dark he could make out the humped shape of a German artillery battery, 88-mm guns. Eighty-eights were designed for anti-aircraft defense but were powerful enough to make short work of a submarine.

Poole peered ahead toward the long narrow neck of water that stretched for miles in the dark.

"Filled with nets and mine fields," he said. "There are only two ways of getting through. First, with charts and maps furnished by our intelligence sources."

"Are they reliable?" Beatty said, detecting something in Poole's voice.

"Yes. Unless the Germans have decided to change the mine field patterns. You never know till you try."

"What's the second choice?"

"We forget about our charts completely, and follow right behind a tanker or freighter. Sort of piggyback our way in. They always know the safe way."

"I hope you've done this before," Beatty said flatly.

"No," Poole admitted. "But one of our oldest commanders assured me it works."

"Nothing personal, but why didn't we get him to take us in?" Beatty asked.

"Frankly he was lost in action on this kind of thing, I'm afraid," Poole said.

"Radar reports ship approaching on the quarter, sir," said a sharp voice from below.

It was a Swedish freighter. The submarine dove and waited, motionless, until the ship passed overhead. Then, barely a hundred feet behind and as close to the surface as possible without showing itself, the sub followed the freighter into the sound.

Within the *Barracuda*, Beatty suddenly thought he heard something wrong, like a loose valve or fitting, and darted a glance at the crew, expecting one of them to track it down and fix it. From the look on their faces, they obviously heard it too, but nobody made a move. They all shifted their eyes to their captain, who was listening just as intently though his face remained expressionless.

The noise, which began as an uneven tapping, became louder, a hollow thump from the exterior of the hull. Beatty guessed it was near the bow. He held his breath. Shanks gripped an overhead pipe, his hands unaware of the heat.

Everyone feared it was a mine and most of the crew had seen what mines did to submarines, blowing them open like tin foil.

The thumping began to move. It seemed to crawl

down the hull, each thump louder than the one before, as if whatever was out there wanted to find some weak spot, some vulnerable place to smash its way in. Beatty glanced again at Poole. Poole's expression was as calm as before, but his neck glistened with sweat.

"A mine?" Beatty almost whispered.

Poole's eyes flickered to Beatty, then back to the noise. The thumping changed to a fierce scraping aft, like a huge, primitive claw screeching its nail back and forth across the steel plates.

Beatty imagined the dread thing out there, entangled by net or chain to the hull, ready to explode when jarred at the right angle. It was a miracle that it hadn't exploded already.

Poole ordered the sub's forward motion stopped. The dead screeching ceased gradually, slowly, but they all knew it was still out there. In the silence, Poole's pale blue eyes narrowed and Beatty could sense his thoughts. Continuing ahead with a tangled mine banging against the hull would be suicidal. To surface and try to dislodge it in the narrow sound, no wider than a river and filled with enemy shipping, was just as dangerous.

Yet they couldn't stay here.

"Prepare to dive," Poole commanded.

The engines whined, the bow nosed down and the deck beneath Beatty's feet tilted crazily as the sub dove.

The thumping aft started again, louder than before, faster, with an almost personal fury as if there were a consciousness behind it and it *wanted* to kill the *Barracuda*.

Beatty wiped a stinging drop of sweat from his eye. His jaw tightened for the inevitable explosion, the fatal rush of water. He heard a wrenching, tearing sound and the submarine seemed to jerk and whatever it was . . .

mine, sunken log, part of a ship . . . was gone, torn free by its natural buoyancy from the diving submarine.

A few minutes later Poole turned to Beatty.

"We're in the Baltic," he said.

CHAPTER 5

At 4:46 A.M., the *Barracuda* broke the black surface of the Baltic.

The hatch swung open. Fifteen men emerged. They entered a world even more sinister than the ocean below. No moon, no light, just heavy fog that concealed the *Barracuda*'s bow from the bridge. The Baltic lay still. They couldn't see it. They couldn't hear it. The submarine could have been floating in the fog.

The men climbed down from the bridge. Their sea boots grating on the ladder sounded startling in the unnatural quiet. They inflated a German life raft to which they mounted an outboard motor and a wireless. They lowered the raft into the sea. It was all executed swiftly, silently, by the numbers.

Poole waved from the bridge, trying to hide what he felt, that he'd never see Beatty or the others again. Beatty sensed it anyway as he waved back and joined his men in the raft. Hammond pushed off with an oar.

The raft and submarine drifted apart and they heard the *Barracuda*'s diving alarm ring, the air roar from the buoyancy tanks, the bridge hatch bang shut. They turned and watched the sub's bow dipping. Before it was fully submerged, the *Barracuda* vanished in the fog.

They were alone.

The outboard sputtered into life and the raft nosed northeast. Crouched in the bow, Beatty wore leather pants, a blue pea jacket with gold buttons and U-boat insignia on the sleeve, and a white cap, which by unwritten law in the German Navy only a U-boat's commander was permitted to wear. The others wore sweaters, pants, overalls, oilskins. Beatty knew that he and his men were still a bit too tanned for men who spent their lives in a submarine but that could be explained by being adrift in a raft under a blazing sun. Otherwise, in the German uniforms, they should pass. For two days, diesel oil particles had clung to their clothes, matted their hair, seeped into their nostrils and pores. They not only looked authentic, they smelled authentic, of oil and sweat and mold.

Beatty nodded to Perth to get the radio working, then turned his eyes to the sea. It was calm, flat, a lifeless gray. The glassy surface wasn't even disturbed by fish jumping for food. Except for the whine of their outboard, the Baltic was wrapped in sepulchral silence.

A dead sea, Beatty thought. No movement, no life anywhere.

Although there seemed to be no wind either, a fog bank shifted and Tanner pointed to port. Something in the water, drifting their way. Finally they made it out. A blasted crate. Charred timber. Pieces of a lifeboat. Spars. Silver-gray patches of oil. Insignias of death on a dead sea.

"A steamer," Hammond muttered.

A body, face black, the skin peeled and blistered with

burns, glided past like a specter, showing its teeth in a ghastly smile, as if it knew something about death which it didn't choose to reveal.

"Must've happened six, eight hours ago," Hammond said.

The men put the corpse out of their minds as the raft edged into another fog bank so thick that Beatty was almost surprised he could breathe. From the bow he could barely see Falco in the stern or the water below. The raft was engulfed in a world of fog again. As minutes crawled by, Beatty felt a rising tension. If it didn't lift, they'd never spot the *Ludendorff*. Their few gallons of petrol would soon be exhausted. They'd be stranded in the middle of the sea with no food, no water. For a moment the white stuff seemed to part, then the raft plunged again into more heavy, rolling fog.

At first Beatty wasn't sure he heard it . . . the low growl of a ship's engine. Not deep or loud enough for a battleship, but some kind of craft not far off.

He signaled Jenkins. Jenkins cut the outboard motor. The raft drifted as the engine rumble off the port bow drew closer. The men huddled down motionless, knowing that to be spotted and rescued by another ship would end the mission, that to be returned to Germany would mean certain exposure and a firing squad.

The unseen ship's whistle gave a piercing blast to warn other sightless ships, and Beatty heard another whistle, another engine rumble to starboard. There were two ships out there. A moment later, an engine's throb seemed to drift from off the stern and Beatty feared the raft was ringed by three ships.

Then the sounds fused into just one off the bow again and he realized they were bouncing off the drifting walls of fog, duplicating themselves like a single object reflected over and over from different angles in mirrors.

The ship's engine seemed closer now. Beatty's only hope was not to be seen.

A shape appeared off the bow. Not even a shape. A dark shadow, like a patch of denser fog, accompanied by an ear-splitting blast from its whistle. Since Beatty didn't know the size of the craft, he couldn't tell how far away it was. It could've been a hundred yards, it could've been almost near enough to touch. The men held their breath. Only their eyes moved. They watched it glide past with a terrible slowness, like a phantom wreathed in mists.

Then some combination of wind and water temperature cut through the fog, forcing it partially to lift and Beatty saw the receding stern of a German patrol boat. It wasn't a clear look across more than sixty yards of mist, but to Beatty it had a startling clarity. The low broad stern. The needle nose of an unmanned machine gun mounted aft, pointed skyward. Hunched figures in the small cabin amidships.

The moment froze in time for Beatty, the raft and the patrol boat so close and in full view of each other.

The fog swiftly closed in again, beginning to obscure the German boat, which hadn't seen them yet. As if by force of will, Beatty tried to urge it to descend faster, to swallow the raft or the patrol boat or both.

Suddenly a shout carried across the water. Followed by the sound of feet running across a wooden deck.

"No . . . *there!*"

Beatty saw a figure dash to the stern, pointing straight at the raft a second before the fog turned the patrol boat into a vague shadow and then swallowed it completely. He heard engines slamming into reverse, digging the patrol boat around. The Germans were coming to rescue them!

Beatty had to make a quick decision. He could try eluding the patrol boat, but once the Germans heard his outboard kick over, they'd zero in on it, and there was no way he could escape a boat capable of doing better than twenty knots. Or, he could stay here, quietly hidden, hoping the Germans would eventually give up without finding them. Unless the fog lifted, which was highly likely.

Beatty shuddered at either option but they were the only ones he had and he decided on the second. By remaining hidden and silent, he'd know where the Germans were and they wouldn't know, at least not yet, where he was. It wasn't much, but it was the only advantage he had.

He heard voices coming over the water.

"Yell . . . Give-us-a-yell," the Germans shouted.

The boat's whistle blasted repeatedly now, signaling. Beatty couldn't see but he knew the crewmen were at the gunwales trying to peer through the cottony fog. The boat was so close that the British could hear the Germans' voices distinctly, in one even the trace of a stutter.

"You sure?"

"Yah, yah. A raft. A white U-boat cap. I s-s-saw."

"Why don't they yell?"

"How the h-h-hell do I know?"

Aboard the patrol boat, the Germans looked at each other questioningly. It didn't make sense, U-boat men stranded on a raft not wanting to be rescued. Not if they were really U-boat men, really Germans. Uneasy, the stutterer ducked into the cabin and emerged with a Mauser rifle. Another took position behind the machine

51

gun in the bow. The patrol boat swung around. Eyes probed the fog.

The Germans were no longer looking for the raft. They were hunting it.

Beatty felt his shirt stick damply to his back. It was too late now to call for help, innocently board the boat and hope to overpower it. The Germans would be too wary. As soon as they spotted the raft, every gun would be trained in its direction. The patrol boat had to be handled in some way and he could think of only one. It was so dangerous, he gave it only the slimmest chance of succeeding but he had to try it.

"Weapons," he whispered, turning to his men. "Anything we have."

Carefully, as if the flutter of a pocket would carry across the water and give them away, the English fished out two screwdrivers, a bone-handled knife, a Stillson wrench. Beatty looked at them grimly. It wasn't much.

"The strongest swimmers?" he asked.

Falco slowly raised his hand, then Jenkins. Hammond looked around, perhaps to see if anyone else followed, then nodded briefly.

Beatty stripped. Without a word, the other three did the same. Falco threw his clothes aside, but Hammond folded his neatly to make a point that he intended to survive and come back for them.

They waited for the sound of the engine to get louder as the search pattern carried it closer to the raft again. Their only chance was to reach the boat when it was moving very slowly or had stopped. Beatty had more reason than the others for wanting to be as close to the boat as possible when he entered the water. He wasn't an exceptionally strong swimmer. As commanding officer, in fact, he could've ordered another man to go instead. But his men might not follow him all the way later unless he showed the spine to lead them now.

From its muffled throb, Beatty judged the patrol boat was swinging in a closer arc again. Tying the knife to his forearm with a strip of cloth torn from his shirt, Beatty silently slipped into the water. Falco, Jenkins and Hammond followed. The Baltic was so cold it hit their bodies like a burning shock and for a moment Beatty felt his heart stop beating. He started to swim before the frigid cold paralyzed his muscles, breast-stroking away from the raft toward the oncoming sound of the unseen German boat. Swimming on his right was Jenkins, to his left Hammond. Falco, swimming so fast he seemed to have flippers, was up ahead, already lost in the fog. The raft itself vanished behind them.

Beatty tread water to listen for the boat. It was off to the right now, its engines idling again. He swam in that direction, Hammond and Jenkins following. He knew they were stretching the distance between themselves and the raft. If they couldn't reach the patrol boat, they'd probably never be able to find the raft again either, and would swim until they became exhausted and drowned.

A shape loomed in the fog. They struck out for it. It wasn't moving and soon Beatty could see, as if through a pane of frosted glass, the gray hull twenty yards away. Suddenly its idling engine coughed and the boat inched forward diagonally ahead of them. Forced to stay with a slow breast stroke because it made no noise, Beatty tried to catch up with the boat, his lungs gasping for air. He was in the boat's choppy wake, which made swimming harder, and it was outdistancing him. He lashed the water with a desperate frog kick, but slowly the boat chugged further into the soup and disappeared.

Beatty didn't know how much strength he had left. But he was prepared to use it all in a final effort to reach the German boat. Signaling Hammond to follow, he struck out with the most powerful stroke he could.

His breathing soon became labored, so loud he was afraid that the Germans might even hear it as he swam through the rollers. His arms and legs were beginning to lose synchronization, were wearily thrashing, and he knew he was near total exhaustion. He remembered hearing somewhere that the quickest, most merciful way to drown was to blow out all the air from one's lungs and immediately dive under, and he was prepared to do it when, incredibly, the German patrol boat loomed directly ahead, so close it almost ran over him.

Beatty spun away to the side, and as the boat chugged slowly past, reached up and grabbed hold of the vertical steel ladder near the stern. He saw, near the bow, Hammond grabbing a short line hanging from the deck.

Beatty and Hammond held on, letting the boat trail them through the water, catching seconds of rest.

Suddenly, Beatty felt a heavy cold hand clamp on his shoulder. He wheeled and saw a huge set of teeth bared in a smile. It was Jenkins, who'd reached the boat before them and had been hanging, out of sight, at the stern.

"Falco?" Beatty asked with his lips.

Jenkins shrugged negative.

Cautiously, Beatty tilted his head back and tried to see what they'd be up against on the boat. In the cabin, the commander, a big man from the way he towered over the wheel, jut-jawed, eyes straining directly ahead into the fog. In the bow, a German at a belted Spandau machine gun with its low-slung muzzle aimed at the water. Almost directly above Beatty's head, in the stern, another German at another tripoded Spandau. Beatty could see a fourth crewman near the rail amidships and hear the thud of footsteps on the other side of the boat. That made it five that he was sure of. A patrol boat this size might have two or three more.

Beatty shot a look at Hammond. Hammond swiftly tore loose the screwdriver tied around his wrist. Jenkins freed his Stillson wrench. Beatty gripped his bone-handled knife.

He signaled and Jenkins let go of the boat, thrashing wildly.

"Here . . . help . . . over here," he cried in German.

"Slow . . . slow," someone shouted from the deck to the cabin.

"There . . . there he is."

The boat stopped, rolling and pitching in the sea. A German on the starboard side threw Jenkins a line. Thrashing weakly in the water, Jenkins reached for it but missed. The German snaked the line to him again. Jenkins lunged for it but a wave pushed him away.

The German straddled the rail and reached down to Jenkins while the other two at the machine guns watched closely.

Behind them, clinging below out of sight on the opposite port side, Beatty and Hammond waited.

Jenkins tried to grab the outstretched hand but missed, choked on a lungful of water, disappeared beneath a rolling wave, struggled to the surface. He lifted an arm again feebly, crying for help. The German reached down further, leaning far over the gunwale. Jenkins' fingers touched his. The German leaned out even more. Their hands locked. The German pulled, but Jenkins, feet braced against the hull, pulled harder. The German plunged into the sea. Jenkins' wrench, held out of sight in his other hand, flashed.

Beatty and Hammond on the other side heard the German's startled cry and the splash. They swung aboard, Hammond coming up from behind, leaping for the machine gunner in the bow, Beatty, knife held low, springing for the machine gunner in the stern.

Beatty moved as fast as he could but his muscles were cramped from the cold water and he felt as if he was struggling against a gale force wind. The German heard him and spun around. The Spandau snarled past Beatty's face as he plunged the knife in a low arc, hit bone, plunged again, heard the German grunt, smashed him away from the gun and swung it around at two crewmen near the starboard rail reaching for their rifles. Beatty squeezed the trigger and the Spandau snarled again. The Germans crashed to the deck.

Beatty heard another staccato blast from the bow. It was Hammond, spraying the wheelhouse with bullets. Wood splintered. Glass shattered. The wheelhouse door burst open and the commander, his face blood-streaked, stepped out slowly, looked around as if puzzled about something and sank down to a sitting position against the wheelhouse, dead.

Beatty and Hammond rushed to the rail to haul in Jenkins, who'd dispatched the German in the water. It was a mistake.

An automatic weapon opened up on them from the engine room hatch. They dove to the deck but there was no cover and without guns they were defenseless.

Something scuttled fast toward the hatch. Falco. The Frenchman, hearing the noise, had somehow caught up with the patrol boat. Like a giant lizard, Falco slithered toward the hatch and dropped inside from behind, pulling the German down with him.

Beatty heard muffled shots within the engine room. Then silence. Falco's head emerged. He looked as if in great pain.

"You hit?" Beatty called.

"No. But *something* was hit down here," Falco answered, darting a look into the engine room vomiting smoke. "It's going to blow."

The three of them instantly dove back into the sea, joining Jenkins, and swam hard against the rollers to get as far as they could from the boat before it blew up, far from the debris which could kill them or the underwater force of the explosion which would crack ribs, crush chests, rip intestines.

Jenkins, in the water so long he was nearly drowning, had nothing left and the others had to keep him up and drag him along. Beatty shot a look over his shoulder. The boat was still awfully close. Flames had burst from the engine room hatch, advanced across the planking, engulfed the bullet-stitched wheelhouse. If it exploded now they'd die. Jenkins saw the look in Beatty's face and thrashed his legs desperately.

Behind them, the patrol boat listed heavily, the frothing sea marching up the port deck, dense black smoke concealing the flames for a moment, then the flames cutting through, mounting higher.

The explosion ripped open the hull's belly and hurled the deck, shattered into thousands of pieces, into the sky.

The second they heard the explosion, the four men dove down, dove as fast and as far as they could. On the surface, where they'd been a moment before, came a lethal rain of smashed wood, searing hot metal. They hadn't had time to dive very far and just a few feet down, they saw steel whooshing around them on all sides like plunging spears. A jagged piece of boiler plating scythed straight for Beatty. Automatically he pulled his head back and it hissed past an inch from his throat.

When the four broke the surface again, the patrol boat was gone.

Beatty and the other three lay motionless in the raft, which had immediately followed the sound of the explosion and managed to pick them up. They were too weak to move, and with the exception of Hammond, who seemed to be so well insulated with heavy flesh, their bodies trembled involuntarily from the cold and exhaustion.

Now that it was over and Beatty was still alive, the terrors of running into the patrol boat were gone and he could afford to be almost thankful for it. He'd proved to himself that when necessary he could kill swiftly and efficiently. Strangely, he could also do it without emotion, even without hatred. He had killed the German machine gunner impersonally because the machine gunner had been a faceless, impersonal threat to his life. No different, really, from killing a dangerous insect except that in this case the threat that had to be eliminated was human. Now, however, Beatty felt almost ashamed, ashamed not so much for having been able to kill so coldly but for being able to look back on it so coldly.

Without warning, the raft emerged into blinding sunlight that exposed raft, sea and men, making them feel very visible, very vulnerable.

Beatty shot a look at Perth on the wireless. Perth shook his head. Nothing.

At three knots, the raft nudged through another cluster of debris, apparently from the same torpedoed steamer they'd seen earlier that morning, and Shanks spotted another body, half-submerged, wearing only an undershirt. The man had probably been asleep when his ship was hit and woke up only to die.

Nobody spoke, but Perth suddenly signaled for silence, clutching the earphones to his head.

"The spotter plane," he whispered to Beatty. "They put the *Ludendorff*'s position twelve kilometers, bearing zero-six-five relative."

"Come about to zero-four-zero," Beatty ordered Jenkins at the rudder.

The scar-faced soccer player swung over to zero-four-zero. Suddenly, they heard something faint, a cry. They turned in its direction, but saw nothing.

"Could've been a bird," Ayles speculated.

But then another cry, and about a hundred yards away they spotted a man clinging to a smashed spar with one arm, the other waving. Over the whine of their outboard they couldn't make out the words, or even the language, only the hoarse desperation as the survivor waved to them frantically.

Jenkins shot a look to Beatty. Beatty knew if they rescued anyone who saw their motor and radio it could give the whole thing away. But to ignore the cries was to sentence a helpless man to death. What he had to do wasn't easy, but after what he'd done on the German patrol boat it was easier than it would've been before. He felt a tightening at the back of his neck as he said, "Maintain course, Jenkins."

"Aye, sir," Jenkins said, as matter-of-factly as if ordered to steer clear of a piece of driftwood.

The distance between man and raft widened. Sinking into a trough, his head disappeared behind a wave, bobbed up, disappeared again. The cries grew fainter and fainter until the British couldn't even be sure they heard him any more.

But Beatty could still hear the cries in his mind, and he had to shut them out as he swept the eastern horizon with his Zeiss glasses. The sea was as empty as the sky. The raft rolled starboard to port, port to starboard in a monotonous rhythm that blurred time. The waves, like mirrors smashed into a million pieces, reflected the sun, dazzling, blinding. Unaccustomed to prolonged use of binoculars, Beatty felt a dull ache pressing in his left eye. He had a sinking fear that he might have miscalculated direction and missed the *Ludendorff*, or perhaps, for reasons of its own, it had changed course. Beatty cursed himself for not supplying the raft with food and water against such a possibility. Unless they were picked up, they could all die out here. The *Ludendorff*, a violent threat to their lives, was also their only chance to survive in this damn sea.

Scanning the horizon with trained eyes, Shanks muttered, "No sign of her, lads."

The others shifted uneasily. Hammond darted an accusing look at Beatty.

And then Beatty saw something . . . an ethereal, shimmering presence created by the optical distortion of sun and heat and sea. It was barely a speck, so far away he was afraid that by blinking he'd make it disappear. For a moment it seemed to vanish in the glare of the sun burning on the sea, but then it rose higher on the horizon, still distant and unsubstantial, almost ghostlike, but no doubt of it . . . a ship!

"Tanner!" Beatty commanded.

"Sir." Tanner instantly slammed a flare gun into his hand.

Beatty raised the flat-barreled gun and squeezed the trigger. Nothing happened. For an instant, Beatty thought the firing mechanism was broken and that the *Ludendorff* would sail unawares right past them. Then he noticed, hoping that the others didn't, that in his excitement he'd forgotten to release the safety. He fired again. The flare arrowed into the brilliantly clear sky and burst into red and white magnesium stars.

They waited.

Emerging from the haze rising off the water, so small at first it could be a fishing boat, the ship changed course, heading straight for them. Jenkins ditched the outboard, Perth the radio. The men grew silent as the ship climbed the horizon. For the first time they could make out the superstructure flashing in the sun. The ship bearing down on them was the *Ludendorff*.

On a cue from Beatty, the men began to cheer and wave their arms wildly, shouting in German though the battleship was much too far away to hear.

The dreadnought loomed steadily larger, and each moment that brought her closer magnified her to a size they could never have conceived. Not because they'd never seen a battleship before, but because from a bobbing raft no fifteen men had ever seen a battleship they planned to hijack. Her superstructure towered over them now like the skeleton of a skyscraper while the great forward turret guns thrust ahead and the ensign, red and white with a black swastika, fluttered at the main mast. The English, without knowing it, grew silent again. The enormity of their mission became real to them for the first time.

Quietly studying the *Ludendorff* through his glasses, Beatty was aware of a strange sensation. Unlike most men, he'd rarely been stirred by military displays, or felt his blood race from martial bands and great parades. But now, watching the *Ludendorff* crash her way through the sea, her camouflage of broken diagonals of gray and blue matching the bleakness of the Baltic, the clean sweep of her lines from bow to stern communicating speed and power, he couldn't help feeling admiration. There was something magnificent, majestic about the *Ludendorff*, even if she was an enemy ship on which he might soon die.

Beatty pushed aside his feelings, a strange mixture of awe and dread, and forced his mind to race through all he'd committed to memory from Naval Intelligence about the battleship he planned to capture.

Displacement: 50,000 tons fully loaded.

Dimensions: 817 feet at the waterline, 836 feet overall, 120½ feet width.

Machinery: Twelve Wagner extra-high-pressure boilers, three shafts, Brown-Boveri geared turbines, 140,000 horsepower, 30 knots.

Protection: Main belt armor 12¾ inches, main turrets 7 inches.

Armament: Eight 15-inch guns (four turrets, two guns each), twelve 5.9-inch guns (six turrets, two guns each), sixteen 4.1-inch A.A., sixteen 37-mm A.A., seventy 20-mm A.A.

Total armament weight: 7,652 tons.

Builder: Blohm and Voss, Hamburg.

Naval architect: Manfred Ruge.

The statistics were formidable enough. Translated into brute power, they meant the *Ludendorff* could hurl a one-ton shell over twenty miles with astonishing accuracy. Her eight 15-inch guns four forward, four aft, each capable of firing three rounds a minute, could sink ships or level cities without even seeing them, while her orchestration of small guns filled the sky with a lethal protective shield against attacking planes. She was a super-battleship, the single most powerful weapon yet devised, a creation of man at his most modern and most primitive . . . science and savagery.

All by itself, the name of the naval architect, Manfred Ruge, was enough, Beatty knew, to guarantee that the *Ludendorff* would be a terror on the high seas, and he'd learned as much about Ruge as he could, as if by understanding the man he'd perhaps be better equipped to overpower the man's creation. It wasn't easy, for the Germans had cloaked Ruge in secrecy, but from bits and pieces a charter profile had been constructed by British Intelligence.

The son of a poor Munich family . . . his father slaughtered pigs for a sausage factory, his mother took in sewing . . . Manfred Ruge was born on May 18, 1907, with a twisted spine and a cleft palate. His devout parents suspected the infirmities came from some sort of spell or curse, and out of shame kept him in the house except for allowing him to limp to school. There he showed extraordinary aptitude for mathematics, but only mathematics. History, biology, art were all studies of human imperfection and the cruelties of God or nature. Numbers, equations, geometrical theorems were pure and perfect, his only liberation from the prison of his body.

At seventeen he became aware of desire, and after weeks of tormented and sleepless nights, took himself to a brothel, half-expecting to be thrown out. Instead, two of the girls insisted on seeing his hump and fought over the chance to experience what it was like to have sex with such a creature. It was the first and last time Ruge ever sought a woman or any other sexual partner.

He plunged deeper into his books, graduating with honors and winning a scholarship to the Marinekirche, the school of marine engineering at Flensburg. The design of great and powerful warships fascinated the deformed youth, perhaps as projections of his own unexpressed hostilities and aggressions in a world where people averted their eyes when he shuffled into a room. In the late 1920s while supporting himself as a draftsman, Ruge began to design on paper huge warships, an exercise in futility because after its defeat in the First World War, Germany under the terms of the Versailles Treaty was prohibited from building capital ships. But in 1935 Hitler denounced the treaty, started to build a *Kriegsmarine* for another war and Ruge's prophetic designs soon came to the attention of the Navy's Commander-in-Chief, Admiral Erich Raeder.

The admiral decided that the hunchback must never be seen at the *Übermenschen* rallies in Nuremberg, or at the parades of Aryan might through Berlin. But Ruge was given a secluded studio and a staff in Hamburg and told to design warships, warships of great power, and if necessary, radical design, that would dominate the seas.

The *Ludendorff* was the dwarf's ultimate creation.

The battleship swung so close, now Beatty could see the tilted derricks, the domelike gunnery controls, the decks alive with men. Somehow a skeleton crew of only three hundred and fifty looked like a threatening horde when seen from a raft, and though the sun was intense, the English felt their flesh tighten with cold. But at a signal from Beatty they resumed their hoarse shouting, shipwrecked Germans grateful for rescue, for safety.

They barely heard the sound behind them.

Beatty spun around and saw someone in a life jacket

swimming toward them, the same man who'd cried for help before. His arms rose and fell almost in slow motion, as if strapped with lead weights, and his legs trailed behind him, too weak or too numb to kick any more. With barely enough strength to lift his head, he choked sea water with every gasp. Desperately, he reached for the raft, missed, was washed away by a wave, thrashed himself back again and grabbed hold with a white, trembling hand.

"Let me hang on. Let me hang on, please," the man gasped. "Please . . ."

His face was a bluish gray from the cold, his skin prune-wrinkled from being in the water too long. His eyes, burned red by salt, narrowed with fear that the men in the raft who had ignored his earlier cries for help would refuse to help him even now.

"Just let me hang on," he choked again. "I won't be any trouble."

Beatty's impulse was to reach for the man's throat and hold him under because he was a danger to the mission. But the *Ludendorff* was too close. The Germans watching the raft through binoculars would see him doing it. He nodded to Maltin, who reached over to haul the man in. He was all dead weight and nearly tipped the overloaded raft, but finally Maltin and Shanks heaved him in. He lay on his back, trembling, spitting water and yellowish bile, his eyes swollen nearly shut.

Beatty studied him swiftly. He looked shrunken and close to fifty because of the ordeal in the sea, but was probably still in his thirties. Spoke English. Wore a plaid sports jacket under his Mae West. Must be strong to endure half a day in the sea, especially the cold Baltic, and still be able to swim. There wasn't much else

Beatty could tell at a glance. A few hours in cold water washes away all individuality.

"Ver sind sie?" Beatty asked as the *Ludendorff* maneuvered to port.

"American," came the reply. "Uh . . . *Ich bin ein Amerikaner.*"

From the halting way he said it, Beatty could tell that though the American wasn't fluent in German, he at least knew his way around enough to communicate.

"Your name, *bitte*," Beatty asked slowly in English with a distinct German accent.

"Walker."

Walker tried to raise himself on his side and Beatty got a glimpse of a gold Patek Phillipe wristwatch, which indicated a certain degree of wealth, or an attempt to give the impression of a certain degree of wealth.

"The name's Terry Walker . . . American and neutral," he added eagerly. "I got nothing against anybody, sir."

Beatty knew the American was too afraid to ask why they ignored his cries for help back there, but just in case the question ever arose, he decided to give a reasonable explanation.

"I had water enough only for my own men."

"Yeah, that's okay, that's okay," Walker said, obviously willing to accept any explanation as long as he was allowed the safety of the raft until the battleship, only a couple of hundred yards away now, picked them up.

Despite his manner, there was something about Walker's shrewd, alert eyes and naturally aggressive jaw, Beatty suspected, which suggested that even if it were necessary, Walker might be a hard man to handle or kill.

As Walker leaned his head over the side to retch up more sea water, Hammond shifted closer to Beatty, speaking low in German.

"What do we do with him?"

"Nothing now," Beatty whispered. "I don't think he saw anything, anyway."

At one hundred yards, the battleship changed course slightly to windward, bringing the raft to the lee side, protected from the wind and waves, and allowing the current to push the ship gently toward the raft, a flawlessly executed textbook maneuver for taking on survivors that brought a grunt of professional approval from Shanks. Falco was less impressed. It meant that full crew or skeleton crew, the *Ludendorff* was in the hands of skilled, disciplined and therefore dangerous Germans.

Shanks and Tanner broke out two oars and paddled toward the *Ludendorff*. The men could now clearly make out the rivets on her heavy armor, the rotating radar equipment making a 360-degree sweep at the top of the superstructure, the caliber of each gun from the 15-inch monsters to the needlelike 20-mm antiaircraft weapons mounted almost everywhere. As they drew closer, the *Ludendorff*'s superstructure blotted out the sun. A swell nudged the raft against the battleship like a minnow against the side of a whale.

A Jacob's ladder snaked down from the upper deck.

Falco grabbed it and was about to climb—despite a certain natural apprehension he felt a jolt of excitement at the prospect of standing on the deck of a German battleship—when he remembered Beatty's instructions. As if weakened by too much exposure, he purposely let the ladder slip through his fingers before grabbing it again. Then he struggled up the ladder on unsteady legs.

As Germans on the upper deck peered down over the guardrail like disembodied heads, Shanks came next, then Perth, then Tanner, all looking authentically exhausted. Tanner felt his heart pound. He didn't know whether it was from climbing, or fear, or both. He had never really thought they'd get this far. He half-expected to have been blown out of the water while still in the raft. Now he expected to be shot as soon as he reached the upper deck.

Below in the raft, Beatty nodded to the American. Grateful, Walker worked himself over to the ladder, looked up at the battleship towering above him, solid and immense, and whistled to himself.

He turned to one of the men in the raft, and muttered, "If you're not safe on that baby, you're not safe on anything."

"*Schnell*," Hammond grunted at him.

The rough hemp cut the flesh of Walker's hands softened by hours of sea water as he labored up the ladder that trembled under his weight. He knew enough not to look down, but looking up made him just as queasy so he kept his eyes straight ahead on the battleship's armor plating. Hammond followed closely behind him.

The *Ludendorff* pitched, the ladder swayed dizzily and Walker felt it whip out from under his feet. He hung on, kicking desperately for a footing, and came down heavily on Hammond's hand.

"Shit!" Hammond hissed instinctively in English as pain shot through a mashed finger.

The American stared down at Hammond for a frozen moment. Their eyes locked.

CHAPTER 6

Walker was sure he heard it. Shit. But he couldn't have, yet . . .

Suddenly, the *Ludendorff* pitched again and Walker, teeth clenched, could only think of clutching the ladder until it stopped swaying. He scrambled up, his mind racing.

He pulled himself over the rail of the *Ludendorff* and stood on the immense forward deck. The first thing he saw, between the two giant anchor chains running across the forecastle, was a huge painted swastika, black, on a white circular background. Across the swastika fell a shadow, the shadow of the battleship's big guns. Two guns in each turret, they pointed straight ahead, almost in Walker's direction. He had the feeling of being in front of a huge firing squad, and without even knowing it, he took a step away to the side.

Out of the corner of his eye he watched Hammond coming over the rail. Sinking down apparently exhausted on the deck, Hammond ignored him as if nothing had happened.

Walker felt a coarse blanket thrown over his shoulders and was aware now of dozens of German crewmen in rubber-soled canvas shoes and blue denim dungarees, some bare-chested, others in faded denim shirts, milling around him and the men from the raft. They handed out whiskey, blankets and cigarettes and jabbered away in German, asking where the raft came from. The raft men, including the big guy whose hand he'd stepped on, answered in excited German, pointing to the southwest, their gestures indicating some kind of battle or explosion.

Walker tried to make some sense of it all. His head was throbbing from the long hours in the sea, his eardrums still ringing from the pounding they took in the waves. Maybe he hadn't heard the big guy saying something in English after all. Maybe he was hearing things. Yeah, that was it. Nothing to get his balls in a sweat over.

But he knew he was conning himself. Shit. That's what he heard. Well, so what? The German spoke a little English. Nothing suspicious about that. A sailor could easily pick up some English. But would it jump out like that when he was in sudden pain? Wouldn't he have automatically cursed in his own language?

It was broad daylight, but Walker felt as if he were locked in a dark room and could hear things, awful things, slithering across the floor toward him.

From a distance, he noticed the big redheaded man from the raft struggle back to his feet and sidle over to his officer, but he couldn't hear the brief exchange.

"He knows," Hammond whispered through motionless lips.

"Are you sure?" Beatty asked.

"He knows. Get rid of him."

70

Beatty nodded imperceptibly and Hammond moved away.

Walker sensed they were talking about him and that they knew he knew something was going on. He had to do something or his ass would be in a tight sling . . . if it wasn't already. Never taking his eyes off Hammond, Walker accepted a slug of whiskey from a crew-cut rating and maneuvered around the milling crowd of sailors to Beatty.

"Listen, Captain, can I talk to you?" Walker whispered.

"Yes, Herr Walker, what is it?" Beatty replied, still behind the cover of a German accent.

"Look—I'm not interfering in anybody's business."

"Business?" Beatty shrugged. "What business?"

"Whatever business." Walker gave him a meaningful look. "I don't know anything about anything, okay?"

"I don't know what you're referring to, Herr Walker," Beatty said. "Perhaps you have had too much of a shock."

"Only from hearing the big guy speak English," Walker answered. "But like I said, you don't have to worry about me."

"You were in the water too long," Beatty said, turning away indifferently.

Walker felt a surge of desperate anger because he knew he was being fucked over, and he tried to fight it down because he sensed the danger, but he was exhausted, his nerves raw, and before he could stop it, his anger spurted out.

"Listen, you tried to screw me out there," he rasped, jerking a finger at the sea. "So start leveling or I'm gonna screw you right here!"

Beatty glanced around. Several Germans were dangerously close.

"We'll talk later," he said.

"I may not be alive later!" Walker snapped. "I . . ."

"*Achtung!*"

The command behind them brought the *Ludendorff*'s crew and the men from the raft to immediate attention, forcing Walker to break off.

A tall, impeccably tailored figure in the uniform of a *Kapitän,* with four gleaming stripes on his sleeve, strode across the deck accompanied by his executive officer. Beatty watched the Kapitän carefully. He'd briefed himself on the commander of the *Ludendorff*'s personal life, habits and career, but was not quite prepared for the cool, controlled power of the man whose pale blue eyes, almost the color of the sky, surveyed the survivors from the raft.

Emerich Ziegler, Beatty knew, hadn't been given a coveted command through high connections in the Nazi party. He commanded the *Ludendorff* because he was the best. He graduated third in his class from the German Naval Academy at Flensburg, where ancient tattered flags hung from lofty corridors, inspiring the young cadet to carry on their glorious tradition. During the First War, twice wounded, twice decorated. As a young gunnery officer on the battle cruiser *Lützow,* Ziegler, resenting the German Navy's inferiority complex over Britain's alleged invincibility on the high seas, poured withering salvo after salvo at the enemy at the battle of Jutland, and in a duel at 9,000 yards the *Lützow* cut the British battle cruiser *Invincible* in half. Out of a crew of 1,031, only five survived. Jutland proved that the German Navy could fight, but the German nation lost and Ziegler witnessed the humiliation of the fleet's surrender at Scapa Flow.

Now, over twenty years later, Germany again wanted to crush England, and though Ziegler had an image of himself as a man of breeding and culture, the finest product of German civilization, the catalyst of war, Beatty suspected, was bringing out his true nature, which was as deadly as the armament on his ship.

"Heil Hitler!" Ziegler saluted, gloved hand upraised.

"Heil Hitler!" everyone responded, except for Walker, who didn't know exactly what to do.

The executive officer, Commander Paul Drau, bristling with military efficiency and decorated with a rather too-perfectly-placed dueling scar on his jaw, inspected their *soldbucher* with an eye trained for detail. Ziegler turned to Beatty.

"Kapitänleutnant von Brennerman, Viktor. Commander of *U-117*, sir," Beatty said, handing him his *soldbuch*.

For the moment Ziegler just held it.

"Are you all right? Your men?" he asked, shaking Beatty's hand.

"Some chapped lips, some nicotine pains . . . nothing serious," Beatty replied, keeping one eye on Walker, who stood uncomfortably close and white-lipped.

Ziegler glanced at Falco and Ayles, who were slumped on deck as if weak from too much exposure.

"Those two, can they stand?"

"I think so, sir," Beatty said.

"Then let them."

The dead calm in Ziegler's voice was so commanding that Falco and Ayles immediately shuffled to their feet.

Satisfied, Ziegler turned back to Beatty and inspected his papers rapidly, but thoroughly.

"How long were you on the water?"

"Forty hours."

Ziegler raised an eyebrow. "You never spotted another ship?"

"A couple. But our flares were wet and misfired. Fortunately, one of them dried out . . . unlike my cigarettes." Beatty crushed a wet pack from his shirt pocket.

Ziegler nodded and offered him a fresh Gauloise.

"One of the minor bonuses of conquering France," he said.

Beatty inhaled deeply. So far so good.

Ziegler turned to Commander Drau, who was inspecting young Tanner's papers.

"Everything in order, Drau?"

Drau looked up with a frown. "I'm afraid not, sir!"

"Oh?" Ziegler stepped closer.

Beatty's men tensed. Walker looked as if he was about to leap overboard and swim to Miami.

Drau held out Tanner's *soldbuch* disapprovingly. "This man has not had his final shots. Typhus, diphtheria, smallpox."

"Yes, yes, Drau. See that he gets them," Ziegler said.

The color returned to Hammond's beefy face. Shanks felt the icicle in his stomach melt. Beatty breathed again. Only Tanner looked unhappy at the thought of more needles.

Ziegler now turned to Walker, eyed him from sopping sports jacket to white flannel slacks.

"And what do we have here?" he asked.

"An American, sir," Beatty answered before Walker could. "We picked him up."

74

"What happened to you?" Ziegler asked in the precisely enunciated English that he'd learned at the naval academy, and which he'd honed by reading every book he could find on British naval strategy and tactics.

"I was on a steamer, sir," Walker said. "A German steamer. We hit a loose mine. At least I think that's what it was."

"Any survivors?"

Walker shrugged that he didn't know for sure.

"Inform the watch of possible survivors," Ziegler told Drau, then returned to Walker. "The steamer's name?"

"I don't know."

"You don't know?"

"Well, you see, I . . . uh, got on board in a hurry," Walker explained vaguely.

"Your passport, please," Ziegler ordered.

Walker fished into various pockets and finally came up with a soggy passport, which Ziegler inspected carefully.

"So, you were being deported from Germany," Ziegler noted, harder this time. "Why?"

"Nothing political, Captain, nothing political," Walker answered. "Just . . . well, I got into a card game with some big shots in Wiesbaden, and I sort of won one of the guy's wives, which didn't go over too good."

Walker tried to smile man-to-man over this, but Ziegler regarded him glacially. Walker was afraid that Ziegler would now ask what brought him to Wiesbaden in the first place, and that he'd have to go into the whole business of the thirty-eight-hour bacarrat marathon in Monte Carlo that left him near broke, and the countess at the same table who was so proud because she'd just had the first complete face and body lift in Germany and wanted to show it off before the whole thing collapsed again, and how she'd invited him to see it in her chalet in quiet Wiesbaden, still undisturbed by the war, and then him finding out that she wasn't a widow as she'd claimed but had a husband, a colonel in the Wehrmacht, and how all he needed was a Wehrmacht colonel dropping in on them while he was getting his cock sucked, so he eased himself out like a gentleman before he got caught and became involved with an interesting crowd at a nearby spa, and found himself in a card game, this time with an aging fertilizer tycoon from Argentina and got eyes for the guy's wife, a nineteen-year-old girl with long, tight-skinned legs that gleamed, and . . .

"What are you doing in Europe to begin with?" Ziegler probed.

"Bad breaks. I had some union negotiations. Only they negotiated with baseball bats and I lost the night club I had in Frisco," Walker explained. "So I thought I'd spin my wheels in Europe awhile."

"What kind of spinning was that? The authorities list you as having no visible means of income."

"Uh . . . I sort of free lanced."

"You left on a tramp steamer instead of a regular liner. The free-lancing must have been getting slim."

"I got a little short of cash. . . . It happens."

"I see." Ziegler turned to Beatty. "Any questions, Commander von Brennerman?"

"No, sir. I have a very clear picture," Beatty said.

"Since America is not at war, Herr Walker," the captain said, "I must accord you all courtesy required by the good relationship between our countries . . ." He smiled icily. "So be careful!"

Suddenly, the *Ludendorff*'s *glocken,* the alarm bells, erupted with an ear-splitting ring.

Walker didn't know exactly what it meant, but years of living by his wits had sharpened his survival instincts to a fine edge. He was one of the first to run as two British Hurricanes bolted out of the sun.

The pilots must have known they couldn't do any real damage against a battleship, but just attacking one would make a good story back at the pub on base, so for the hell of it they dove down, their twelve Browning machine guns snarling.

The crew raced for battle stations, swiftly donning flak helmets. A German rating plunged off a ladder as if struck by a hammer. Two of the English, Maltin and Ayles, sprinted for cover but staggered under a burst of gunfire.

Another burst zigzagged across the deck, ricocheting against the armor plate as it headed straight for Walker. He raced against it for the shelter of a winch and dove head-first under it, hunching himself into a ball as the bullets hammered into the steel all around him. The noise was shattering, and Walker was certain that within a few seconds he would be dead. His life didn't pass before him, just a stark image of himself huddled in the same position as now, only gone, finished. The image was so terrifying that he didn't hear a new sound.

The *Ludendorff*'s 37-mm A.A. guns barked, firing tracer bullets that seemed to float slowly in white, green, orange and red arcs toward the attacking planes, the arcs crossing paths with the tracers fired by the Browning machine guns. The sky hummed with steel, was pockmarked with brown shellbursts. Empty ack-ack casings rolled clanging across the decks.

Walker felt a stab of pain in his head that made him

cry out, and thought he was hit. It was the ear-splitting crash of a 4.1-inch gun.

One of the Hurricanes, screaming in again at 350 mph, swept the *Ludendorff*'s bridge with machine-gun fire, then Rolls-Royce engines straining, tried to outrace the tracer bullets. Its shadow darted across the ship as it pulled out of its dive, the tracers pursuing it. A filigree of black smoke showed from the wing, a tongue of flame, and the fighter disintegrated in a fiery ball, pieces raining into the sea. The other veered off, disappearing into the clouds.

When it was certain that the Hurricane wasn't returning, the cease-fire gong sounded and Ziegler snapped out orders.

"Resume cruising speed. Fall out action stations. Inspect for damage!"

The humming turbines and the vibrations of the great ship filled Beatty's ears, but it seemed like silence after the fury of the attack. He rushed over to Ayles lying on the deck. Though his body was still twitching, Ayles was already dead, half his face gone, his brains splattered on a barbette behind him. In a moment, the twitching stopped.

Beatty turned to Maltin. Maltin breathed heavily, one hand clutching his jacket where a red splotch on the right side of his stomach oozed blood that formed a scarlet rivulet on the deck. Another bullet had torn a patch of hair and skin from the top of his head. Maltin tried to say something, but choked on a mouthful of blood. Two medical corpsmen rushed over and stretchered him away.

Beatty rose slowly from one knee, spotting Maltin's blood on his hand and attempting to rub it off on his leather pants, but it only smeared. In front of the Germans, he tried not to look the way he felt. For the first time in his life he had seen someone he knew, Ayles, alive one moment, dead the next. Another wounded, probably dying. Two men lost, and it was he who had led them to this. They'd been aboard the *Ludendorff* barely ten minutes.

In the aftermath of the sudden violence, Hammond recovered first, dashing over, his eyes hunting.

"The Yank," he whispered low.

Beatty wheeled, searching for the American. "Herr Walker!" he called. No answer. "Walker!"

Walker, still under the winch, peered out.

"Yeah, what?" he asked flatly, almost as if he preferred the lethal fighter planes to Beatty.

Beatty and his team, along with Walker, were escorted by Commander Drau down a steep companionway to quarters below deck. Walker had never been on a warship before and had a sudden feeling of being trapped as they were led through a labyrinth of steel passageways with no windows, almost no headroom, the only light a cold glare from bare bulbs bouncing off gray bulkheads. He was still weak from his ordeal in the sea and was hit by numb exhaustion from the long trek through the *Ludendorff*'s main deck. But the anticipation of danger started his adrenalin pumping as he was led through the lethal monster, past machine shops, boiling steam counters in a huge galley, a diving locker, an optical shop and compartments filled with equipment he couldn't possibly recognize. Everywhere, the *Ludendorff*'s passageways were crisscrossed by networks of other passageways, as if the battleship were a huge steel hive.

They descended by ladder to the second deck, two

levels below the upper deck. Walker could hear the constant hum of unseen generators, the slam of watertight doors, which made him feel even more trapped.

He wanted to get the tall U-boat commander . . . or whatever the hell he was . . . alone again, but there was no chance right now. There was even less when they reached a large, empty compartment with strung hammocks. Beatty said something to Drau, who nodded and had Walker, as a civilian and a foreigner, separated from the others and ordered into a small compartment of his own. The door was slammed behind him.

Walker looked around. It was barely a cell. Bunk, washbasin, no head, no portholes. Walker slumped on the bunk that was covered with a rough green blanket and a hard pillow. He had a desperate urge to sleep, but fought it down. He rose again, pressed his ear to the door and tried to hear the others in the compartment across the passageway. He could only hear muffled sounds over the *Ludendorff*'s incessant engines. Walker cursed to himself. Being unable to eavesdrop increased his feeling of defenselessness.

Beatty's men were changing into black work pants and heavy black sweaters, under the watchful eye of a big, soft quartermaster with a pink face.

"Please, nothing must be thrown away. Everything must be signed for," said Alex Schnaubel, as he passed out gear, delighted to be of service to the new men. "No, no, that doesn't fit," Schnaubel told Tanner, who'd put on a loose T-shirt. The German came up with another.

"Don't bother. This is fine," Tanner said, surprising himself at how easily he shifted into the German of his grandparents, the German which had been such an embarrassment to him as a boy in England.

"No, no, no," Schnaubel clucked. "You listen to me. A good-looking boy like you must look just so."

Wanting no trouble, Tanner pulled off the loose shirt, baring a tightly muscled chest and ridged abdominals, and put on the new one, which was just a bit tight.

Schnaubel played it cool but didn't miss any of it.

"Nice," the pudgy German said, lifting an eyelid slightly.

Tanner, innocent and not quite sure of what Schnaubel was all about, shot the German a puzzled look.

Across the passageway, alone in his cubicle, Walker nervously fished into his pockets and removed a handful of soaked bills, dollars, Deutschmarks, liras. He unfolded them, laid them out neatly and carefully dabbed at them with a towel. He did it as much from nerves taut as banjo strings as from a desire to preserve all he had left in the world. Through his fatigue he had a rising urge to let the *Ludendorff*'s captain know something was coming off and that he sure as hell wasn't part of it. Yeah, he thought sourly, maybe honesty is the best policy. It had never been before but maybe he should try it now.

To see if he could, Walker peered through a crack in the door. Two of the men from the raft were in the passageway, keeping an eye on his compartment. They could have guns, and he wouldn't stand a chance making a run for the deck.

He silently closed the door again and swore to himself. If the English and the Germans wanted to kill each other, fuck 'em. He had no interest in European politics or any politics at all, in fact had never voted even in an American election, regarding all politicians as crooked bastards, guilty until proven innocent and then don't be too sure. Every year or so, it seemed to Walker, a new one popped up with big promises, and the country would jerk off over him and think how they'd finally found themselves a real leader, and then he'd turn out to be like all the others, and the country would wait for the next election, the next guy, and if it had any jism left it'd start jerking off all over again. They believed because they wanted to, because they had to, because the truth was too scary. Walker, however, liked to think of himself as a realist. The only difference between the local assemblymen he'd encountered in San Francisco . . . they'd usually come to his night club with bimbos clinging to their arms . . . and the clowns in Washington, was that the Washington boys used fancier words, made bigger promises, wore more expensive suits and humped more expensive hookers. And could steal more. Then, when they got caught with their hands in the till, the judge, who was usually in somebody's pocket, let them off with a suspended sentence and a character reference for a nice soft job. It was a realism, or cynicism, about people that came naturally to Walker.

He expected and wanted nothing from anybody. He had a way about him, a smile that could charm a nun. But that was camouflage, self-protection. We live as we dream, alone, he'd read someplace. It always stuck in his mind.

There was a rap on the compartment door and Walker quickly scooped the money together and sat on it as the two men who'd been guarding the passageway . . . Falco and Hammond . . . stepped inside. They were so big they practically filled the entire compartment. Without saying anything, Hammond, the bigger of the two, nodded for Walker to follow them. He saw they meant business.

Trying to look calm, Walker stuffed the damp money

into his pockets and started for the door, but the men opened it first, getting an all-clear sign from Shanks, who was keeping watch in the passageway. Hammond took Walker's arm with a heavy grip.

"Be nice!" Walker warned, peeling Hammond's fingers off, figuring that if he played it hard they might not be so quick to push him around. It didn't work. The hulking giant grabbed him in a wristlock and the other shouldered him against the wall so he couldn't move. He knew enough to see they were pros at this kind of thing.

Clamped between Falco and Hammond, he was escorted down the passageway and hustled toward another compartment, Hammond using hands and elbows to keep him moving fast.

"Don't handle me," Walker hissed, losing his temper again in spite of the danger. "I don't like being handled!"

They were unimpressed.

Walker found himself confronted in the second compartment by Beatty. Beatty nodded for the others to leave, but the American knew they'd stand guard outside.

Alone, Beatty regarded Walker coolly for a moment.

"You wanted to know the drill up there," he said, dropping all pretense of a German accent. "All right," he continued quietly. "We're hijacking the *Ludendorff*."

Walker stared. The suddenly perfect English combined with the meaning of the words dazed him and he stood there speechless.

"We're taking this ship," Beatty repeated.

"Oh," Walker replied, not believing him. "Yeah, well good luck."

"We are taking this ship tonight," Beatty repeated, harder this time.

"You gotta be joking," Walker said, though he suspected now that maybe the Englishman wasn't joking.

Beatty let it sink in by not saying anything, just meeting Walker's stare.

"Well, look, you don't have to worry about me," Walker said quickly. "Like I told you before. I know how to keep my mouth shut. I'm a *shtummy*."

"I know you are," Beatty agreed.

"You do what you want," Walker said somewhat relieved. "I'm only interested my ass isn't sticking out."

"But it is. Whether we succeed or not, the Germans will assume you're part of it. You were picked up on the same raft with us."

"I could tell them . . ."

"You could tell them what you want. Once the shooting started they wouldn't hear you over the noise."

Walker knew it was true and realized he had to do some awfully good talking or things would start hitting the fan. But what approach could he take with a guy who, if he was completely in his right mind, wouldn't be here in the first place talking about capturing a battleship. Sincerity! He was always good at that when he needed it.

"Look, let me level with you," he said. "Whatever I say, it's for my own skin. Okay, fine. Nothing wrong with that. What guy isn't worried about his own skin? But think about yourself, too. You had an idea. You were gonna take over a battleship. Okay, fine. You're a ballsy guy."

He paused a second to see if he was reaching Beatty. It was hard to tell, but at least Beatty was listening.

God, how he'd like to ram his fist down the English-man's throat.

"I admire guts," he continued sincerely. "But now that you're here, you see the size of this thing, and what've you got? You just lost two of your men up there. That hadda throw your whole plan off. You don't have enough men to take over a Chinese laundry."

"You're perfectly right about the number of men," Beatty conceded quietly.

"Exactly." Walker was encouraged. At least the cocksucker isn't crazy, he thought. "Just for openers you'd need more men."

"That's right," Beatty conceded again.

"Sure I am. We're in the middle of the ocean. Where're you gonna get more men, even one m . . ." Walker's voice trailed off as it dinged in on him. The throb of the *Ludendorff*'s engines pounded in his ears. "Ohhh no," Walker said. "No you don't."

He backed up instinctively until his heels banged against the door. Beatty didn't say a word, just fixed him with a look.

"Listen, man," Walker shook his head. "You got the wrong guy. This isn't my kind of thing. I'd be scared shitless. I'm scared shitless already."

"Night clubs, union hoods, tangling with the German police, who knows what else," Beatty said. "You'll do."

"You're crazy. For your own sake I'm telling you," Walker pleaded. "I'll fuck it all up. I don't know a damn thing about boats, your plan, nothing."

"There isn't much you have to know. What there is, I'll show you," Beatty replied.

"I don't want on-the-job training. I'm a neutral. Know what that means? It means someone who doesn't fight."

"Too late for that, Walker."

"Too late hell. I've stayed alive keeping out of other people's problems. The minute someone starts talking about their problems, I go take a piss."

"All the heads are full up," Beatty said firmly. "I could kill you right now. But I need you to pull this thing off."

Walker slumped down on an iron stool, trying to figure some way out of this, some way of tricking the Englishman.

Beatty studied him closely. "If you're thinking of conning me by saying okay," he said, "and then running to Kapitän Ziegler first chance, I wouldn't advise it."

"Hey, man. That's not my style," Walker said.

"Perhaps. But I still wouldn't advise it, because Ziegler'd throw all of us, including you, in the brig and take us back to Germany for an investigation."

"That'd be tough shit on you, not me."

"Don't be so sure. An investigation would take months," Beatty pointed out. "By that time America could be swept into the war, she's almost in it already, and you'd be sent to a concentration camp. The Germans send you to one of those camps, and you disappear forever."

Beatty's words tolled like a bell for Walker. Open his mouth to the Germans and he'd wind up, maybe forever, behind Nazi barbed wire. Help the British and some Kraut bullet was bound to drill him another ass hole. Either way he was screwed.

"Why should I risk getting killed for you?" he asked. "You were gonna let me drown out there."

"Because I'll make it worth your while," said Beatty, who'd suspected it would come down to this. "Throw in with us and you'll get $15,000 out of my pocket. Deposited to a number in a Swiss bank."

"You think I'd risk my life for a lousy couple of dollars?"

"You want to go back to the States broke, a loser?"

"Who's a loser?" Walker shot back.

Beatty knew he'd touched a raw nerve.

"Bumming around Europe, deported, you had a night club and lost it . . ."

"Not lost. Pushed. By union hoods," Walker said grimly, remembering the taste of being muscled out after seven years of nothing but sweat, first as a waiter, then as a bouncer, wearing cheap Bond suits and living in a rat's nest so's to save enough money to buy a piece of the action. A lot of good it did him.

A lot of good he got from anything he'd done since then, too. Getting thrown out of Germany, in fact, for balling a big shot's wife the way he did was one of the *better* things that happened. Had he stayed in Germany, or if he were returned now in the *Ludendorff*, in another few days, a week, something *else* was bound to catch up with him. Nothing that awful really. At the time he pulled it off, it was rather profitable and nobody, not even the German baroness, really got hurt. Hell, in a way it was even kind of funny. But once they found out, the German authorities wouldn't see it that way. It was the kind of thing they gave you, especially a foreigner, fifteen years in the slammer for, and he could just see himself pushing fifty, getting out of a Deutsche jail with no money, no prospects, a wipe-out.

Walker shuddered to himself. Now here was this shmuck across the room, waiting for his answer, offering him a lot of money to risk his ass. Really risk his ass. He could remember as a kid, he wasn't even twenty, during Prohibition driving a truck, delivering stuff because they said it was safe, everyone was paid off, and one time in Jersey getting the bottles in back riddled with machine-gun bullets by another outfit and from then on riding with, though he never had to use it, a .32 under the dash. That was for thirty-five bucks a week. Now he was talking fifteen thousand.

"You don't have that kind of money," Walker said.

"I own a good part of the home counties," Beatty replied matter-of-factly.

Walker, who'd always had a nose for the rich, sensed it was true. Beatty watched as he circled the bait like a trout.

"What if you got knocked off?" Walker asked.

"My men'd see that you were paid."

"What if you *all* got it?"

"Then so would you," Beatty replied simply.

Walker turned it around, trying to see all the sides. "What if we . . . what if you could grab this thing?" he asked. "Then what?"

Beatty caught himself before mentioning the *Ludendorff* attacking the U-boat base at Skagen. That's all the American would have to hear.

"Under a German flag, we'll race it to a port," he answered generally.

"Just like that, huh?"

"No, but that's what you'd get paid for."

Walker paced the narrow compartment. Beatty knew he had to hook him now while the vision of the money was as strong as the prospect of the danger.

"You've been looking for a bundle all your life," Beatty said. "Now here's your chance. In one jump."

Walker stopped pacing. He could hear the slap of a

high wave as the *Ludendorff* crashed her way through the sea. He turned to Beatty and let out a deep breath.

"Raise the box tops to twenty-five thousand and you've got yourself a boy," he said.

CHAPTER 7

A harsh rasp, like a man trying to cough up sandpaper lodged in his throat, filled the *Ludendorff*'s sick bay.

Hearing it, Beatty could feel with every raw nerve in his body just how close the mission was to disaster. He stood at the side of a cot, looking down at Maltin's face, which was almost as white as the bandages that swathed his head. The dark eyebrows were in a tight straight line, knit together in pain. Except for Maltin, the other cots in the sick bay were empty, which only seemed to magnify the sound of his labored breathing.

Beatty observed Maltin with Leutnant Mark Preisser, the battleship's surgeon, whose bifocals and neatly trimmed beard and mustache gave him the appearance, oddly, of a young and vigorous Sigmund Freud.

"A perforating stomach wound," he told Beatty, "and a subdural hemotoma."

Beatty looked up at the doctor.

"Brain concussion," Preisser explained.

Beatty nodded. "How serious?"

"Either wound is serious. Together . . ."

Preisser didn't have to complete the sentence. He tapped his stethoscope against his leg in the nervous gesture of a surgeon who has done all he could but wished he could do more.

Maltin's eyes remained closed but his body twisted spastically, and he moaned, a low moan that rose in pitch and strangled itself in a tormented sigh.

"Stomach wounds . . ." Preisser shook his head.

Beatty wondered how much agony Maltin could take and still keep his senses, still play a role in front of the Germans. No man, not even a young bull like Maltin could maintain absolute control under sufficient pain and certainly not under delirium.

Afraid of what Maltin might do or say, Beatty turned to Preisser.

"Whatever you can do to ease the pain."

"Of course," Preisser nodded.

It occurred to Beatty that he personally liked Maltin, a sturdy Yorkshireman who combined an aggressive, combative streak with an unexpected sensitivity that expressed itself in big, bold, splashing paintings that he sold for next to nothing while studying art on a meager scholarship in Austria before the war.

Maltin stirred and opened his eyes. Beatty leaned over to catch Maltin's attention first.

"How do you feel, Kleist?" he asked.

"Head aches," Maltin said. Weakly, he tried to shift on the pillow. "But I'll be all right . . . be all right, Herr Doktor."

He said it in perfectly controlled German to Preisser but it was meant for Beatty.

"I will be all right," Maltin repeated almost insistently, sensing what he knew had to be Beatty's concern.

"You'd better leave now," Preisser told Beatty.

"I don't mind staying," Beatty replied, afraid of leaving Maltin alone with the German. He could see the same fear in Maltin's face.

Preisser shook his head firmly.

"He's better off resting."

Beatty couldn't insist on staying without making a dangerous issue of it, but he still made no move to go.

"I assure you, Commander von Brennerman," Preisser said with an edge of impatience, "I shall keep a very careful eye on him."

"I'd appreciate that," Beatty said.

He touched Maltin's shoulder encouragingly. Feverish sweat had soaked the sheet covering his body.

As Beatty turned to leave the sick bay, Maltin's tortured breathing followed him out the door. In the passageway, Beatty flinched at a terrible wish. He wished that Maltin had been killed outright. And since he hadn't, Beatty feared that he might have to kill Maltin himself.

Muscles gleaming with sweat, shoes crashing in unison, four rows of bare-chested Germans were doing morning drills with Germanic discipline on the quarter-deck, led by a petty officer, Rheinbolt, who had the thick sloping shoulders and scarred face of a boxer. There probably weren't more than twenty-five or thirty sailors lined up, but to Walker, seeing them swinging arms and legs with such precision, they looked like the whole fucking Navy. Their brush cuts made them appear all alike, gave them a unity, and they had the tight-mouthed, fixed-eyed look of men trained to face battle. He had already seen what they did against the British planes, his right ear still ached from the vicious crack of the 4.1-inch ack-ack gun, and he could imagine the swift violence they'd unleash against any threat aboard the *Ludendorff* itself. And he couldn't blame them. Hell, it was their ship. But it was his life, and though he'd never killed anyone before, he figured that if he had to, he could. But could he do it fast, efficiently, as many times as necessary without losing his head and walking into some goddamn bullet?

"Liegestütz!" Rheinbolt barked.

From a rigid, standing position, the Germans fell straight forward, landed on their hands and in one smooth motion began doing push-ups, some of them, the real *shtarkers*, balanced on their finger tips or clapping their hands together between each push-up.

Although they were supposed to be exhausted from two days on a raft, some of the British had joined the drill because the Germans, they knew, would expect that kind of Spartan grit from U-boat men. It was a treat for the German fag, Schnaubel, who was exercising near young Tanner and giving him kittenish smiles. In the middle of a push-up Tanner noticed it and almost collapsed, but he caught himself and kept going, his head angled away from Schnaubel.

Midway through, Rheinbolt increased the tempo and Shanks, trying to pass himself off as young enough to be in the Navy, strained his milk to keep up with youths barely one third his age. At the count of forty, most of the Germans had pooped out and at fifty push-ups Shanks's arms began to bind up. But he burned out the last ten and then eased himself up, slower than some of the others but not much slower, with a very pleased-with-himself look on his face. Off to the side, Walker threw him a nod. A smile flickered across Shanks's face.

Suddenly, the *Ludendorff*'s loudspeaker crackled to life with the blast of a whistle and the metallic voice of the bosun's mate from the bridge. "All hands fall in for muster and inspection."

The inspection on the fantail, delayed by the attack of the British planes, brought out nearly a hundred more crewmen, and though Walker knew about them, seeing a hundred Germans massed together tightened his throat. He mentally divided fourteen, the number of English with him included, into three hundred and fifty, to figure how many Germans he'd have to handle by himself. It came to something like over twenty. Jesus, he thought.

Then came the crash of boots at double time and twenty-five men, all over six feet, appeared in black helmets, blue combat uniforms, carrying bolt-action Mauser rifles. At an order from their lieutenant, as one man they fixed bayonets with the clash of metal on metal. They were obviously from some kind of elite fighting unit and their precision chilled Walker. He approached a young officer with a clipboard, inspecting lifeboats amidships.

"Sharp outfit," Walker said casually.

"Marines," the officer said. "They hitched a ride to Kiel."

"Oh, marines," Walker nodded. He tried to smile admiringly. "Sharp."

"Ya. Very sharp," the German said, returning to the lifeboats.

Walker glanced back at the crack marine unit, then saw Beatty above on the boat deck. Beatty had an eye on the marines, too. Walker climbed a ladder to the boat deck and motioned Beatty behind a twin 20-mm machine-gun mount.

"You said this was a skeleton crew!" Walker whispered low.

"It is," Beatty answered.

"There's a lot of meat down there for a skeleton crew."

"Later!" Beatty snapped.

"How do you know there ain't a whole fucking division down in the basement?"

"I looked," Beatty said dryly.

"What about them? You didn't even know about them," Walker said, his eyes drawn back to the marines.

"I'm figuring them in now," Beatty said.

"Now," Walker repeated sourly. "Terrific."

Beatty concealed his own concern about the marines, but in fact was just as worried about Maltin in the sick bay as he was about the marines on deck.

Below on the quarterdeck, Kapitän Ziegler, flanked by Commander Drau, carefully inspected the crew.

At the end of one line, Ziegler stopped, spotting dirt on a cleat at the gunwale. He turned and quietly asked, "Who is responsible? Whose detail is this?"

The question was addressed to Drau but was meant for the men. After a long moment, a boy with ink-black hair and gaps between his front teeth stepped forward, frightened.

"Your name?" Ziegler demanded.

"Helmreich, Herr Kapitän," the boy said.

"Well?"

"It's . . . it's the height, sir," Helmreich said. "Every time I go near the edge, I get sick."

"There is only one cure for fear. Conquer it," Ziegler said, almost kindly. But then, with a nod to the guardrail, he ordered, "Over!"

"Yes, sir." The sailor seemed to will his body to move, but it refused.

"Over," Ziegler repeated.

Terrified, Helmreich moved stiff-legged to the guard-rail and climbed over the rail backward so he wouldn't have to look down at the churning sea. He held onto the rail, hands clenched white, too paralyzed with fear to bend down. Ziegler fixed him with a glare that was an order. Helmreich slowly unwrapped one hand, fumbled for a handkerchief, kneeled and tried pathetically to wipe the cleat clean. His body shaking, he was drawn irresistibly to look down at the dizzying rollers, and panic crept into his eyes.

At a glance from Ziegler, one of the marines stationed himself at the rail to prevent Helmreich from climbing back. His panic rising, the boy inched his body as far from the edge of the ship as possible, until his back touched the point of the marine's bayonet. The marine automatically withdrew the blade an inch, but at a look from Ziegler moved it back. Helmreich, cringing in blind fear, didn't even feel the bayonet go through his shirt.

From the boat deck, Walker and Beatty could see a patch of blood form on Helmreich's shirt, heard a low whimper come from his chest, carried faintly across the deck by the wind. The boy dropped his handkerchief. It fluttered down to the sea, was snatched away by a wave. He sank back to his knees, clutching the guard-rail, eyes tight shut, moaning now like an animal. Ziegler left him there to continue the inspection.

Walker felt sick. So did Beatty, who had to force himself not to turn his eyes away. But in a sense he was grateful for the scene. It gave him a better idea of the kind of man he was up against in Kapitän Ziegler.

Now Ziegler stopped at the Frenchman, Falco. Falco stared straight ahead, not daring to meet Ziegler's eyes, afraid that somehow the Kapitän suspected he wasn't German. Ziegler's hand reached out for Falco's throat.

"Sloppy!" Ziegler snapped, tearing off the bandanna around Falco's neck. "Where were you trained?"

"At the Heilgenhaffen, Herr Kapitän," Falco said.

"That's not the way they taught you at the Heilgenhaffen," Ziegler snapped.

Under the Kapitän's glare, Falco started to retie it, then hesitated. He'd been thoroughly drilled at S.O.E. on the German Navy's regulations and dress codes, and he thought he remembered everything. But in the excitement and tension of boarding the *Ludendorff*, he'd forgotten how to tie a lousy knot. He wanted to dart a look at a nearby German but was afraid that would be a giveaway. Ziegler was looking at him, waiting. What if he couldn't tie a regulation knot a second time? The Boche would become suspicious, see through the men picked up on the raft. Falco felt a drop of sweat trickle down his crotch. If he was going to die, he had the sudden urge to take Ziegler with him, to smash the German's jugular with one quick chop.

"That is correct. Next time don't forget," he heard Ziegler saying.

Puzzled, Falco looked down. There was a perfect knot. As his brain whirled, without his even knowing it, his hands had automatically, instinctively, tied a second knot correctly. Even so he could still feel sweat trickling down his balls.

Ziegler stopped at Perth. Blond, blue-eyed, skin pulled tight across his cheekbones, he looked like an enlistment poster for the German Navy.

"Your name?" Ziegler asked.

"Hochmuth, Emil. Torpedo man, Herr Kapitän," Perth snapped out.

"Excellent, excellent," Ziegler smiled. "You're the kind of man we need."

"Heil Hitler!" Perth saluted.

Falco's eyes swiveled, giving Perth a withering look. When it came time to kill Germans, he would keep a very careful eye on Perth.

The inspection over, Ziegler climbed back to the bridge, signaling Beatty to come with him. Face stern and set, the Kapitän said nothing as they mounted the ladders, and Beatty wondered whether the German had seen or sensed his revulsion over the incident with the boy at the guardrail.

They entered the Kapitän's sea cabin aft the wheelhouse, with deep plum-colored carpets and dominated by a magnificently carved rosewood desk from eighteenth-century Spain. Pointing Beatty to a chair, Ziegler put a record on the gramophone behind the desk, filling the cabin with the sparkling first movement from Mendelssohn's violin concerto.

"That's better," Ziegler smiled, easing himself into his leather chair. He studied Beatty a moment. "I hope you did not misunderstand what I had to do down there."

"Do?" Beatty asked.

"Putting the boy over the rail."

"I saw it only as discipline," Beatty replied carefully.

"And that is all?"

"That's all."

"Come now. Let's be frank. I detected something else in your face," Ziegler said, watching him closely.

Beatty shrugged, giving himself another second to think of an answer.

"It's not pleasant to see a German sailor cower or show fear," he said.

"I see. . . . You don't think that came easily to me, that kind of brutality, do you?"

"I'm not sure I would call it brutality, sir."

"But why not? I went against my upbringing, my class, even against my nature. It was very brutal. I had to steel myself to do it."

"I'm not sure I follow you."

"Von Brennerman, young as you are, you must know Germany is filled with men who indulge in barbarism for its own sake. I do it as a *political* necessity. They do it as an emotional, personal necessity."

"I imagine there might be a few like that," Beatty said. Ziegler obviously meant men like Hitler, Himmler, Goebbels. Was he trying for some reason to lure Beatty into a slip of the tongue?

"More than a few," Ziegler said. "And the longer this war lasts, the further entrenched they become. That's why, before it's too late, we must end this war quickly, ruthlessly, before like Dr. Jekyll and Mr. Hyde, Hyde takes over completely, forever."

"Barbarism in the name of civilization."

"If you wish. For if we can be brutal to ourselves, think what we can be to our enemies," Ziegler said, his cold eyes on Beatty.

In that moment, Ziegler let slip his pretense of civilization. Intelligence reports had indicated that Ziegler, like his chief, Gross-admiral Raeder, considered himself a professional military man superior to the gutter rabble that'd come to power in Germany. Before the war such officers even raised an occasional mild voice against Nazi excesses, the street violence and political terrorism. But they supported Hitler because they said he was a historical necessity. The Austrian corporal possessed the power to tap the wellsprings of insecurity and resentment of the German masses. Now, they were all reaping the harvest, a Germany rising from ashes, on the march again. Now they, the Zieglers, raised their voices no longer because that had been their dream, too, all along. They and Hitler, to whom they'd ransomed their souls, were created in the same image.

The music on the gramophone behind Ziegler unfolded in a rhapsodic passage.

"Ah, just listen," Ziegler smiled to Beatty with genuine pleasure. "Whenever I attend a concert in Berlin these days, I am bombarded with Wagner. Heavy, Teutonic Wagner. Frankly, he gives me headaches. Thank God out here I can listen to Mendelssohn. . . . A Jew of course, but . . ." Ziegler shrugged. "I hope some of them are left after this war to entertain us."

The *Ludendorff*'s great forward engines beat in Hammond's ears, and hearing them this close while hidden out of sight in a deserted passageway gave him an almost illicit thrill, as if he were spying on a woman who didn't know he was there.

Hammond had feigned exhaustion to avoid Ziegler's inspection on deck and had slipped below to check out the engine room through an open hatch one level above. The engine rooms were one of the most crucial targets in the take-over, and before the British could make any move that night, a careful bead had to be drawn on them. From years of dealing with complicated machinery, Hammond knew that it was one thing to get some idea of a battleship from Intelligence reports and diagrams pieced together back in London. It was another thing to plant his feet down here, to get the feel and smell and his own hard look at what he'd be going up against.

Even now Hammond could only see a small part of the vast humming room below. But from what he did see, he filled in the whole picture of the intricate dungeon. The officer of the watch, the chief of the watch, the throttle man, eyes trained on revolution indicators, thermometers, gauges. The ninety-degree heat that invaded the body and sapped energy. The high-pitched whine of the turbines that invaded the eardrums and obliterated sound, so that the men, like mutes, communicated by a private system of hand signals. Out of sight, below the control room with its throttle board, which regulated the ship's speed, was the operating level, which controlled the pumps, and below that the bilge, which controlled the valves, a three-level network of great power and finely balanced complexity.

Though it was an enemy ship, Hammond felt strangely at home down here, for he loved engines. Engines were comprehensible, which was more than he could say for so much else in his life.

Boilers, pressure, shafts, turbines, screws, they were predictable, direct, clean, and he resented the popular conception of engine rooms as dank, dirty, greasy places operated by dirty subhuman men. Grease and dirt were fire and accident hazards and not tolerated in modern engine rooms, which were kept clean and spotless as hospital corridors. Cleaner. Hammond had only one emotion toward marine engines. Admiration. He was going to enjoy taking over the *Ludendorff*'s great engines and making them his.

He glanced up and down the empty passageway and spotted what he was looking for, a large fuse box. He swiftly opened the steel door and scrutinized an electrical panel, a maze of switches and circuit breakers. He understood the function of each instantly. Engraved on the inside of the door was a schematic circuitry diagram of the *Ludendorff*. Swiftly, expertly, Hammond copied key details with a pencil stub on a scrap of paper.

Suddenly, he heard a sound. With no time to hide the paper, he crumpled it in his hand and turned innocently. A tall, wiry boilerman with a large pitted nose had rounded a corner in the passageway. The German noticed the panel door ajar. He stopped.

"What're you doing?" he asked.

"Nothing. Just curious," Hammond shrugged. "I've never been on a battleship before."

"But this is forbidden. You're not ship's company."

"Sorry," Hammond said meekly. He turned and started to leave.

"What have you there?" the German demanded, pointing to Hammond's closed fist.

Hammond didn't answer.

"You come with me to the exec," the German ordered.

"Ah, I have nothing," Hammond said with a smile, stepping closer, holding his hand open.

The German brought his head down to look. Hammond drove the heel of his hand into the German's jaw, snapping the head back, then smashing his elbow at the exposed neck. It landed too low and the German lunged back. They crashed against the panel, the German tearing at Hammond's face with thick powerful fingers. Hammond clamped a hand across the German's mouth, stifling a cry for help, and tried to wrestle him to the deck. Thrashing wildly, the German inched a hand toward the heavy brass nozzle of a fire hose hanging from a hook. Hammond spun him around, but too late. The boilerman got to the nozzle. The brass club glanced off Hammond's shoulder with a sickening thud and clanged against the sweating bulkhead.

In the engine room below, one of the machinists looked up from the control panel. He thought he heard something over the turbine whine but hearing nothing again, returned to work, adjusting a valve.

In the passageway above, the German swung at Hammond again. He caught the nozzle in his hand and twisted it away. Afraid to use it as a club because of the noise, he jammed it against the German's windpipe. The German, back pressed against the bulkhead, lashed out with his feet, but Hammond put all his weight behind the nozzle against the boilerman's throat. His eyes stared wide. His mouth twisted open, tongue turning blue. Trying to signal for help, he banged his heavy boots against the deck.

In the engine room, the machinist was sure this time that he heard a muffled banging from somewhere. He closed off a valve, stuffed his rag into a pocket and climbed the ladder toward the level above.

Hammond, struggling with the German, heard boots ascending the engine room ladder. He wrestled the boilerman down the passageway away from the hatch, foot by foot, inch by inch, their mingled gasps muffled by the engine's roar.

Coming through the hatch from below, the machinist looked up and down the passageway. It was empty, except for the fire hose which seemed to have fallen from its rack. With an irritated shrug, the machinist replaced it and clumped down the ladder to his control room.

After a long moment, the door to a store closet in the passageway opened a crack. Hammond peered out. One arm propped up a sagging corpse.

CHAPTER 8

"I had to," Hammond told Beatty, voice low and tense.

"Who?"

"Some boilerman, name's Borgmann. He's off watch now so they won't miss him. Least not for a while."

The door to Beatty's cabin suddenly opened and Walker, who'd seen Hammond surreptitiously signaling to Beatty topside, slipped in. Walker sensed trouble and came to see what it was for himself.

Beatty turned back to Hammond. "Where is he?"

Hammond opened Beatty's clothes locker. The corpse inside started to slide out, the face a ghastly grayish blue, one glazed eye staring sideways.

"Oh, Jesus," Walker muttered.

Hammond slammed the locker door in time.

"Why'd you bring him here?" Beatty said.

"I couldn't leave him there," Hammond replied sharply.

Walker, staring at the clothes locker, shook his head. "Oh, Jesus," he muttered again.

"Stop saying that!" Hammond snarled, his nerves jumping. "In a minute I'll croak *you*."

Beatty forced himself between them. They peeled off angrily to opposite sides of the compartment. He turned to Hammond again.

"You say they won't miss him. For how long?"

"With the tubes being tested, no boilerman's gonna be off watch too long." Hammond shook his head. "He'll be due back tonight."

Beatty swiftly calculated the consequences of Borgmann not showing up. He'd be reported missing . . . an investigation would be held immediately . . . every crewman questioned . . . the machinist from the forward engine room would mention what sounded like a fight, a struggle . . . the ship would be searched far into the night. Every German would be awake. Impossible for fourteen men to take over the *Ludendorff* under those conditions.

Even if they could devise a cover for Borgmann's disappearance . . . a big if . . . any cover Beatty could think of would still keep the battleship awake. There was no way around that. There was no way, he was forced to realize, to catch the battleship off guard that night. His carefully integrated plan for the take-over would have to be delayed, put off to the following night.

That meant staying aboard a German-held battleship twenty-four hours more, increasing danger at every turn, so many unpredictable dangers that he couldn't worry about them now. He had to solve the problem of the dead German in the locker.

"When you were down there, did anyone else see you?"

"No," Hammond said.

Walker gave a sigh of relief.

"But a couple of 'em had to've seen me heading that way," Hammond admitted. "They couldn't help but."

"Oh, Jesus," Walker gasped.

Night. Two figures emerged through a blackout curtain and came out on the *Ludendorff*'s upper deck forward. One of them supported the other, who seemed to have difficulty keeping his feet as the battleship pounded through a choppy sea and a cold mist of rain.

The rain didn't fall. It hung in the air, whipped by the wind at the two men and up ladderways and across decks. The decks dripped, as if sweating even in the cold. In the moonlight, the wet armor plating looked like wax.

The two men stood on the swaying deck, the rain driving against their bulky pea coats. One of them was Hammond. He supported what looked remarkably like the dead German, Borgmann. Actually, it was Jenkins, wearing the boilerman's clothes with the jacket collar turned up against the weather and concealing most of his face. They saw four machine gunners at their watch behind a nearby 37-mm ack-ack mount.

Jenkins sagged, wobble-legged.

"Easy, Borgmann," Hammond said, loud enough for the Germans to hear. "You've been seasick before. You won't die."

At the same moment, below deck, Shanks stepped from Beatty's compartment, shouldering a large canvas laundry bag with a very heavy-looking load.

He hefted the dead weight for better balance and headed aft down the passageway. He saw a radioman approaching in the opposite direction. Shanks forced a

106

half-smile and nodded to the radioman. The German returned the nod as they passed.

Shanks could already feel the strain of the weight on his arms and wrists. He hoped the bag was strong enough, that the seams wouldn't split open.

On the upper deck, still in view of the ack-ack mount, Hammond led Jenkins to the rail, where Jenkins pretended to be sick. He eased Jenkins down against the flag bag, a fifteen-foot steel locker holding signal flags, and patted his shoulder. One of the machine gunners drifted over and looked at Jenkins, head bowed, face buried in his jacket collar.

"Take him to the sick bay maybe," the German suggested.

"Ach, all Borgmann needs is some air," Hammond said.

With some dry heaves that sounded surprisingly authentic, Jenkins nodded in agreement. "Yah, just air."

"Why suffer? Better go to the doctor," the gunner said.

Jenkins shook his head no.

"If you don't want to go to the doctor, Borgmann, you know what sometimes helps?"

"Uhh?" Jenkins groaned.

"Beating your meat. It takes your mind off it," the gunner said seriously. "It helped me."

"It's *still* helping you," another gunner deadpanned, approaching. He leaned over to help Jenkins up. "Come on, let's get you to the doctor."

In another second he'd see Jenkins' face.

Jenkins swiftly made the impossible effort to swallow his own tongue, gagged and vomited over the German's boot. The German drew back in disgust. "Borgmann, you son-of-a-bitch," he swore angrily.

"Leave him here," Hammond advised, with a wave of his hand. "He'll feel better after he vomits some more."

The German didn't move.

"You want him to get your other boot?" Hammond said wryly, moving toward a hatch.

With a sour look, the German stepped away carefully in his squishy boot.

"Borgmann" was left alone on the pitching deck.

Laundry bag slung over his shoulder, Shanks stopped for a moment to catch his breath and ease the load tearing at his wrists, then cut down another passageway. With head bowed low against the weight, he almost bumped into a barrel-chested petty officer coming out of his compartment. The petty officer looked at the bag.

"Laundry this late?"

"Our gear was so damn dirty," Shanks said. "The commander told me to get it washed."

"Wait!" The German ducked into his quarters and came back with two soiled denim jackets. "As a favor, *bitte*."

Shanks couldn't say no. But he needed both hands to manage the heavy bag and to take the jackets he had to put it down. He eased it off his shoulder and lowered it gently so it wouldn't thump, but the movement shifted the body inside so that an elbow strained at the seam. Shielding it with his chest as much as possible, Shanks opened the bag. The German stepped around Shanks to put his bundle in by himself, but Shanks swiftly speared it away and dumped it into the bag, tying it closed again before the German could get a glimpse of a clawlike hand and a pair of staring, sightless eyes.

"Danke," the German said.

With a nod, Shanks carefully heaved the bag back on his shoulder and trudged down the passageway.

"Hey!" the German called out sharply.

Shanks froze and turned slowly.

"No starch!"

On the upper deck, Jenkins slumped against the signal flag locker. The machine gunner at the ack-ack mount, not wanting to risk more vomit on his boots, called from a distance, "How do you feel, Borgmann?"

Jenkins groaned. He stole a swift glance at the luminous hands of his watch. Exactly two minutes to eleven.

One deck below, Shanks knocked softly on an armored door. It opened just enough for him to squeeze inside with his bundle. The door clanged shut behind him. He was in the anchor chain room, a huge dark cavern housing the giant steel links that held the *Ludendorff*'s stern anchor. His back aching, Shanks dumped the sack at the feet of Beatty and Walker. It landed with a thud. He turned to go, remembered something and reached into the bag for the two dirty denim jackets and left.

Beatty and Walker dragged Borgmann's corpse from the bag. Beatty didn't have to choose Walker for this night's work, any of his other men would do, but the busier he kept Walker, the less time the American would have to think, to panic. Even more important, Beatty needed to know how Walker performed under pressure. The next twenty-four hours would be harrowing. If Walker couldn't hack it, now was the time to find out.

The body resisted stiffly as Beatty grabbed hold of the legs, Walker the arms. They lugged it to the hawse pipe, the shaft through which chain and anchor shank were drawn. There was just enough space left in the shaft for a body to slip through and fall into the sea. They lifted the corpse to the lip of the hawse pipe and lowered it, holding it back by the legs. Beatty glanced at his watch. One-half minute before eleven o'clock.

On the upper deck, Jenkins let his head slump to the side and checked his watch. Almost eleven. But he still couldn't make his move. The machine gunners at the mount could still see him out of the side of their eyes. He waited. He'd have to chance it. Soon. One of the gunners lit a cigarette, hunching over the match to hide the flame. Another gunner hunched over with him to make it two on match. Jenkins quickly darted for the nearest hatch.

He prayed the gunners hadn't seen him.

At almost the same moment, Walker and Beatty let go of Borgmann's legs. The body dropped down the hawse pipe. With a scraping sound, it squeezed through the narrow hole. It landed on the *Ludendorff*'s anchor fluke, high above the sea. It hung there, stuck between the anchor and the ship's side, limbs twisted crazily. Walker stared down the hawse pipe at the body hanging in full view.

"Get him off there," Beatty ordered.

"Whatta you mean, get him off there?" Walker asked.

"Climb down. Get him off," Beatty rasped.

110

Walker peered down the hawse pipe again at the body wedged on the anchor, the sea racing below it. "Why don't you climb down!" Walker whispered hoarsely.

"Move!"

"Shit!"

"Move!"

"Don't rush me."

Very slowly, Walker eased himself into the hawse pipe feet-first and inched his way down, hugging the anchor shank. The ship's vibrations, magnified in the narrow steel tunnel, surrounded him like an angry presence. He glanced up. Beatty flung a signal at him to keep going.

Walker emerged from the lower end of the hawse pipe. He was in the open now, high above the dark waves, and a blast of wind threatened to tear him off the anchor. He clung to it, pressing himself against the stern of the great ship as it crushed through the sea. He tried to steady his breathing but felt his heart leap when something seemed to reach out of the sea to snatch at him. Without moving his head, he peered down. It was only the waves, as the bow cut through them, flashing with phosphorescence. For a moment the eerie glow hypnotized him, but then he saw the body just below him, framed in the strange light, as if the glow came not from the waves but from the body itself. Christ!

Walker tried to reach the body with his foot to lever it off. Suddenly the *Ludendorff's* bow nosed into a deep trough and a wave slammed at Walker, nearly sweeping him into the sea. Choking salt water, Walker started to scramble back up into the hawse pipe but he could dimly see Beatty at the top, blocking the way. He inched down again, stretched out a foot and shoved at the body. It moved, but only to become wedged more firmly between the anchor and the side of the ship. Walker let himself down a bit further and pushed harder at the body. It didn't budge this time. He had jammed it in.

The *Ludendorff* rolled and pitched in the rough sea and Walker, hands numb with cold, didn't know how much longer he could hold on. He kicked the corpse. It wouldn't fall. He could hear the dull thunk as his foot landed against the head and chest.

"You bastard," he muttered, furious at the dead body, kicking it repeatedly. "Fall, you mother-fucker, fall."

The body resisted as if it had a will of its own and refused to relinquish its hold on the ship.

Walker wiped a hand across his eyes half-blinded by sea salt and stretched out one foot, forcing the tip of his shoe under Borgmann's chin. He tried to pry the body loose. The body didn't move but the head did, tilting away sharply. Walker wedged his foot in deeper now between the body and the anchor and pried some more.

Suddenly he realized. His foot was stuck. He had pushed it down too deep. He tried to pull his foot free. But Borgmann had hold of him and wouldn't let go. He and the corpse were locked together on the anchor high above the sea.

With desperate strength, clinging to the anchor shank, Walker wrenched at his wedged foot. His captured ankle, twisted at a sharp angle, shot with pain, but he had to get loose. Had to. The wind beat at him. A wave lashed him. The corpse trapped him, clung to him.

Then he felt something, something give. The body, as if alive again, stirred, scaring the hell out of Walker. He pulled again and the body came unstuck, scraping against the armor hull plates. As it began to slide off the anchor, Walker, to make sure, kicked at it one, two more times. It plunged into the sea, its impact in the waves creating an enveloping phosphorescent shroud.

"Man overboard!"

On the upper deck, Hammond, concealed behind a vent, dashed to the guardrail shouting. "Man overboard!"

The alarm spread across the decks.

On the bridge, the helmsman immediately spun the wheel in a full rudder turn. The *Ludendorff,* instantly responding, swung sharply, but a warship that huge had to make a wide and time-consuming circle.

Men from the ack-ack mount rushed to Hammond's side on the quarterdeck. In the moonlit darkness, they could barely make out a figure floating away from the moving ship.

"Borgmann . . . I saw him at the rail!" Hammond shouted. "He must have been sick again."

Boots thudded on the deck, rushing to a starboard davit. It creaked shrilly as a rescue boat was lowered rapidly into the sea. Engine snarling, it swung around sharply in the direction of the body.

Hammond could only stand there helplessly with the others and watch. What if the body didn't sink in time?

The rescue boat cut the distance to about eighty yards.

The body rode high up the crest of a wave directly in front of the rescue boat and plunged into a trough. When the sea flattened out again momentarily, the body was gone.

The boat circled the area repeatedly, but in the darkness it was impossible to see anything and they reluctantly had to call it off and return to the *Ludendorff*.

"God," the machine gunner who'd cursed Borgmann muttered to himself guiltily.

Hammond patted him on the shoulder to console him.

Down below, Walker shimmied up the anchor shank, through the hawse pipe and squeezed back into the anchor chain room.

"At least that's over," he breathed.

Beatty didn't reply. He was less worried now about the dead than about the living.

CHAPTER 9

In sick bay, Maltin's condition turned for the worse.

The stomach wound racked his body in cruel waves. But he didn't scream, didn't cry out. The only outward signs were his fingers clawing the sheets, his head pressed back rigidly against the pillow, an involuntary trembling of his face.

"Extraordinary courage," Dr. Preisser said after observing the wounded man through most of the night.

"Exactly what I expected of him," replied Beatty. He had hurried down to sick bay to check on Maltin under the pretense of wanting to ask "Kleist" if there was any message he'd like to send to his family. Now he could see that Maltin's silent suffering was more than simply courage under pain. Maltin was trying to keep himself under rigid control to prevent any kind of slip in front of Preisser or one of the medical corpsmen.

"Please . . ." he said in a choked whisper.

Preisser leaned over and took his pulse.

"Give me some more," Maltin said. "Anything."

They followed his urgent glance to a steel drug cabinet at the other end of the sick bay.

"I'm sorry," Preisser replied firmly.

"Please," Maltin asked again through clenched teeth, his eyes blurred and hollow.

Preisser shook his head no.

Beatty drew the doctor aside.

"For God's sake, why not?"

"I've already given him an analgesic for the pain," Preisser said.

"Give him some more. Better off totally unconscious than what he's going through."

"Are you questioning my professional judgment?" Preisser retorted, peering at Beatty closely through his thick glasses.

"I'm not questioning anything, Doktor," Beatty answered. "But surely morphine could . . ."

". . . kill the pain from the stomach wound. Of course. But with a brain injury, morphine inducing unconsciousness could kill him as well."

"I see," Beatty nodded. "I'm sorry."

"Accepted," Preisser said curtly.

As Beatty left the sick bay, out of the side of his eye he saw Maltin's whole body grow taut again, then slump back weakly. Maltin was losing strength, even looked smaller, frailer under the sheet than he had before. How much more could he endure before losing control? Could he hold on until the next night?

Beatty couldn't answer that and wondered whether he should find some way to kill Maltin now. The idea, killing one of his own men, filled him with a sickening dread. But what stopped him for the moment was not the dread but the risk. Trying to kill a patient lying in full view in a sick bay staffed by a doctor and corpsmen was dangerous, so dangerous that the only reason to chance it was a greater danger, that Maltin was on the verge of breaking. But Maltin was hanging in there, so far. Meanwhile, at least one of the other men would always make a point of being near enough to the sick bay now to keep a tab on him. If Maltin's condition became even worse, Beatty, regardless of the risks, would have to kill him.

Beatty reached the upper deck. To the west, it was still dark, but light bled over the western horizon and spilled across the sea.

To Beatty, the light was a glaring reminder of time slipping away and of all the intricate preparation that should've been done by now but which had to be delayed after Hammond killed the German. The take-over, scrubbed the night before, had to be pulled to-night because the battleship was scheduled back at Kiel the following morning. This was their last chance. And before night fell, there was still a lot of work to do.

Beatty took a deep breath and headed up the ladders leading to the bridge and to Kapitän Ziegler.

Ziegler smiled to himself. Standing alone on the wing of the bridge, the wind hitting his face, he felt the battleship's power surging under his feet and watched the bow cleave the Baltic. The *Ludendorff* was doing it, but he was her commander and the *Ludendorff* was there-fore an extension of his body and his will, and her power was his.

"Flank speed," Kapitän Ziegler ordered, stepping into the wheelhouse.

The lee helmsman, standing near the helmsman at the wheel, rang up flank speed on the engine room tele-graph, which communicated the order to the telegraphs in the engine rooms in the bowels of the ship. The engineers opened the throttles and the *Ludendorff* lunged ahead at her top speed of thirty knots.

Ziegler felt the ship's mounting thrust and nodded. Normally, he would have to subject the *Ludendorff* to the strain of flank speed only in battle, and so far the new boiler tubes were functioning superbly. But to make sure, he didn't want to hurry. Before entering battle, Ziegler wanted to push the *Ludendorff* mercilessly at maximum speeds as an ultimate test.

"Maintain flank speed," he ordered, and as the battleship plowed through the oncoming waves, he stepped out on the wing again. Despite the wind that tugged at his collar, it was hot for June and Ziegler felt the early morning heat building up on the sea. The sun would bake the *Ludendorff*'s armor plating. His crew's movements and reaction time would become a fraction of a second slower if he let them, which of course he had no intention of doing. Ziegler himself, no matter how oppressive the heat, would remain in full uniform, starched white shirt, tie, jacket, cap. That sort of thing, unimportant in itself, was strangely effective in commanding a crew's respect.

As Ziegler's sea-blue eyes traveled across the *Ludendorff*'s great bow, he looked forward with anticipation to picking up his full complement of two thousand men at Kiel, to breaking out of the Baltic, to marauding the Atlantic as commander of a battleship that was the most powerful weapon ever devised by man, the culmination, the highest achievement in some four thousand years of naval warfare.

"A magnificent ship, Kapitän," Ziegler heard behind him.

. Ziegler turned. The U-boat commander had reached him on the bridge.

"Thank you," Ziegler said. "If Germany wasn't so infatuated with the Army we'd have ten *Ludendorffs*. We'd send England back to a nation of shopkeepers in six months."

"Absolutely," Beatty said, fearing that Ziegler might be right.

"Your wounded man, Kleist. How is he?" Ziegler asked.

"Critical," Beatty said matter-of-factly, masking his concern without overdoing it.

"A shame."

"Yes."

Beatty waited another moment, then apparently just happened to glance down to the boat deck where he saw Walker, who seemed to be looking for someone.

"He's probably looking for me," Beatty said, making a weary face to Ziegler.

"Oh?"

"Ever since we rescued him, he's been thanking me, tripping under my feet, like a kid asking 'what's this, what's that?' "

"My condolences," Ziegler said. He turned and passed a message to the helm. "Standard speed."

In a moment, the battleship, charging ahead at flank speed, would start to slow down.

"I wonder, sir," Beatty mused as if the idea had just occurred to him. "If I showed him around, do you think I might get him off my back?"

Ziegler looked down at the American staring at a 20-mm gun like someone admiring a hunting rifle in a store window.

"We're conquering the world," the Kapitän shrugged,

119

"but still not spared the company of fools . . . I suggest you confine him to his compartment till we reach Kiel."

Beatty smiled as if he had already considered doing just that.

"Of course, but it turns out he's one of our American sympathizers."

"We can easily do without that kind of sympathizer," Ziegler smiled thinly.

"Agreed. Except for one thing, sir, which I'm sure you've considered. When we reach port, the American wire services will jump on the story of an American being rescued in the Baltic by a German battleship. It'll make front pages for a day or two. . . . Now who knows? If we gave him the standard tour, a few messes, a few machine shops, make him feel important, it might encourage him to spread the word about how impressive our warships are. . . . It certainly couldn't hurt," he noted.

Beatty didn't mention it, but indirectly he was reminding Ziegler, shrewdly putting him on the spot, about the Reich's desire to impress upon Americans, from Ambassador to England Joseph Kennedy and Charles Lindbergh . . . who were easy sells . . . to the average citizen, that Germany would be a fatal enemy.

Ziegler gazed down at Walker without saying anything, and Beatty hoped he hadn't pushed too hard.

A bell shrilled and Ziegler, before turning to a phone, looked back at Beatty briefly and said, "Very well. But he's your responsibility. Make sure he doesn't wander into a boiler. I don't want more paperwork."

Beatty led Walker to the forward deck where the

American pretended to admire the massive dimensions of the *Ludendorff*'s superstructure that skyscrapered over them.

Walker's mind already reeled trying to grasp, during what had to be a quick walk-through of the battleship, the intricate details of Beatty's scheme. How they planned to get their hands on weapons from the ship's armory while jamming all the other guns there so they'd be useless to the Germans. How they planned to catch the crew off guard after lights out. How they expected to overpower the gunners at the machine-gun mounts. How this was all timed down to the minute, the second, so that each of the fourteen men fanning out through the labyrinthian warship would know precisely what the others were doing.

Now Walker was stunned when Beatty, his face a perfectly bland mask, added, "Your job's to take the bridge."

Walker turned from Beatty and his eyes slowly traveled up past the looming guns of "A" turret, past the higher guns of "B" turret, to the bridge towering over them, its wide expanse of windows flashing back the sun like a huge shield. Then his eyes slowly made the same trip back down until they met Beatty's.

"Come on, man," Walker said, shaking his head.

"Taking the engines, boilers, radio room is too technical. Up there's the easiest job," Beatty replied, nodding to the bridge.

Walker squinted at it again. Technical or not, it was still awfully big, awfully high.

"Once I'm up there, then what?"

"Steer."

"You want me to *steer* a fucking battleship?"

"There's nothing to bump into out here."

121

Walker nodded. It made some kind of sense, but he still looked like a basset hound being neutered and Beatty, not wanting him to dwell on the dangers, pressed on.

"I wouldn't recommend a fight up there without knowing your way around," he said.

"How do I do that?"

"They won't give you a floor plan," Beatty said. "Get up there and find out for yourself."

"Yeah, how?"

"You've conned people before," Beatty said. "How else have you stayed alive all these years?"

"By staying out of deals like this!" Walker answered.

At that moment, they heard hurried footsteps behind them. It was Jenkins. The soccer player's craggy face was taut with tension. His eyes darted around to make sure nobody was in sight.

"Maltin," he whispered, going right past them. "Very bad."

With a look at Walker, Beatty turned and headed below for the sick bay.

Walker found himself standing alone below "A" turret. He didn't fully understand what Jenkins meant about Maltin, nobody had told him how seriously wounded Maltin was, but he suspected the worst.

With that hanging over his head, Walker, trying to look loose and casual about what he was doing, began to climb the five levels of the superstructure to case his target . . . the bridge.

CHAPTER 10

Walker reached the broad boat deck and waited till he saw Kapitän Ziegler leave the bridge for an inspection below decks. He knew he didn't stand a chance of nosing around with Ziegler up there.

Then he started up again fast, but checked himself, forced himself to slow down. Come night, he might have to fight his way up these same ladders, and he figured the more he remembered about bulkhead angles, corners, protection, the better. He made a mental note of all the places where he, or a German with a gun, could hide.

On the upper deck, on both sides of the ship, were lifeboats and the secondary batteries, three 5.9-inch turrets. Lots of protection there, as long as he remembered that it could just as easily conceal a Kraut.

Above that, here on the boat deck, clusters of lifeboats and launches on raised platforms, the base of the funnel, on either side of the funnel a towering derrick, and along the entire level, the 4.1-inch ack-ack mounts and the smaller 37- and 20-mm machine-gun mounts.

Some of the machine guns, Walker saw, were manned around the clock in case of a surprise air attack, but Beatty had assured him they were absolutely harmless in case of a fight on the ship itself. Something about them being fixed for safety so that while they could fire anywhere into the sky they couldn't, by accident or panic, be swung to hit anything or anyone on the battleship itself. At least that's what Beatty said . . . maybe to make Walker feel less jittery. But Walker remembered how those machine guns tore apart the British strafing plane like a butterfly and he made a mental note to stay away from those guns, fixed or not.

He noticed, as he climbed, the number of ladders on each level decreased. From the upper deck to the boat deck, lots of them, lots of choices. From the boat deck to the next level, four ladders. Then only two ladders . . . so that anyone on the bridge expecting trouble from below had only two approaches to worry about and guard.

"Hey!"

Walker looked up. A crewman was descending the same narrow vertical ladder Walker climbed and he had to step down to get out of the German's way. The German gave him a dirty look. "Not up," he said, jabbing a finger at the ladder. "Down. Up . . . other side."

"Oh, yeah," Walker said. "Sorry."

Walker made another mental note. There were regulations to control traffic flow on the ladders. The ones here on the port side were for going down. The starboard ladders were for going up. He went around and took the last starboard ladder and reached the wing of the bridge.

At that moment he heard the rattle of gunfire somewhere below and froze. Terrifying images flashed through his mind. Hammond had got it into his head to kill another Kraut. Falco was going berserk or the Germans had gotten wise and were massacring the English. He'd get it next.

He dared a glance down over the chest-high splinter shield. Saw nothing forward or amidships. Leaning far out, he could see aft. At the fantail, three Germans were blasting away with rifles at targets floating off the stern. Probably part of some kind of landing party or assault group practicing. Walker drew back, noticing his hand resting on the splinter shield was still trembling, and ordered it to stop.

The wind, stronger up here, chilled the sweat through his shirt and from this height the sea surrounding the *Ludendorff* was even larger, more alien. The water near the far horizon seemed unmoving, solid, sculpted in wrinkles like the hide of an alligator, but the closer it came to the ship, the more it came to life, blue-green waves rolling toward the *Ludendorff*, across her bow, then past the ship and as they receded toward the opposite horizon becoming solid and wrinkled again.

Walker looked down once more at the upper deck with its huge painted swastika and felt a rush of dizziness. It seemed a mile away.

He wet his lips which were suddenly dry, jammed his hands in his pockets for his most confident and sporty look and strolled into the wheelhouse.

"You can't stay here. It is *verboten*," the deck officer immediately said, turning from the window and striding over across the wood grating. Leutnant Dietrich was a big, dark-jowled man who always looked as if he had just shaved yet still needed another shave.

"Just wanted to get a look at the view," Walker

smiled, all charm. "The Kapitän said it's really something to see."

"The Kapitän allows you here?" Dietrich asked dubiously.

"Well, the Kapitän said Commander von Brennerman could take me around. But since he's busy right now, I thought I'd come up myself a second. I'm sure it's all right with them."

Dietrich recalled seeing the American with the U-boat commander, but a civilian, a foreigner on the bridge in wartime still offended his naval sensibilities.

"It's not all right with me," Dietrich said firmly.

"Then call Kapitän Ziegler," Walker said, braving it out, knowing the German reverence and fear of authority. "Let him tell you."

Dietrich studied Walker a second after reaching for a phone. Then he remembered. The Kapitän was inspecting the after engine room, which had to be shut down until they reached Kiel because of trouble with the reduction gears. Ziegler was very intense at such times and hated to be interrupted by petty details Dietrich himself should be handling.

Dietrich had a nagging suspicion that Ziegler didn't give him the respect he gave other officers, and it might be for exactly this kind of reason, which stuck in a captain's mind and chipped away at his confidence in a deck officer. Slowly, Dietrich cradled the phone.

"But you can't stay long," he told Walker.

"I'm on my way out already," Walker said, staying.

He stepped to the window. It had a commanding view of the forward deck. One pistol shot down there at the wrong time, and they'd be wise to it up here in a second. He gazed out and whistled softly, as if awed.

"Christ, what a view. Almost as high as the Eiffel Tower from here."

"I take my leave in Paris," said the pimply-faced helmsman.

"You'll love it," Walker winked.

"Two weeks," the helmsman said proudly.

"Only one thing about Paris. It costs. They charge a Frenchman one price, you another," Walker warned, knowing this was the kind of thing Germans loved to hear about France, whose food, style and women they secretly envied.

"I have heard," the boyish signalman nodded. "The French are not very honest."

"Isn't that the truth. Never trust them," Walker agreed.

The helmsman looked worried.

"I will have my leave pay. But I don't want to be cheated."

"Your best bet then," Walker advised, "is to have a French broad with you who can read the prices."

"Yah, that is what I must do," the German said, smiling through greenish, mossy teeth. "Get a girl."

"Listen . . . a guy like you doesn't need it but maybe I could give you a couple of numbers. Nice stuff."

Walker searched through his pockets and produced a small address book, still a bit damp from the sea, as the helmsman, navigating lieutenant and the signalman tried not to watch too enviously. His fingers searched the pages, but with his head lowered his eyes swept the bridge. Behind the wheelhouse, and connected by a short passageway, was another compartment, from the look of the maps and charts most likely the navigator's.

Beyond that, another cabin apparently, probably the captain's.

"Here she is," Walker said, his finger tapping a name. "Nicole Buisson. Rue Miromesnil. Said I was her best. But ahh, who believes her."

"I *never* believe them," the helmsman said morosely.

"Come, come Seidman," the navigator said. "If you ever saw pussy, you'd hit it with a stick."

"I beg your pardon, sir," Seidman protested. "I would never hit it with a stick."

All the Germans laughed except for the bosun's mate of the watch at the other end of the bridge. He couldn't hear but he sensed it was about women. *"Vas, Vas?"* he called out.

The navigator motioned for him to be quiet.

"Tell me, Herr Walker," he said, "you have been so many places . . ."

"Mmmm," Walker shrugged with cool modesty.

"Which ones are the best? On the Kurfürstendamm?"

The Kurfürstendamm, Walker knew from experience, was Berlin's Park Avenue, filled with classy girls who weren't worn out yet, who were clean, stylish and knew their business in a cool, efficient way, but still awfully overpriced for what you were getting. Ass, after all, was just ass. However, he didn't want to knock anything German. Not here.

"Oh, yeah, you get some great pussy on the Kurfürstendamm," he agreed.

"I'm tired of German women," said the navigator, who wore a wedding band on his finger. "All they talk about is the war. And don't bring home syphilis from the French."

The others chuckled from their own experience with

the familiar refrain and Walker chuckled along with them sympathetically.

"I'll tell you," he said with authority, "if you want girls who won't give you any shit, the Swedish broads are the end. No question. Blond hair. Long legs, they wrap around your neck, you can die."

Walker noticed Dietrich had stepped away for a moment, issuing an order to another part of the ship through a telephone. There were telephones all over the bridge. He'd have to keep the bastards away from the phones to stop them from spreading an alarm.

"But I'll tell you something else," Walker leaned in confidentially, playing for more time. "It'd be worth knocking over America, just for some spade pussy I know in Harlem."

The Germans raised their eyebrows, intrigued with the lust of Aryans who secretly suspect that non-Aryan girls, especially the darker ones, are wilder and capable of mightier orgasms.

"*Vas, Vas?*" the bosun asked, sure that he was missing something from the other end of the bridge.

"Shhh," Seidman waved him off. "*Schworzen, schworzen!*"

"Oh," the bosun exclaimed eagerly. "*Schworzen.*"

"Let me tell you what happened to me one night on Lenox Avenue," Walker said, as Seidman and the bosun's mate gathered around.

"No. No more," Dietrich said, motioning for Walker to leave. "You have been here enough."

"Oh yeah, right," Walker said quickly. "But just let me finish." He turned back to Seidman. "This girl, her name was Jewel, she would shove a little roll of silk ribbon up your keester and when you were coming she'd draw it out, real slow, and you'd come till you damned near passed out."

As Walker embellished on Jewel and her silk ribbon, he filed away in his mind all the dangers of the bridge. The exposed approaches that led to it. Its broad view of the forward deck. The telephones. Some kind of microphone which Walker suspected connected to the ship's loudspeaker system. Close, confined area. A big steel desk and a compass platform. Bulkheads and doors in the back with at least two more cabins. A German with a gun could be hiding anywhere.

Christ, he thought. What a fucking place for a fight.

CHAPTER 11

"Oh, Jesus, I'm drowning . . . I'm drowning."

Maltin's words strangled to a gasp. Despite the racking pain, Maltin from some automatic sense of discipline under danger still spoke in German, but his grip was slipping.

"The doctor'll be right back," Beatty warned, keeping a comforting, and restraining, hand on Maltin's shoulder. Preisser had been called away for a moment and they were alone in the sick bay.

"How're you doing with . . . ?" Maltin's eyes indicated the decks above.

"Tonight," Beatty said.

"Hurry. Just hurry."

Beatty held a cup of water to Maltin's cracked lips. He took a feeble sip, most of the water trickling down his stubbled chin, and collapsed back on the pillow, hands pressed against his stomach.

"If he can sleep it's a blessing," Preisser said coming through the door.

"Docs he stand a chance?" Beatty asked low, stepping away from the cot.

"Hard to say," Preisser answered.

Across the sick bay, Maltin convulsed in an uncontrollable shivering.

"Cold . . . very cold . . . another blanket." He said it in German. *"Kalt . . . sehr kalt . . . noch eine Decke."*

But then, close to delirium, in slurred, barely intelligible English, "I'll be all right, Commander. Just hurry, just . . ." He trailed off quickly as he saw his mistake reflected in Beatty's eyes.

A terrible silence filled the sick bay. Beatty was aware of Preisser looking quizzically from Maltin to him.

"What did he say?" Preisser turned back to the cot.

"Another blanket."

"No, after that."

"I didn't catch it," Beatty replied evenly.

He watched as Preisser approached the cot with another blanket, the doctor's ear cocked slightly, waiting to hear if Maltin said something again. If he muttered anything else in English, Beatty would have to kill Preisser on the spot. Maltin stirred under the added weight of a second blanket. Preisser waited, studying him. Maltin remained silent.

"Mmm," Preisser finally shrugged, as if he'd probably imagined hearing something.

"Since he's quiet," Beatty said, "if you don't mind I'd like to stay close by. Just to give him whatever support I can when he wakes up."

"Of course. Call me if necessary." Preisser left the bedside and stepped into his adjacent office, leaving the door open. He was out of sight, and in a moment his typewriter filled the sick bay with a nervous tat-tat-tat.

Beatty sat again at Maltin's side, and with a small towel gently wiped the perspiration from his waxen face. Maltin's eyes half opened. Beatty shot him a warning glance toward Preisser's office. Maltin seemed to understand.

"I must've fallen asleep again," he said.

Beatty nodded.

Maltin darted a look at the office and with his lips silently formed the words, "I didn't say anything?"

"Don't worry about that now," Beatty replied.

"I feel better, Herr Commander. Rested."

"Good," Beatty said. "That's good, Kleist."

"I'll make it," Maltin said, searching Beatty's face, knowing what Beatty had to be thinking. He clutched Beatty's wrist. "I'll-be-all-right."

"Sure."

Maltin winced again and his eyes shut. Soon his breathing became deep, a guttural undercurrent to the metallic clacking of the typewriter in the nearby office. His body jerked as if tormented by invisible electric wires.

Beatty knew there wasn't much time. If Preisser had said Maltin was definitely dying, it would've made Beatty's decision if not simple then at least easier. But he had to do it anyway. He felt a momentary stab of anger at Maltin. It was *Maltin's* fault for getting wounded, for putting everyone in danger, for forcing Beatty to do what he was going to do. But it wasn't Maltin's fault at all, he knew, and now Beatty's anger turned on himself. He wished he'd never heard of the *Ludendorff*, never thought of capturing it, never presented the plan to S.O.E., most of all never made the decision to lead it. He wished . . .

133

Beatty stopped himself. Whatever he wished didn't matter on the *Ludendorff* and he was flooded with a deep sorrow for Maltin, who had trusted and followed him into an enemy sea. But even that emotion Beatty forced himself to shut off before it paralyzed him, preventing him from acting. He had to do it now.

But with Preisser just a few feet away, how?

He looked around and spotted the steel drug cabinet on the opposite bulkhead.

"Easy, Kleist," Beatty said to the unconscious figure, loud enough for Preisser to hear. "I'll get a cold towel."

Beatty rose, turned a faucet on full so that the splashing water would cover the sound and gently clicked open the cabinet. His eyes swiftly scanned the shelves of bottles, tins, ampules. He had almost no knowledge of chemistry and only seconds to decide. Ether would leave a powerful, telltale smell. From somewhere he seemed to recall, though he wasn't sure, that metallic poisons like mercury were corrosive, left burns that might be easily detected. Morphine and strychnine . . . he didn't know whether they were detectable but because of their reputation was afraid they were.

Nothing in the cabinet seemed usable. Shutting it softly, he returned to the bed. What he dreaded most appeared to be the only way. His hands. Strangling would normally leave bruises, marks of violence, but he wouldn't have to use that much force.

"Be all right," Maltin suddenly mumbled incoherently in English, delirious again. "Surprise . . . be all right . . ."

"Does he need me, Commander?" Preisser called from the office, hearing the indistinguishable babble of words.

Beatty could hear the typewriter stop and the chair squeak as Preisser started to rise.

"No, it's all right," Beatty called back.

The typewriter clacking started again as Preisser said, "I'll be there in a minute."

"You'll see . . ." Maltin continued, his English becoming sharper, clearer. "Timing . . . timing . . ."

Beatty consciously willed his hand to move.

"Tell him . . . tell Comman Beatty . . . the *Luden* . . ."

Beatty firmly pressed his thumb into the soft area above the chest at the base of Maltin's neck. The words stopped.

Beatty held his thumb against the neck. It would take, he knew, more than a minute. Maybe two. He could hear the typewriter and his own breathing.

Suddenly Maltin's eyes opened, startling Beatty, almost making him release the pressure. He couldn't tell whether Maltin was conscious enough to see him, to know what was happening.

One of Maltin's hands reached up and clutched Beatty's wrist. The hand was cold. The nails dug into Beatty's flesh. Maltin's eyes, immense, staring, met Beatty's.

Beatty pressed down hard.

CHAPTER 12

Christ, but he wished it was time. Time to make their move now and not have to wait another twelve hours, Perth thought as he came out on the wind-swept quarterdeck.

Emotionally, Perth had been trying to pace himself, to build himself up, so that when the time came, he'd be ready, prepared to do anything necessary, no matter how dangerous. But he was ready now and every few minutes he felt a muscle jump with nervous tension.

He warned himself to be careful, to slow himself down before the tension wore away his edge and his energy.

He peeled off his turtleneck sweater and sat as if he'd come up here to get some sun, which was routine for off-duty crewmen. Through the corner of his eye, however, he studied the changing of the watch at the machine-gun mounts, from the forenoon to the afternoon watch, which would stand guard until four. The Germans all had a snap, a discipline that he recognized as all too familiar from his childhood in Germany.

Perth tried not to think about that, regarding it as self-pity, as weakness. But watching the crewmen triggered too many long buried memories. Katrina Perth, his German schoolteacher mother, in her own way had the same kind of efficient discipline, a discipline that his British father, a gentle antique dealer, never had and could never live with, which was what led to their divorce. That and his mother's sudden enthusiasm for the Nazis.

He thought of his mother now, still in Berlin, still undoubtedly beautiful, still helping to turn out obedient young Nazis, like the crewmen on the *Ludendorff*, who wanted to destroy England, just as he wanted to destroy Germany. And though he dreaded to think of it in personal terms, in a way his mother was trying to kill him, just as he was trying to kill her. God, how he hated his mother. How much he still loved her.

Across the quarterdeck a handful of Germans sat in a circle, a couple of them singing a stirring military song, *"Heute Wollen Marschieren"*—Today We Will March."

One of them waved Perth over. Perth shook his head and rose to go, but the German insisted with another wave and Perth, rather than risk bringing attention to himself, went over.

"Cigarette?" one of them offered with a smile.

"Danke," Perth said.

"Come on," another said, making room for him.

He sat as the sailors launched into another chorus of *"Heute Wollen Marschieren."* Perth didn't know the words, but military tunes, English or German, are as easy to grasp as a gun barrel and he faked it by aggressively humming the melody. He felt a revulsion for the song . . . marching, fighting, conquering . . . and despised the Germans for singing it so proudly, so fiercely, the veins swelling in their necks. Which one of them, he wondered, might have gone to school in Berlin and been his mother's protégé?

The song ended but one of the boys, his close-cropped hair making him look even younger, kept singing, his clear liquid tenor gliding into "*Ich hatt einen Kamerad*"—"I had a Comrade." The other youths, their faces hard a moment ago, listened quietly to the sad song of loyalty and loss. They took up the words, linking arms, and Perth felt hands on his shoulders and sang along with them. The words, the melody, moved him without his realizing it, until he looked around at the faces of the boys. He turned away. Was it actually going to happen? It was one thing volunteering for a mission to prove loyalty to his adopted country and strike back at the land of his birth for the wounds it had inflicted on him. But it was another to sit here on a deck and know that he would soon have to kill these Germans who spoke the same language as he, who had gone to the same schools, played in the same streets, who were so much like himself. Could he do it? One of the young Germans smiled at him and Perth had to smile back. He felt unclean.

Then, something made him look up.

He saw on the boat deck, arm resting against an ack-ack shield, Falco. The Frenchman, his face a mask concealing implacable hatred, was watching Perth singing in the circle of arm-linked Germans. Their eyes met and locked.

Falco had been watching Perth since the beginning of "*Ich hatt einen Kamerad*" and had a black urge to turn a gun on the whole bunch down there on the lower deck and see Perth die with his *Kameraden* in a pool of

138

blood. Suddenly he was aware that the Germans, all of them, were glancing up at him. If he turned and left it wouldn't look right, so he stayed where he was. But why were they watching him?

"Your pal looks lonely," one of the Germans said to Perth. "Call him over."

"I don't think he'd want to," Perth said quickly.

"Why not?"

"He's a loner anyway," Perth answered.

"Then some company'll do him good. Go on," another German insisted.

Perth waved to Falco.

On the boat deck above, Falco wondered what Perth was up to. Now a couple of the Germans waved to him, too.

Falco casually descended a ladder and strolled over to Perth and the others.

"Rest your butt," one of them said, shoving over.

Falco sat down between him and Perth as the Germans swung again into a final chorus of "*Ich hatt einen Kamerad*." Perth was singing so Falco joined in, hoarsely and off-key, hitting the word *Kamerad* as loud as he could. He was beginning to enjoy himself. It was a new experience. Singing with Germans he was going to kill.

He felt a friendly arm thrown around his shoulder and turned to look at the German, a gunner.

The gunner smiled at Falco.

Falco smiled back.

At the same time, Beatty climbed to the Kapitän's sea cabin aft of the bridge, trying to anticipate why Ziegler had unexpectedly summoned him.

He was still shaken by the nightmare in the sick bay,

his fingers pressing against Maltin's neck, Maltin's breathing stopping almost instantly, his body growing rigid then sagging back, perfectly still, Beatty calling for Preisser, the doctor rushing in and listening for a heartbeat that had stopped forever, then looking up and shaking his head. Beatty tried to bury it but the scene kept flashing into his mind, especially Maltin's hand, perhaps as an automatic reflex, perhaps in a feeble attempt to struggle, reaching for Beatty's arm as he died.

Beatty feared Maltin's death might be behind Ziegler's summons. Could Ziegler be suspicious about a U-boat commander insisting upon spending so much time with a wounded non-com in the sick bay, and then that man dying so suddenly? Beatty told himself there was no reason for Ziegler to be suspicious, but it didn't erase the fear.

A guard stepped smartly aside and Beatty entered the Kapitän's sea cabin. Ziegler, going through a stack of reports, looked up from his desk. Beatty noticed that everything on it, reports, writing materials, a log, was arranged in a precise geometry as precise as Ziegler himself.

"You sent for me," Beatty said, matter-of-factly.

"Oh yes, I have a surprise for you."

"Surprise?"

"In a minute," Ziegler said, checking his watch. "Please. Sit down. A drink?"

"Thank you," Beatty said. Was the Kapitän trying to throw him off guard?

Ziegler jabbed a bell and a steward entered with a bottle and two crystal glasses on a tray.

"Kirsch," Ziegler said, offering him a glass of the colorless liquid.

Beatty sipped the kirsch, as fiery as he remembered it

from his days in Berlin. He had to make sure not to take more than one glass if he wanted to keep his mind clear.

Ziegler drained his own glass and placed it carefully on his desk. He leaned back and looked at Beatty.

"How would you like to talk with your father?" he said.

"I'm sorry, sir. I don't understand," Beatty replied, hoping he'd kept the shock out of his voice.

Ziegler must've seen something in his face, however, and reacted, a reaction that Beatty couldn't interpret.

"Surprised, hey?"

"Well . . . yes."

"When your father received word that you were rescued he wanted to find out how you were, wanted to talk to you if possible. And when the Secretary of Economic Development wants something the Navy obliges."

Ziegler led Beatty below decks, past the ship's radio room, and held open the door to the transmitting room. Beatty stepped inside.

The transmitting room was filled with huge banks of *Telefunken* equipment with glowing dials and barely enough space in the aisles between to walk through. The door shut behind them.

It was a trap, Beatty thought. Ziegler, suspecting something, had contacted shore and set this up to test whether he was actually U-boat Kapitänleutnant Viktor von Brennerman. But even if it wasn't a trap, how could he carry off a conversation with an absolute stranger who was supposed to be his father?

An operator saluted and showed them to a small steel desk surrounded by transmitters.

"Sorry we couldn't patch it into your cabin, sir. But it's so far, it took a while to build up a frequency," he said. "I think we've got it as clear as we can."

Ziegler stepped aside and gestured Beatty to a stool bolted in front of the desk and its microphone. He heard the crackling of the ether, then a voice, scratchy and distant.

"Viktor . . . Viktor?"

Aware of Ziegler standing directly behind him, Beatty had to answer, and once he started there'd be almost no time to think, to calculate what to say. He took the microphone. His hand was as cold as the polished steel.

"Yes . . . Hello, hello, Father?" Beatty replied.

"Viktor, thank God, thank God, how are you?"

"Fine, fine. Very well," Beatty said over a high transmitter whine.

"What?"

"Fine," Beatty had to raise his voice.

"Are you sure?"

"Yes, Papa. Yes," Beatty reassured. The less he said, the less chance of a slip or of the German recognizing even over the interference and distortion that the voice wasn't his son's. At the same time, if he seemed unemotional or distant, it would appear unnatural to both the father and Ziegler. He had to do a delicate balancing act.

"You weren't injured?"

"No, just scared," Beatty said, trying to joke.

"Thank God."

"Yes. Thank God."

There was a pause.

"You sound different," the voice stated suddenly.

Beatty's pulse raced.

"You sound different, too," he replied. "A lot of interference on this wave length."

"Yes . . . I guess that's what it must be."

Another awkward pause. Beatty tried to shield the transmitter directly in front of him with his body so that Ziegler and the operator couldn't see it.

"We got your last letter," the voice said through an explosion of static.

"Oh . . . good," Beatty said, terrified of being asked about something in the letter.

He knew damn little about transmitters but did know that it could take as many as a dozen dials to build up to certain frequencies. On the pretext of trying to hear better, he leaned in and stealthily turned one of them, hoping to break the connection, but . . .

"What should we do this time with Maria?" the distant voice asked.

Beatty froze. Who was Maria? Wife, daughter, niece, dog? He had to answer.

"Uh . . . why not do what we've always done?" he managed.

"Are you sure?"

"I think so."

"If that's what you want," the voice said, for some reason disappointed.

"That'll be fine," Beatty said. He knew he couldn't keep this up much longer. He tried another dial which only seemed to increase the treble, sharpening the static.

"Viktor, since you are safe . . . I haven't even told Mother yet, I wanted to make sure . . . I think we'll take her to celebrate, at that restaurant. You know, your favorite . . . which one?"

Beatty forced his mind to race back to his summers in Germany. He must have eaten in a hundred Berlin restaurants, but now with the question coming over the static and Ziegler standing right behind him, he drew a terrifying blank. He reached down into his memory and there was nothing except the famous Hotel Adlon. Before the war, spoiled, rich foreigners inside, fifteen-year old prostitutes, cocaine dealers and transvestites outside. But it was the only one he could think of.

"The Adlon?" he said.

"No, no, you never liked the Adlon." The voice seemed surprised at Beatty's answer.

"The food, yes. The prices, no," Beatty said, trying to take the curse off a bad answer.

"I mean the one you took us to when you got your commission."

Beatty could feel Ziegler's eyes on him. His brain reeled. He got a vague image of a rustic place, almost a farmhouse, that his own father had liked, a great favorite of diplomats and officers though it had been much too stuffy for Beatty . . . *Krug* . . . *Der Alter Krug.* It was a long shot but he had to say something.

"*Der Alter Krug,*" he said.

"Ah, yes of course. *Der Alter Krug* . . . I hope we're not taking up too much wireless time."

"Well . . ."

Ziegler signaled to Beatty to take as much time as he wanted.

"Just one more thing, Viktor, since you may not be home for a while . . ."

Beatty's hand stole to another dial, brushed it swiftly. The voice changed to angry static. The most beautiful sound Beatty ever heard. He turned to Ziegler. "*Ach,* lost him," Beatty frowned.

"The British must be jamming. I'm sorry," Ziegler said.

"That's all right. It was still a wonderful surprise."

Beatty was sure nothing more harrowing could possibly happen.

He was wrong.

CHAPTER 13

"The armory," Falco shook his head. "We can't get in. We can't jam the guns."

The British, hunched over a poker game as a cover for gathering below decks in their compartment in mid-afternoon, stared at him, stunned. Beatty had been checking with each one on how they sized up their targets . . . Hammond the forward engine room, Perth the radio room, Walker the bridge . . . when Falco burst in on them, his dark brows clenched in a frown.

"It's impossible," he said.

"What's wrong?" Beatty demanded.

"Those marines. They have no watch, no duty," Falco replied. "They lie around in that compartment pulling their meat all day, exactly next to the armory."

"Terrific," Walker said dryly. "A ship full of live guns."

Perth turned to Beatty.

"Maybe I can find a way to divert the marines long enough for . . ."

"Stay away from the Germans," Falco growled, the

image of Perth singing with them fresh in his mind. "I'm not sure which side you are on."

"And I am not sure you're here to capture a ship," Perth slashed back. "You just want to kill people."

"Only Germans, *German*," Falco snarled, in his frustration and anger making a sharp move toward Perth.

Perth, smaller but faster, sprang up to meet him.

Beatty was between them in a flash and just in time. They heard footsteps passing on the other side of the door. Whoever it was would've heard the fight and anything incriminating said in anger. Beatty waited until the footsteps died away, then spun on Falco and Perth.

"Anything like this happens again, I'll shoot one of you," he snapped. "And I won't care which one it is."

A silence gripped the compartment. They might not have believed him before, but they believed him now, after what happened to Maltin. Not that they blamed him for what he did to Maltin. They'd have done the same thing. He had become as ruthless as any of them.

Beatty let his words sink in, then without saying any more, wheeled out of the compartment. A second later, Walker hurriedly followed. He slowed up a moment in the passageway . . . he didn't want any German to see how alarmed he was . . . and ducked into Beatty's compartment right behind the Englishman.

"Look," Walker began, trying to keep his voice low and calm. "Let's be reasonable. It's not working out. You can't jam the guns. Your men're crazy, they're fighting. Call it off before we all get killed."

"We can't," Beatty said.

"Why not? In five, ten years some clowns'll sign a treaty and you and the Krauts'll be friends again anyway. That's the way things are. Why die for it?"

147

"That's not the point. We're already here. Either we take them tonight or they take us."

"Not if we put a boat over the side and cut."

"They'd spot it."

"Then find another way. That's your department."

"There is no other way."

"You don't *want* there to be another way," Walker said with a rising anger. "You've run around in velvet pants all your life. Servants wiping your ass. Now you're trying to be a hero on other guys' blood."

"That's enough!"

"What do you want, Viscount? A statue of yourself in Hyde Park? The pigeons have enough to dump on already."

Beatty drove his fist into Walker's stomach. The American doubled over, gasping, catching his breath, and Beatty, wanting to hit him again, stopped himself. He already had had to kill Maltin, had just threatened to shoot Perth and Falco. Now this. If things kept unraveling, he'd have half the men turning against him.

"Sorry," he said, stepping back.

"Okay, okay," Walker nodded, apparently accepting the apology.

But as soon as Beatty lowered his hands, Walker smashed a hard fist into the commander's kidney.

"We're even," Walker said, satisfied.

Beatty slowly straightened himself up, his side clenched in pain. There was something typically American and insane about Walker wanting to even a personal score with all the danger around them, but if Beatty had to, he'd deal with that, too.

"All right, we're even," he said.

"Look, do you really need me?" Walker asked plaintively, already knowing the answer. "Do you absolutely need me?"

"I'll find a way to handle the armory," Beatty said, ignoring the question. "You ever handle a submachine gun?"

Walker shook his head no.

"Then you better learn."

Nine-millimeter Parabellum bullets smashed into an empty paint can bobbing in the *Ludendorff*'s foaming wake. The can jerked as if tugged from below, tipped over on its side, and within seconds sank.

Two members of the *Ludendorff*'s landing party were practicing marksmanship off the fantail with their Schmeisser MP-38s. Very serious about it and very expert, they planted their feet wide, not locking their knees, firing in economical bursts. As one of them removed an empty magazine, he noticed the American stroll across the quarterdeck and sit near the guardrail with an old issue of *Das Reich*.

Walker couldn't read it well, though he seemed fascinated by the pictures. He winced nervously at the submachine-gun bursts.

At first the Germans ignored him, but they were soon secretly amused that they could make the American squirm uncomfortably every time they fired. With a wink, one of them nudged the other, then held out his Schmeisser to Walker . . . would he like to give it a try? Walker hastily shook his head and waved back as if to say thanks, but I'm chicken with guns. The German, prematurely bald but with huge hairy ears, was really enjoying himself now. He approached Walker, who had started to rise and leave.

"Come. There is nothing to be afraid of," the German, whose name was Steeger, said.

"Thanks. But I'll pass," Walker replied.

"Every man should know how to fire a weapon. Is that not so, Junack?"

Junack looked around uneasily. There were no officers in sight, but handing your weapon to someone else, especially not a crewman, was not a good idea. Still, he didn't want any hassles with Steeger, who had the reputation of being violent and impulsive and even resented being drafted into the Navy because he'd had ambitions to be in the S.S. In fact, he was still trying to transfer into the S.S. Junack hated pulling duty with Steeger and all he wanted to do now was avoid trouble.

"Better not, Steeger," he said, low.

"Christ, you're an old lady," Steeger shot back. "You should've been an air-raid warden."

"I just meant don't because . . ."

"Air-raid warden," Steeger ridiculed nastily. Up until this moment, he hadn't really meant to hand the Schmeisser to the American, he just wanted to have some fun with him. But Junack's "don't" rubbed him the wrong way. Where did a chicken-shit like Junack, a peasant from an ass-hole village like Neckarsulm, who probably fucked sheep, come off telling him don't. He swung back to Walker.

"Just try," Steeger smiled, thinking he was concealing his contempt for the American. "You may have hidden ability."

"Come on, fellas." Walker shook his head as Steeger elbowed him over to the fantail and thrust the gun at him.

The Schmeisser's nine-and-one-half pounds felt surprisingly heavy and thick in Walker's hands. As a kid

150

he'd done a little hunting, but a .444 Marlin had a smoothly polished and carved stock, a comfortable grip, a long, graceful barrel. Hunting guns were made to look beautiful to disguise their true function, killing. But a Schmeisser, with its cold steel shoulder support and snout of a barrel looked exactly like what it was—a machine for tearing flesh and smashing bone. The reality of a gun battle aboard the *Ludendorff* came one step closer to Walker, chilling and concrete, as he clutched the weapon.

"Shoot," Steeger said. "I'll make it easy for you."

He threw into the sea the largest target piled on the quarterdeck, a battered garbage can, knowing that Walker couldn't hit it anyway.

Obediently, Walker took a deep breath, stepped to the rail and nervously raised the submachine gun to his shoulder.

"Watch out for the birds," Junack cautioned seriously, pointing to several gulls dipping astern as he stepped behind Walker for safety. "The Kapitän does not like us hurting them."

Walker nodded that he'd spare the birds and raised the Schmeisser again. The can, looking smaller by the second, bobbed nearly sixty yards away by now. The Schmeisser's sights were too crude, the barrel too short, to aim effectively. Trying to keep the gun steady on the rolling deck, he squeezed the trigger. The Schmeisser blasted, a sharp, nasty, jarring blast, each shot jerking the barrel upwards until he was almost shooting into the air. At the same time, the recoil jolted Walker off balance, driving him a few steps back across the fantail, his right foot twisted behind his left. He could see his shots, looking harmless in the distance, zipping far behind the can.

"Just as I thought." Steeger smiled his bully's smile. "Hidden ability."

Walker had the hook set. Now he had to reel Steeger in, carefully.

"All right, all right," he said with hurt pride. "But with some practice I'd do as good as you any day."

"*Ach.*" Steeger dismissed him with a wave of his hand.

"*Ach,* bullshit yourself," Walker said, taking a chance on needling him.

"*Auf wiedersehen,*" Steeger singsonged with an edge of contempt, taking the Schmeisser away from Walker.

From the corner of his eye, Walker saw a handful of sailors gathering around, listening.

"What do you want to bet?" he challenged Steeger.

Steeger turned his back on him contemptuously.

"I throw this time, Junack. You shoot," Steeger said, reaching for another can.

"Come on," Walker said louder, so the others could hear. "What do you want to bet? You afraid?"

Steeger peered back at him. Walker took off his gold wristwatch. The sea water that got into it the day before would soon corrode its delicate mechanism, but for the moment it still ticked and sparkled beautifully.

"This against that," he said, pointing to the Iron Cross on Steeger's jacket.

"Come on, Steeger," Junack cautioned. "Quit screwing around with him."

Steeger glanced at the nearby crewmen. It was becoming a matter of face. He held out his hand to look at the watch, and Walker, for the first time since he'd bought the Patek Phillipe on a crazy impulse when he was almost broke, was glad that he'd spent two hundred bucks on the damn thing. The watch impressed Steeger.

He nodded. He locked in a fresh magazine, banged it with the heel of his hand for good measure and passed the Schmeisser to Walker.

"We will each fire three magazines," he said.

"Uh-uh. Show me first," Walker said. "Fair's fair."

The German shrugged impatiently and took back the gun.

"There is nothing to know," he said, removing the magazine. "This is the magazine. It holds thirty-two rounds. You put it in . . . so."

He locked the magazine into the underbelly of the submachine gun, then pulled back and released the breech bolt.

"Wait a minute. What'd you do?" Walker asked, watching intently, remembering every step.

"You must pull back the breech bolt to bring the first bullet into the chamber. Otherwise it won't fire."

"Suppose I want to fire just one shot at a time?" Walker asked.

"No one shot with Schmeisser," Steeger condescended. "Fully automatic. As long as the trigger is pulled, it continues to fire." Greedy for the gold watch, he handed the gun back to Walker. "Now you fire."

Walker took the submachine gun and raised it to his shoulder again.

"Point low," another German said from behind. "The recoil rides it up."

Steeger gave the German kibitzer a dirty look, but Walker nodded gratefully. He saw a can arc into the sea and fired a long sustained burst, the shots kicking up spouts wide of the mark, the can bobbing, teasing and untouched, further and further away, till he heard a click. Out of ammunition.

At his side, another Schmeisser cracked, Steeger firing again. The German's bursts hit the water and chased the can, zeroing in and smashing it.

Walker shook his head and whistled softly to himself as if awed by the German's skill. He said nothing about it but noticed that Steeger had got the range not by emptying the clip in one long blast but in short bursts.

Walker inserted a fresh magazine—no problem there, it just slipped right into place—and pulled back the breech bolt, hearing a bullet click into the chamber. The Schmeisser might be blunt and ugly but it was constructed simply, just stock, barrel and magazine. At least he'd never have any trouble firing it. Hitting something might be another story.

He stepped to the rail and like Steeger fired quick short bursts at the next can. He saw the first one fall short and used the splashes to find his way closer and closer to the target. The gun clicked empty again before he hit anything, but he knew he was getting the hang of it. He had to stop the smile that threatened to cross his face as he glanced up and saw Beatty watching him from the boat deck aft. Beatty, not in the Germans' line of vision, nodded to him imperceptibly.

Walker inserted the last magazine, sure that he'd hit something this time. He squeezed off a couple of rounds . . .

"That's enough!"

The sharp command spun him around. It was Ziegler, striding across the quarterdeck, his face tight with anger.

"What is this man doing with a weapon?" Ziegler demanded.

The Germans were too scared to speak.

"Well, you see, Captain," Walker said. "I . . ."

"Point that away!" Ziegler ordered as Walker, trying

154

to explain, unintentionally leveled the gun cradled in his arm directly at him. Walker hastily lowered the gun. One of the marines grabbed it away.

"It wasn't anything, Captain," Walker said. "I bet this watch against . . ."

Ziegler with sudden fury snatched the watch from his hand and threw it into the sea. Walker saw it disappear with a flash of reflected sun in the *Ludendorff*'s boiling wake.

"Take him below," Ziegler commanded.

The chunky marine moved to Walker's side and shoved him toward a nearby hatch.

"All right, I'm moving," Walker said. "I'm moving."

But not fast enough. The marine jabbed him in the back with a billy. The pain shot down Walker's side, but he made for the hatch as fast as he could. The marine slammed him again, this time harder, taking his breath away, scrambling his senses and triggering a surge of anger he knew he had to control, but when he saw the club coming a third time, Walker, who'd spent most of his life acting on impulse, darted a hand out and the next thing he knew the club was spinning through the air over the guardrail and the Germans were staring at him. Enraged, the marine charged Walker. They crashed down. Two more Germans jumped in and slammed him to the hard deck.

"Throw him in a cell!" Ziegler ordered.

The Germans led Walker away. Despite the stabbing pain in his side, he was aware of a strange feeling, almost a feeling of relief, and then he knew why. Everything had been going wrong, from the English losing two of their men as soon as they stepped on board, to the guns in the armory still not taken care of. But now he was out of the whole mess. He felt a pang about losing the chance to collect the money from Beatty, but the odds on the take-over working and him living to collect had looked longer every minute. Now the English and the Germans could cut each other's balls off up here. He'd be out of it and neither side could involve or blame him. He'd be safe in the brig.

"Just a moment!"

It was Ziegler, his command slicing across the quarterdeck.

Ziegler had watched Walker being led away and realized that he'd made a mistake. Throwing Walker into a navy jail for a few weeks for assault when the ship reached Kiel wasn't quite satisfying. The punishment wouldn't be personal or immediate enough for Ziegler. Walker had breached ship's discipline, created an incident and had made him angry. There must be some better, some more satisfying way of personally dealing with the American.

"Bring him back here," Ziegler ordered.

Walker was spun around and led back to face the Kapitän.

"Since you are so combative, Herr Walker . . ."

"I'm not comba . . ."

"Be quiet!" Ziegler commanded. "Since you are so combative, I think I'll give you a choice between facing assault charges and jail, or what you can really do against a German."

"I got nothing against Germans," Walker replied. It was one of the few completely honest things he'd said since coming aboard the *Ludendorff*.

"But we have something against you," Ziegler said coldly. "We hold boxing matches from time to time on the *Ludendorff*. If you are willing, I can arrange something this afternoon. You can fight Rheinbolt."

"Rheinbolt?"

"The middleweight champion of the *Ludendorff*. You against him. That should be both entertaining and symbolic."

CHAPTER 14

Below deck, Walker got into a pair of gym shorts and sneakers from the ship's supply. They were both tight, but he'd have to live with them. He swung his arms and danced nervously from foot to foot, trying to loosen up. The past winter, with the fancy crowd he'd hung around with, he'd done some skiing in Garmisch and was in fairly good shape, at least his legs were, but skiing, he knew, was one thing and getting into a ring another.

Shanks came in with a couple of towels and a pail of water. "I'm your cornerman," he said.

"Thanks," Walker replied glumly. "That'll be a big help."

He slumped down on a hammock and held out his hands for Shanks to wrap them. To his surprise, Shanks did it swiftly and expertly, hooking the bandage to his thumb, then wrapping it around his wrist, thumb, fist and back again, making his fist a compact package. Shanks reached into a box and took out a pair of Everlast gloves.

"Mother-fuckers," Walker muttered.

Shanks didn't have to say anything. Instead of the sixteen-ounce gloves generally used in gym fights, the Germans wanted them to use these. They looked like ten-, maybe even eight-ounce gloves, hard-packed and punishing.

"Better do some warm-ups, lad," Shanks said, patting his shoulder.

Walker rose and started bobbing and weaving to get his blood moving.

"Where's the head guard?" he asked.

"No head guard," Shanks said.

Walker stopped jumping.

"What're they trying to pull? This isn't a pro fight."

Shanks shrugged.

"Terrific," Walker said sourly, heading for the door.

With tin mugs of coffee and pretzels, the Germans, laughing and shouting across the ring, died to a hush, a murmured undercurrent as Walker, with a towel thrown over his shoulders, accompanied by Shanks, came across the quarterdeck. They had to step their way over and across the crewmen sitting around the ring, and ducking under the rope, Walker could sense their eyes sizing him up. He thought for a moment of flexing his muscles to look bigger, but figured fuck it, it wouldn't accomplish anything and might only make his muscles tenser than they were. Shanks was already kneading the back of his neck to keep it loose. They stood in a corner a long moment, the Germans just watching him. Rhein-bolt was nowhere in sight.

"Where is the son-of-a-bitch?" Walker whispered low.

"Keeping you waiting," Shanks whispered back.

Walker gnawed his lip.

"Easy, lad, it's just a corny trick."

Walker looked out over the crowd. Ziegler was standing off to the side, near the big turrets. It was too far to see, but Walker could imagine the look on his face.

The crowd stirred and broke into a cheer. Rheinbolt came across the quarterdeck, swinging his head, pawing the air with his fists. He slipped into the ring and removed a bulky sweater. His heavily muscled body was already covered with a fine sweat. The *Ludendorff*'s crew howled for action.

Drau entered the ring as referee and approached Shanks, as if Walker was unworthy of a referee's attention. "This man knows the rules?"

"He knows," Shanks nodded.

"Excellent," Drau smiled. He crossed the ring to instruct a yeoman at the side, holding a small dinner bell in one hand, a sweep-second watch in the other.

The crowd grew quiet again.

Beatty watched from near an open hatch some ten yards behind the crowd around the ring. Out of the side of his eye, he could see Lester through the hatch in a passageway on the deck below. Lester waited.

In the ring, waiting for the bell, Walker heard waves slapping against the side of the ship and felt the wind, or was it something else, chilling his body. Shanks exited the ring. Walker never felt so alone in his life.

He turned to face the opposite corner and studied Rheinbolt, who was throwing short warm-up jabs. Bare-chested, Rheinbolt looked even squatter and chunkier than before, with thick, cabled muscles. Probably not fast but powerful, Walker thought, with the heavily ridged forehead and wide jaw of a man who could absorb a lot of punishment. From his days as a saloon bouncer Walker could tell that Rheinbolt was the type who, you prayed, wouldn't get nasty-drunk at 2 A.M.

because if he did it meant lots of broken chairs and shattered glass before it was all over.

Walker figured he had no chance of beating Rheinbolt. Given a choice, he would've taken a few weeks in jail over getting his brains scrambled. But if the crew, the marines, came on deck to watch a fight, it'd leave the armory unwatched, unguarded. It would be, Beatty said, a perfect diversion for Falco to get in there. Their only chance to take care of the guns. Walker had to buy Falco time. Half an hour. Seven rounds. Christ.

The bell rang.

Walker came out cautiously, his guard high up to protect his head. Rheinbolt came out to meet him.

At the same instant, Beatty made an imperceptible hand signal to Lester.

Lester relayed the signal down the passageway to Falco. Falco slipped through the marine compartment, now empty, and tried the armory door. Locked. He made a small tear in the lining of his shirt collar and removed a piece of flexible steel that looked like a small dental pick. With it, he was inside the armory in a second. He quickly closed the door behind him and eyed the dozens of closely racked guns. He went to work.

In the ring above, Rheinbolt, hunched low, circled to Walker's right. The German held his gloves barely waist-high, showing that he wasn't afraid of getting hit by the American.

Walker saw a left jab, blocked it, then reeled back, stunned by a punch he never saw coming. Less than a minute into the fight and he was hurt. The Germans around the ring and standing on the turret roofs howled.

Walker covered up as Rheinbolt moved in, weaving, bobbing, circling, always moving.

Walker threw a jab at the German's cropped blond

head just where the hair ended in a scar. Rheinbolt flicked it off with his right and shot a left that stung Walker's nose, blurring his eyes for a second. As Walker raised his guard, Rheinbolt slipped inside and drove a right to his ribs. Walker had suspected he was in for trouble. Now he was sure of it. Rheinbolt knew his business.

Walker clinched and leaned on Rheinbolt heavily. He outweighed Rheinbolt by at least ten pounds. Maybe with enough time he could make Rheinbolt feel it. Rheinbolt tried to wrestle away, but Walker held on. The Germans at ringside saw what he was doing and they raised a shout and Drau broke the fighters apart. Rheinbolt feinted with a left, raked Walker with a straight right, and as Walker watched for the left hook to follow, hit him again with another right, then a third, the three punches exploding in a fraction of a second. The Germans screamed.

"*Für Volk, Führer und Vaterland,*" a clown bellowed, drawing a big laugh as the bell rang and Walker returned to his corner. He had thrown only one punch, which didn't land. He was breathing hard. His shoulder muscles hurt from keeping his arms up and wrestling the German. He felt pooped, exhausted. It was the end of the first round.

As Walker slumped on a stool and gargled a mouthful of water from a bottle held by Shanks, Beatty near the hatch shot a nod to Lester below, a signal that Falco was safe working in the armory for the moment. For a second, Beatty had been afraid that the fight was going to be over in the opening round and that the Germans would immediately disperse. But now it looked as if Walker was going to last. For a while at least.

Rheinbolt didn't wait for Walker to meet him in the

middle of the ring for the second round. He charged from his corner, head low, swinging. Walker back-pedaled and got in a good jab, his first punch to land and it felt good, with lots of snap to it. Maybe he stood a chance, he thought, if he could stay away from the German's heavy stuff. Rheinbolt, his face red under the left eye from the jab, came in flat-footed, throwing rights again, splitting Walker's lip, bringing the taste of blood.

The crowd saw it and roared.

Walker clinched, forcing the German to support his weight again. Rheinbolt didn't seem to mind. Christ, the cocksucker was strong. Drau started to break them apart. Walker saw a chance and didn't wait. Before Rheinbolt could raise his guard, Walker let go with a roundhouse that caught the German below the ear and nearly lifted him off one foot.

Watching from the roof of "C" turret, Tanner almost let out a spontaneous cheer but caught himself before Schnaubel at his side could hear.

Walker didn't feel like cheering. Rheinbolt had taken Walker's best shot and was still coming in, eyes hard, looking for revenge for the roundhouse. Again, Walker didn't see a right cross. It nearly took his head off. The deck seemed to slam up to meet him. He was on his back, the sky spinning, the deck holding him down like a magnet. He saw Drau standing over him, mouth moving, counting, but heard nothing except the pain in his own head. He tried to rise but the spinning, tilting deck wouldn't let him, and then Drau stopped counting and turned away.

Shanks ducked into the ring and helped him, wobble-legged, to his corner. He sagged on the stool. It was over. He'd been whipped, knocked out. He felt all beaten up, but he had no business getting into a ring in the first place.

"I'm sorry . . . sorry," Walker gasped, spitting blood.

"You're doing fine, lad," Shanks whispered.

Walker looked up. He didn't understand.

"They never counted past six. The bell rang," Shanks explained.

"Ohh," Walker muttered. "Oh, shit!"

"You take a good punch."

"How many more rounds?"

"Only five."

"Oh, Jesus."

"At your age," Shanks said, "I'd go five rounds every day before breakfast."

"Terrific," Walker said, spitting more blood into the pail between his feet.

"Just stay away from him," Shanks cautioned.

Walker shot him a dirty look.

"What the fuck do you think I'm trying to do?"

In the armory below, Falco swiftly stripped down a Luger. Pressing the muzzle against the steel table to release the tension on the recoil spring. Sliding off the complete barrel and toggle assembly. Removing the toggle assembly and breechblock housing the firing pin. Extracting and pocketing the firing pin. Reversing the procedure to reassemble the Luger. Falco was grateful to the Germans for designing an automatic that could be quickly taken apart and reassembled without tools. With dozens of weapons to work on, he'd need every second he could get.

* * *

The bell rang for round three, and Walker heaved himself off the stool.

Rheinbolt met him with a savage attack, driving Walker back across the ring. Desperately covering up, Walker got an idea. He waited for the right moment.

A left hook grazed his temple and he went down. He stayed down to the count of five, resting on his side, taking up as much time as he could. He struggled to his knees at the count of six, shaking his head as if to clear it, and grabbing the ropes, pulled himself to his feet at eight. He just had to hang in there and he'd last longer if he could rest and spend part of each round lying on the deck.

Rheinbolt barreled in, swinging. Walker covered up, threw a couple of jabs to make it look good and the next time a punch glanced off his head, went down again. It felt good on the canvas, restful and safe. But the Germans screamed. They suspected that he was faking it. He had to rise at seven, sooner than he had planned. Drau stuck his face in his.

"The next time, a knockdown like that is a *knockout*," Drau warned. "Fight will be over."

"Whatta you mean?" Walker protested.

"You know what I mean," Drau snarled.

Rheinbolt stepped in and jarred him with another short jab. Walker grabbed Rheinbolt and clinched. The Germans booed. Rheinbolt doubled him over with a right that exploded under the heart. The bell rang. Walker stumbled back to his corner unable to breathe.

Half of Falco's time was up.

He finished with the last of the Lugers and started on the submachine guns. He glanced at his watch. Even if Walker could last seven rounds, Falco didn't know whether he could do it. He pressed the first Schmeisser's trigger, then twisted the pistol grip to the right about eighty degrees, revolving the entire frame, which he removed. At the front of the telescoping tube he found the firing pin. He removed it and dropped it into his pocket. His pocket was getting heavy with firing pins.

The Schmeisser was one hell of a gun, it flashed through Falco's mind. The Luger, with its lethal reputation, had too many exposed parts, which made it unreliable in sandy or muddy conditions. But the Schmeissers were reliable, lovely, he thought, as he pocketed another firing pin and pictured a German confidently raising this castrated gun and trying to kill him with it.

"Keep away from that right," Shanks whispered through tight lips as he worked on Walker's left eye.

"Can't. Legs're too tired," Walker gasped.

"Then keep grabbing him and clinch."

"Can't. Arms're too tired."

Walker stole a glance, a look of hate, across the quarterdeck at Beatty near the open hatch. Beatty shook his head. They needed more time.

Shanks, too, saw Beatty's signal and peered at Walker's eye. Ruptured blood vessels under the eye were pouring blood into the soft tissues. The reddish-purple swelling had just about closed the eye, leaving Walker almost blind on one side.

Shanks fished into his pocket for a German coin, a small pfennig. He pressed the sharp edge of the coin against the lump under Walker's eye. The taut, bruised skin stretched. Walker winced. Shanks pressed harder. The lump burst with a warm gush of blood.

"See better?" Shanks asked, wiping the blood away.

"Think so," Walker muttered.

The bell rang. Walker had to grab the ropes to rise.

Shanks figured even if Walker could see, he wouldn't last the fourth round.

The German moved in on Walker relentlessly, cutting off the ring again, cornering him along the ropes. He wanted to finish the American . . . now. Cold and steady, his eyes drilled into Walker's. His mouth wore a thin smile.

Walker threw a left at the smile. It landed, but had no steam and Rheinbolt moved in straight through it. The next thing Walker knew he was staring up at the *Ludendorff*'s superstructure, on his back again, the ring spinning slowly.

His body felt as if it was nailed to the deck. He fought to one knee, groped for the ropes and lurched to his feet at the count of nine, Rheinbolt coming after him. He tried to clinch and put all his weight on Rheinbolt, who shouldered him into the ropes and as he bounced off blasted him with a right that took him off his feet again.

On his stomach, through blood-blurred eyes, Walker saw Drau counting and the Germans shouting from the turret roofs. Drau didn't have to warn him this time about faking a knockdown. He was hurt. He blinked to clear the blood and make out Beatty across the quarter-deck over the jeering crowd.

He saw Beatty's mouth clenched in a silent scream for him to get up.

Walker's eyes messaged back, fuck you.

Grimly, Beatty pantomimed an order. Get up!

Walker could see a couple of Germans shaking their heads, disappointed at the fight being over. They rose and headed toward a ladder leading below deck. Some others followed. Falco was down there. In another minute they'd discover him in the armory. Walker didn't give a damn about Falco, but if the Frog was caught down there with the machine guns . . .

Spitting blood on the canvas, he grabbed the ropes and hauled himself slowly to his feet. By clutching the ropes, at least he could stand.

Through one eye, he saw Rheinbolt boring in again, a blurred ghost, and behind Rheinbolt, the Germans scrambling back to watch.

Backpedaling, Walker slipped on his own blood and as his arms automatically went down, Rheinbolt threw lefts and rights at a wide-open target, the blows thudding loud and sickening.

The crowd roared as Walker reeled across the ring, Rheinbolt ripping him with a right, another right, a third right that snapped his head back at the bell.

Falco's hands working on the submachine guns slipped with sweat. Now he not only had to remove the firing pins, he had to wipe his fingerprints off the immaculately polished steel barrels. In the right angle of light they showed up and might arouse curiosity, suspicion. As he stripped one of the Schmeissers, the firing pin fell and rolled under the small table. He couldn't risk a German coming across a loose firing pin. He dropped to his hands and knees. In the dim light under the table he couldn't see it so he had to feel for it frantically with his hand. He touched it, but just then the ship rolled and the firing pin was gone again. He groped blindly. Finally got it. Precious seconds lost.

Walker couldn't remember what round it was, whether Shanks had whispered that it was the fourth, or the fifth or the sixth. His breath came in wrenching gasps, his legs had no lift, no spring left, as if they were wading through glue. His arms ached, so heavy and tired that his punches moved almost in slow motion, feeble taps that Rheinbolt didn't even bother to block.

Rheinbolt charged in, throwing bombs with lefts and rights. Walker covered up and tried to duck behind Drau for a second, but Drau shoved him back into the center of the ring.

"Hide behind me," a gunner at the rear of the crowd called out. "It's safer back here."

The Germans at ringside howled.

Walker reeled against the ropes, hearing as if from very far away Rheinbolt grunt with every punch. He was in a fight, he knew, on a battleship. But how he got on the ship, why he was in a fight, he didn't know, couldn't remember.

Somehow over the screaming crowd he heard the bell ring . . . he heard it long after it stopped, a shrill painful echo piercing his eardrums . . . and grabbing the top rope, staggered back to his corner. He collapsed on the stool, his stomach racked with dry heaves.

Shanks darted a pleading look at Beatty.

Beatty shot an urgent glance down the hatch and got a sign from Lester that tore at his raw nerves. He turned back to the ring and scratched an ear with one finger, which was damp with sweat and ice cold.

"Just one more," Shanks whispered to Walker.

Walker shook his head with a muffled groan through shredded lips.

"Sure you can," Shanks said, giving Walker a swig of water.

Walker gagged, shaking his head no. He felt his stomach heave again and tried to keep it down, but knew it was no use and threw up into the pail between his legs. It tasted sour, burning his throat, dribbling yellow and green down his chin, splashing the rim of the pail and his sneakers. His whole body shook. He couldn't stop gagging on his own blood.

"It's up to you," he heard Shanks hissing.

"No more . . . can't," Walker gasped, trying to squeeze off his gloves. If Falco couldn't take care of the guns, if he got caught down there, if the Germans got wise and killed all of them, he didn't care any more.

The bell rang.

"Sorry, lad," Shanks whispered. He yanked the stool out from under Walker.

Walker, bent half over, found himself in the ring, Rheinbolt crouching in, the Germans roaring him on. Walker tried to keep him off with his left, but Rheinbolt threw a right straight through it. Walker didn't know whether the roaring came from the Germans or from within his own head. It stopped every time Rheinbolt hit him, then started again.

A hard right spun him around, draping him over the ropes, arms down, almost helpless. With his own good eye he shot a look at Beatty at the open hatch.

He saw Beatty fire a look down the hatch again and Beatty just seemed to stand there, frozen, not moving, looking down the hatch for an agonizing time, as if he'd never move again, as if he'd stay there forever and Rheinbolt would torment him, Walker, forever on a battleship that would sail the seas forever, and then Beatty slowly turned back to the ring and though his face revealed nothing, he just strolled away from the hatch.

Walker's thudding heart leaped. He knew he could end it now by dropping to the deck. But he'd hung in there and taken too much for seven goddamn rounds just to drop and let Rheinbolt and the other Germans see him being carried out. He didn't hurt any more. He was beyond pain. Rheinbolt couldn't do any more to him than he'd already done. If this thing was going to end, he wanted to end it his way.

Walker stepped in, taking a hard right under the heart—and grabbed Rheinbolt in a tight clinch. Rheinbolt spun him around. Walker went with the spin and ripped his knee into the German's balls. Rheinbolt doubled over with a surprised, strangled croak. Putting his whole body behind it, Walker smashed an elbow into Rheinbolt's eye. Rheinbolt's head snapped back and Walker hit him again in the face. A gout of snot burst from Rheinbolt's nose. Now the German was trying to get away. Walker swarmed all over him, swinging wildly. Drau tried to pull him off but in his fury he didn't even feel it. He caught Rheinbolt against the ropes, clubbed his windpipe with a forearm. Rheinbolt sagged over. Walker hit him on the way down and kept smashing away at him until Drau dragged him off.

Ziegler turned away and stormed from the quarterdeck. The Germans at ringside screamed at the American. A few had to be restrained from climbing through the ropes and attacking him.

Walker didn't care. On trembling rubber legs, he stood alone in the middle of the ring on the quarterdeck of the battleship *Ludendorff*, one arm raised in victory.

CHAPTER 15

The yellowish stream turned pinkish then a gleaming red, splashing against the steel bowl, mixing with the water, gurgling down the drain.

It was the most terrifying thing Walker had ever seen in his life. Instead of urine, blood coming from his penis.

Still wearing only boxing shorts and sneakers, covered with sweat, he felt a stab of pain that almost doubled him over and with his free hand he grabbed at a pipe to keep himself standing in the confined head. He stared until the red stream died to a dribble of red drops, then wheeled and bolted through the compartment for the door just as Shanks entered.

The Englishman saw the wild look in Walker's eye and held him, blocking the door.

"Where's the doctor on this thing?" Walker demanded.

"What for?"

"I'm pissing blood, that's what for," Walker nearly shouted. "My kidneys took a beating."

172

"Easy now. A doctor puts you to bed, you won't be much use to us tonight."

"I'll just get a pill or something."

"Could make you sleepy or drowsy," Shanks warned.

"I might die here," Walker complained, scared.

"Nobody dies from that kind of thing."

"Sure!" Walker shot back. "*You're* not pissing blood. I am."

"Just stay out of sick bay."

"If this keeps up, I'm going and nobody's stopping me. My cock comes first," Walker warned, allowing Shanks to sit him down and begin to clean his badly cut face.

"Easy, lad," Shanks said, keeping his voice low. "Trouble with your generation, you've had things too cushy."

"Why is it you old guys always say that?" Walker asked through raw lips.

"I guess because we're old guys," Shanks grinned. "Bet your dad gave you the same routine."

"He gave me nothing," Walker said flatly.

Shanks felt Walker slamming a door shut and didn't try to enter. The American was an odd one, all right, not a serious chap and therefore not the kind that Shanks normally cared for. But a man showed what he was made of in three ways, Shanks believed, the way he screwed, the way he fought and the way he died, and after the way Walker fought Rheinbolt, Shanks couldn't help liking him.

"You did such a jolly good job up there," Shanks said, "Falco's promised to make you a partner in his cathouse after the war."

"Only if I can wrestle the naked girls," Walker said dryly.

"I'll take it up with Falco." Shanks smiled. He patched a plaster above the left eye. "There. See all right, feel okay?" he asked, concerned.

"Yeah, fine," Walker muttered. He felt awful and knew that in a few hours every part of his body would be stiff, throbbing with pain.

"Meanwhile," Shanks cautioned, "you better stay out of Ziegler's sight. I don't think he likes you any more."

"I fuck him where he breathes," Walker grunted. "Standing there, enjoying it. Most of them did." Something clicked into place. "They like that kind of thing, the bastards."

"That's getting through to you, is it?" Shanks asked.

Walker saw Shanks's meaning and backed off.

"Listen. Go pass your leaflets to somebody else."

He rose and headed for the door, his legs still shaky.

"Better try and get some sleep," Shanks advised, concerned about the American. He glanced at his watch. It was almost 6 P.M. "Less than ten hours to go," he said.

Shanks didn't know it, but at that same moment the timetable, designed to trigger the take-over during the battleship's most vulnerable hour, and upon which their lives depended, was being totally and irrevocably shattered.

"Your man, Kleist," Dr. Preisser said, approaching Beatty on the upper deck. "I'd like your permission to perform an autopsy."

The single word was partially obscured by the wind pulling at their jackets, but Beatty heard it like a nearby crack of lightning.

"With those wounds, there's no question about why he died, is there?" Beatty asked as if it were just a point of curiosity to him.

"None whatsoever," Preisser replied. "If there were, I wouldn't have to ask your permission as his commanding officer."

"Then why . . ."

"An autopsy's the only way a doctor has to officially confirm his diagnosis," Preisser said. "And the only way he can learn to avoid any mistakes he may have made in the past. In the long run it's the living who benefit."

"I see," Beatty nodded.

He could think of no legitimate reason for any commanding officer to refuse Preisser's request. If he did, it would look so singular and unco-operative that Preisser would report it to Ziegler and Ziegler would not only permit the surgeon to go right ahead and perform the autopsy, he'd ask questions about Beatty's refusal and immediately make the connection as soon as the autopsy revealed that the actual cause of death was strangling.

Preisser was looking at him, waiting for a reply.

"By all means, Doktor," Beatty had to say. "And I'd appreciate your letting me know what you find. Just for my own records," he added.

"Of course. And thank you," Preisser said, turning away.

"Any idea when you might be finished?" Beatty asked as casually as he could.

"Hard to say." Preisser consulted his watch. "I won't start until after lights out. No interruptions, nobody getting their fingers mashed in a machine and needing a splint."

Alone again on the upper deck, Beatty swiftly calculated the consequences of an autopsy on Maltin. He had no idea how long a routine post-mortem took, but he had to assume not very long. A couple of hours, conceivably less. If Preisser started after lights out at ten, he'd be finished, with enough time to discover the actual cause of death was not bullet wounds, long before 4 A.M., the hour scheduled for the take-over. Beatty either had to find some way to neutralize Preisser now, in broad daylight, which was too dangerous, or revise his own plans here at the last moment, which could be just as dangerous.

He had the dread feeling that the knife waiting to open Maltin's body was pressed against his own throat.

"Before midnight?" Hammond exploded, shaking his huge head. "The whole fucking crew won't be sleeping by then."

"Before midnight," Beatty repeated firmly. "We can't wait any longer."

Hammond frowned to himself. So did some of the other men.

Beatty turned to Falco.

"Those marines might still be awake next to the armory," Falco said. "It'll be hard to get out the guns."

"Well?" Beatty asked.

"That's all," Falco shrugged. "It will be harder."

As Beatty went around the compartment, checking each man, each job, Walker watched the English begin a strange ritual . . . stripping down and putting on fresh socks and underwear.

"What the hell's this?" he whispered to Shanks.

"Helps prevent a wound infecting," Shanks said. "Might save your life."

Walker would've never thought of it himself, but if Shanks said so, why not? He did the same.

Beatty reached Walker. The American's face looked

worse now than it did just after the fight. Lips puffed up and gorged with clotting blood. Nose swollen out of shape and probably broken. One eye closed and oozing pus. Beatty wondered if Walker had taken so much punishment that he'd be unable to move fast enough if he had to. Even worse, had he taken so much to the head that his judgment, his reactions would be unreliable.

"Now remember, Walker," Beatty said. "We take out the marines first, then the crew and engine room. Then you make your move on the bridge. Clear?"

"Don't worry about it," Walker said tensely. He could see every step up the superstructure to the bridge in his mind.

Beatty nodded and looked around at the men one more time. He'd taken them this far. They trusted him now to take them all the way.

"Everybody knows what to do . . ." Beatty said.

The men's eyes met his.

Evening fell. The *Ludendorff* raced to Kiel under scudding clouds and a leaden sky.

In the wardroom, decorated with forest-green carpets and red leather chairs, Beatty shared a table with Drau and a couple of younger officers, their dinner served on expensive china by efficient stewards who glided in from the pantry with tureens of savory lentil soup and platters of roast pork. Across the wardroom, Beatty saw Dr. Preisser at a table with an engineering officer.

He glanced at the bulkhead clock over Drau's shoulder. Seven o'clock. Barely four hours to go. Across the wardroom, Beatty saw Dr. Preisser finishing a second cup of coffee. Beatty forced himself to finish his own dinner and rose.

"Don't go," said one of the lieutenants. "How about some chess?"

"Too many reports to make out when you lose a submarine, I'm afraid," Beatty said.

In the mess, at a separate table, Beatty's men tried to appear relaxed with Germans all around them. Walker poked at his cold cuts, his stomach too tied up to get anything down.

Tanner wolfed down his food as fast as possible because at a nearby table Schnaubel, encouraged by Tanner sitting with him at the fight, was stealing glances at him. He couldn't have Schnaubel coming after him tonight. Tanner finished a torte and headed for the door. Schanubel hurried up behind him in the passageway.

"You will be at the film tonight?" the German said, keeping pace at his side.

"Film?" Tanner asked, puzzled.

"The advantages of battleship service," Schnaubel smiled. "Films for the crew twice a week."

"Oh," Tanner nodded. "What time?"

"Seven-thirty."

Tanner breathed eaiser. At least it'd be over before eleven.

"Well, maybe," he said.

"And you must tell the others," Schnaubel insisted. "Everybody comes."

At exactly seven-thirty, the film began in the mess. The Germans were punctual even when it came to relaxation.

Since sailors traditionally love movies as a relief from the tedium of sea duty, if none of the British showed up, it would've raised questions and called too much attention to them. So Beatty ordered some of his men, including Walker, to attend. The American looked exhausted. At least sitting in the dark for a couple of hours would force him to rest instead of pacing a compartment. Beatty himself went to keep an eye on him.

A beam from a 16-mm projector stabbed across the mess as Tanner took a bench near the back. He expected a German propaganda film and was surprised when the MGM lion roared from the starboard bulkhead and the title appeared:

GRETA GARBO
in
Camille

"She is the Führer's favorite," a voice whispered in Tanner's ear as Schnaubel slipped beside him.

"Uh-huh," Tanner replied neutrally.

"My favorite, too," Schnaubel added, his breath garlicky, his thigh heavy against Tanner's.

The scenes flew by, meaningless and disjointed for Walker, who could think only of what was to come in a couple of hours. He felt pressure on his bladder and wanted to take a leak, but he kept sitting, afraid of what he might see if he urinated again.

As *Camille* wound down to the last reel, Greta Garbo was nobly giving up Robert Taylor because as a courtesan she felt she wasn't pure enough for him. Her swanlike neck and satin shoulders glowed on the battleship's bulkhead, and Tanner began to feel a lump in his pants.

"So lovely," Schnaubel whispered, meaning Robert Taylor. Schnaubel leaned over. "After lights out, let us talk."

"Leaving quarters after four bells is against regulations," Tanner said, shaking his head.

"No one will know. . . . You like me, don't you?"

"Listen," Tanner whispered. "I'm not that way. Really."

"What way?" Schnaubel asked.

"You know."

"I respect that," Schnaubel said, not wanting to believe him. "Then we will just talk, be friends. I will come and find you."

"Better not," Tanner said.

Schnaubel smiled conspiratorially, ardor undimmed.

Beatty, sitting diagonally across from Tanner, glanced at his watch . . . 9:03.

"Commander von Brennerman."

Whispered from so close in the dark, the words were startling.

Beatty turned. It was Kapitän Ziegler. Ziegler signaled him to step into the passageway.

"An interesting development, Von Brennerman," he said.

"Yes, sir?"

"You are leaving the ship."

"Leaving . . . ?"

"Yes, tonight."

CHAPTER 16

Ziegler's words hung like pistol shots in the passageway.

"Leaving tonight? I don't understand. Why?" Beatty asked.

"It seems experienced U-boat commanders are considered much too valuable to be pleasure cruising in the Baltic. And I agree."

"Of course. But we'll be in Kiel in the morning anyway," Beatty said.

"But you're to fly back to your base at St. Nazaire. With five seaplanes in our hangar we can always spare one when ordered by Naval Group West."

"Kapitän, I've been with my crew since the war started," Beatty said. "With your permission, I'd rather wait and return with them."

"I appreciate how you feel. I would feel the same way," Ziegler replied, handing Beatty a radiogram from Naval Group West. "But as you see, you're to be given a new command immediately."

"Yes, sir," Beatty said. "Uh . . . what time do I leave?"

"As soon as we raise a glass to your new command."

"PREPARE FOR AIRCRAFT LAUNCHING."

The *Ludendorff*'s loudspeaker blared into the night with its hard metallic voice.

"PREPARE FOR AIRCRAFT LAUNCHING."

Beatty, his gear slung over his shoulder, waited grimly nearby on the boat deck as the deck crew swung open the hangar on the starboard side of the funnel. They disappeared into the cavernous shelter and moments later pushed out a small, frail-looking plane, a single-engine Arado-196 with twin floats. They guided the Arado along the shunting rails to the catapult rails fitted athwartships.

In the darkness illuminated by two large beams from above, several dozen crewmen had gathered to watch. They were joined by Walker and most of Beatty's men.

The British realized that without Beatty—he was the only one who had a full command of all the pieces—they could never pull off the mission. Falco felt an urge to grab a gun and start shooting there and now, but even he knew that'd be suicidal. They could only wait until their cover was blown at Kiel and be shot. Losing Beatty meant losing their lives.

To Walker, it meant there'd be no fight and this hit him with conflicting emotions. On the one hand, he was glad. No shooting, no chance of getting killed. On the other, he felt a strange letdown, because it meant he'd gone through all this, especially the beating by Rheinbolt, for nothing. That Beatty and the others would face a firing squad occurred to Walker only secondarily, and however he felt about it, it came nowhere near matching in intensity or sorrow his feeling about having come this far and then losing all that money.

A lieutenant in leather jacket, helmet and goggles climbed to the boat deck, saluted Beatty smartly and scrambled into the plane. The Arado's 900 horsepower BMW engine coughed, then settled into a steady roar, the propeller a flashing blur in the moonlight.

Beatty turned to his men. They saluted and he returned it.

Ziegler strode across the deck.

"Have a good flight. We shall take good care of your crew."

"I appreciate that, sir," Beatty said, saluting, his mind desperately searching for something, anything, to keep him on board. He could find nothing.

He climbed heavily into the Arado behind the pilot and buckled himself in.

"Excellent flying weather," the pilot shouted over the engine's roar, shutting the canopy above them.

"Yes," Beatty said. "Excellent."

He could feel the light craft trembling, eager to lift into the sky. His mind still raced, trying to think of something he could do. Like Falco, his first thought was to start the mission now, but he knew that a handful of unarmed men—even if a few of them could reach the armory—wouldn't last long against all the Germans. After the plane took off, he thought, he could commandeer it if he had a gun, but he didn't, and not knowing how to fly himself just to overpower the pilot in the air was suicidal. Crawford was right. Easy to hatch plans and send others out to die. Now he knew how they felt. After all the detailed research and intricate planning that he'd done, he'd made one fatal oversight: assuming the identity of a veteran U-boat commander, the most valuable resource in the German Navy and urgently needed at all times for active duty.

183

The engine roaring in his ears had the malevolence of fate.

The horizon line swung and Beatty realized the battleship was turning broadside into the wind. The flight operations officer waited for the ship's windward and leeward sides to become level so that the plane would have a horizontal surface for taking off. He signaled. The catapult gear operator pressed the lever. The Arado's engine roared, the forty-foot wingspread shuddered, but the plane remained on the catapult rails. It hadn't moved an inch.

Beatty's body, prepared for the thrust of take-off, felt suspended in a limbo of tension. The pilot shook his head with disgust. Through the closed canopy, Beatty saw the operations officer rushing over to confer with the catapult gear operator, who shrugged, puzzled. The German checked the lever and the rails and gestured that everything was all right. The operations officer waved to the pilot to get ready. Then he signaled again. The catapult operator pressed the lever. The Arado, engine racing, still stayed on the rails.

Beatty watched from the plane, uncomprehending, as half a dozen Germans, motioning excitedly, swiftly checked the catapult gear in the beam of searchlights. One of them reported to the operations officer who took a look and then turned to Kapitän Ziegler.

"Sir," he said, "the compressed air pipe . . ."

Ziegler studied the compressed air pipe in the harsh beam. The pipe had several jagged holes.

"How could this have happened?" he snapped angrily.

"I don't know, sir," the operations officer said, white-lipped and scared. "Mostly likely—uh—when we were strafed by the British planes."

"All deck equipment should have been inspected immediately for damage."

"I'm sure it was, sir. The damage was apparently missed."

Furious, Ziegler signaled to the pilot to cut the Arado's engine. Beatty climbed down from the seaplane.

"My apologies," Ziegler said. "I'm afraid you'll have to wait for tomorrow."

"Quite all right, sir," Beatty replied, stunned by the extraordinary luck, a million-to-one chance that a few random strafing bullets had saved his life.

A moment after Ziegler left, Shanks approached.

"Very sorry, Commander von Brennerman, sir. Bad luck," he said.

"Yes, wasn't it?" Beatty replied, giving Shanks a quizzical look.

As Beatty headed below decks, he saw Shanks casually stroll over to the rail and drop a chisel concealed in his sleeve into the sea.

9:51 P.M.

Barely two hours before the British moved against the *Ludendorff*, Lester silently left his compartment and headed for the German sleeping quarters on the same level.

The passageway was empty. The ship's fans whirred steadily. The battleship was settling down for the night.

Lester took a drag on a cigarette. The deep breath helped ease the tightness in the big factory worker's chest, but not much. It still felt like a weight pressed against his ribs.

Lester reached the German compartment and, slowing down, shot a quick look through the open door. Most of the crewmen were in their hammocks, reading, smoking, talking quietly. A card game was finishing up. Lester didn't see what he was looking for and continued on to another compartment at the far end of the passageway. He wanted to get this over with and had to force himself to slow down, to act as if he just happened to be crossing the passageway with nothing urgent to do.

In the second compartment, again, he didn't find what he was looking for. The weight pressing against his ribs felt heavier now. He didn't have time to search the whole bloody battleship.

He heard the hissing of water off to the left.

Lester entered the long narrow shower room. A lone, naked man stood under a steaming jet of water. It was Schnaubel. The soapsuds streaming down his fat, pink chest and fleshy buttocks made him look even softer and grosser. Schnaubel was making himself fresh and clean for the young U-boat rating he planned to seduce after lights out.

Schnaubel heard Lester's footsteps, glanced at him briefly across the long shower room, then returned to his soap, scrubbing his ears and neck and snorting to clean out his nostrils. Lester felt a slight physical revulsion but nothing more. He'd never thought much about queers. They were just rather sad blokes who lived in a world of their own, and that was fine with him. But this fat one, planning on going after young Tanner after lights out, could get them all killed.

Lester walked toward Schnaubel, stopping just out of range of the shower jet.

"You leave the boy alone," Lester said, his voice dead level, echoing in the deserted room.

Schnaubel turned innocently.

"What boy?"

"You know what boy."

"I don't know what you mean." Schnaubel hastily washed off the soap, reached for his towel.

"Just leave him alone, you hear?" Lester stepped closer, the shower spraying his boots.

"I don't force him to do anything," Schnaubel whined. "He will do what he wants and you leave me alone. This is not even your ship."

Lester stepped straight into the shower and closed a powerful hand around the German's genitals.

"The boy is *mine*," Lester hissed. "Go near him again and I will kill you. Understand, fat bitch?"

"You can't . . ."

Lester's hard hand squeezed and a strangled cry echoed through the shower room. Schnaubel sank to his knees in the water, moaning.

"Now you understand," Lester said from the door. "Stay away."

At precisely ten o'clock, the *Ludendorff*'s bosun's mate saluted Drau on the bridge.

"Request permission to pipe lights out, sir," he said.

"Permission granted," Drau said. Through the bridge window his eyes scanned the lower decks. They were quiet, empty, except for dark clustered shapes hunched in the machine-gun mounts.

Drau felt tired but restless. The *Ludendorff*, steaming south, would reach Kiel in just a few hours and he was anxious to get his feet on ground for a couple of days. He wanted to go on a good long drunk for the last time before the *Ludendorff* went hunting in the Atlantic.

Behind Drau, the bosun moved to the master control of the *Ludendorff*'s loudspeaker system and blew on a small whistle strung around his neck. Throughout the ship, the shrill of the bosun's pipe was followed by his voice, flat, mechanical, commanding.

"Lights out. All hands turn in. Silence will be maintained about the decks."

In compartments, staterooms and crew quarters the lights went out. The engines still pounded but a kind of silence embraced the ship. Miles of passageways became deserted. Nothing moved on the decks.

The *Ludendorff* crushed through the sea, a dark monster.

Dr. Preisser swung open the steel door and felt cold air seeping from the refrigerator unit. He reached in and pulled out a long steel tray that moved smoothly on rollers. On the tray lay Maltin's body covered with a white sheet.

Preisser lifted it under the shoulders and moved it to a white porcelain table with gutters for carrying off blood and body fluids. In medical school he'd been instructed always to handle a corpse with the same respect and dignity as the living but that seemed pointless, especially here, and he transferred it from tray to table as quickly as he could because he wanted to finish this autopsy as soon as possible and catch some sleep before the battleship reached base.

On a smaller table at the head of the larger one Preisser arranged his instruments which gleamed under the light, each one of their curved surfaces reflecting him and the draped corpse in a different distorted way. An autopsy knife for opening the body and removing organs, bone-cutting forceps, serrated-tip forceps for handling soft tissue, intestinal scissors for opening the intestine, stomach and heart, a probe for exploring the coronary arteries, blunt scissors for exposing the arteries of the neck, a metric rule for measuring abdominal fat, organs and tumors, rib shears, retractors, chisel, hammer.

An arsenal for assaulting the dead.

In the British compartment, Shanks flicked out the light. In the muted red glow of the night light that prevented total darkness in case of emergency, he could see the others, still dressed, getting into their hammocks and pulling up their blankets. Falco to his right, Hammond and Perth to his left, behind him Lester, who'd just slipped back into the compartment, the others further away. They all lay there, waiting, not moving.

Shanks tried to close his eyes but he was too on edge, they wouldn't stay shut, and he knew, he could sense without even looking, that the others, too, had their eyes open in the dark.

In the small cabin across the passageway, Beatty checked his watch, then doused the light. By now, he was sure Preisser had begun the autopsy on Maltin. Sweat matted Beatty's armpits, but he was surprisingly calm, almost drowsy, as if his body knew it needed this last brief rest. He felt, especially after the seaplane scare, as if he'd already gone through a grueling battle and it took a second for him to realize that the battle was yet to come. The *Ludendorff* so far was still in German hands.

For some reason his thoughts jumped to his former wife, Evelyn. What happened to them? Simple, really. They were young, they fell in love, they got married and they were unhappy.

Beatty wondered where Evelyn was, and what she would think if she knew where he was and how would she feel if she got word that he'd been killed? It didn't make any difference. Too late for that now.

He pulled his mind away, pulled it back to the *Ludendorff* and all the moves he and his men would soon have to make.

"Expect the Unexpected." That was the melodramatic warning sign on the desk of the eccentric journalist at S.O.E. who talked about writing spy thrillers after the war. Beatty tried at the last moment to detect any flaws in his plan, any element he might have overlooked.

He couldn't think of any. But he'd find out soon enough.

Chief Master-at-Arms Karl Goosens, his gait tuned to the roll of the ship, his big shoulders and immense stomach, almost like a sumo wrestler's, tight against his shirt, moved through the passageway, a solitary figure nearly filling the entire space. At this hour each night, as he made the rounds from compartment to compartment seeing the men were settling down, he always felt the *Ludendorff* was his personal responsibility, his ship, and the Luger on his hip the symbol of his authority.

Goosens looked in on the compartment occupied by the rescued U-boat men. They were in the sack already. Well-trained, well-disciplined, he thought approvingly.

Further down the passageway, he saw a sliver of light through a door crack and pushed it open. The American, the civilian, lay on his back in the tiny cubicle, hands under his head. Walker looked up, startled. Goosens shot Walker a dirty look and snapped out the light.

The door slammed shut, and lying in the dark, Walker felt cold.

Suppose, in another half hour, he was dead? He didn't want to think about that. If you're alive, you're alive and it was a waste of time worrying about death. And when you're dead, you're dead and you don't know it anyway. So there's nothing to be afraid of. At least that's what he told himself. Better to think about what he'd do, if he ever got through this, with Beatty's twenty-five grand. It could be a whole new ball game for him. He could set himself up in something solid and legitimate. And he was smarter now, he'd learned a lot. Before, he'd always thought small. When he had to make contacts, he made small ones, shmeering the desk sergeant at a station house, the shop steward at a local union. That's how he'd lost his bar. By not having clout higher up. And after the war, he had a feeling things were going to change, get even bigger, because there'd be more in the pot. The unions, the big money, the lawyers, Washington . . . they'd all work together. The newspapers'd show them meeting at the Plaza, the Mark Hopkins, the Mayflower, with flags in every corner and a priest saying a prayer to start things off. All first cabin, respectable. But to get anything done, you better have someone there on your side, just to keep them out of your way. That's what he'd have to do. Be smart for once in his life.

His life . . .

Walker almost never thought about his life any more because there wasn't much *to* think about. Father and mother, both dead. No friends, no real friends anyway. No girl. Lots of girls, actually, but all of them a blur. He could remember, if he tried, different shaped breasts, the way some rolled their hips under him, the way some of them moaned. But what those girls were all about, what was going on inside their heads, what they wanted from him he couldn't recall now. Couldn't recall because he never knew, never really cared. What the hell? They didn't care either, most of them. He was probably as much a blur to them as they were to him.

A sea boot grating on a ladder somewhere broke into his consciousness and he stirred uneasily. What was he wasting his time thinking about this for when in another thirty minutes he might die? But it was inconceivable to him that he, Terry Walker, was going to die. He was going to get through this alive, and he had a feeling that he would if he didn't take any long chances.

Then he realized that in another half hour, just going out on the upper deck would be taking a long chance.

CHAPTER 17

Eleven o'clock.

Continental air masses from Russia swooped down on the Baltic, bringing dry, cold winds as the *Ludendorff*, only a few hours from Kiel, steamed under a quarter moon that disappeared fitfully behind low clouds. Her high-flared bow carved through the sea that slapped at her sides, then leaped away as if to make room for the battleship. At the stern, the great screws churned up a plumed wake that spread out and stretched behind under the moonlight in a silver V. A rising wind hummed through the masts and rigging, giving the *Ludendorff* her own eerie voice to answer the rhythms of the sea.

Below decks, the ventilation fans sucking air into the ship droned over the faint hum of electric generators. The bulkheads sweated.

The watertight door of the British compartment opened a crack and Falco stepped quickly into the deserted passageway.

The take-over had begun.

Wearing a bulky jacket, Falco moved swiftly and silently. He had to get where he was going with no delay, without being stopped.

The squat Frenchman felt a stir of eagerness, almost of pleasure. He was making the first move. All the others, Hammond, Jenkins, Perth, even Beatty, would have to follow, were dependent on him. If he failed . . .

Falco wiped the thought from his mind. He wouldn't fail. He'd been on enough missions to know how to get a job done, and none of those jobs meant as much to him as the *Ludendorff*. He wanted the *Ludendorff*, this German battleship, this German prize, more than anything in his life, more than any kind of money, more than any kind of possession, certainly more than any kind of woman. Everything he was, everything he'd ever been led to this moment, and capturing the *Ludendorff* would settle a lot of old scores.

Falco heard footsteps in a nearby passageway, coming in his direction. There was a lone door directly ahead. Closed. The only place to hide. He rushed to it. He had no idea where it led. If Germans were on the other side, he was in trouble, but he had no choice.

Just as the footsteps reached a turn in the passageway and were almost upon him, he ducked through the door and closed it behind him.

He was in one of the crew's sleeping compartments. He could see figures lying there, watching him in the dark, puzzled, suspicious. He expected them to rise in a moment and grab hold of him. Then his eyes became accustomed to the dark and he realized he'd imagined the figures. The compartment, the hammocks were empty.

Cursing himself for imagining things, he waited until the footsteps on the other side of the door passed and receded. Silence again. He opened the door slowly, made sure the passageway was empty and proceeded until he reached the marines' compartment.

Some of the marines, not ship's company and therefore allowed to ignore lights out as long as they kept the noise down, were still awake. A couple in hammocks wrote letters. Others talked quietly. Tuned low, a wireless set picked up a London broadcast, Vera Lynn, the sweetheart of the British armed forces, singing "Someday I'll Find You."

On the opposite side of the compartment was the battleship's armory, its doors closed.

Without any show of hesitation, Falco started through the marine compartment. Several Germans looked up.

Falco shook a handful of requisition forms.

"Papers, forms," he bitched. "They're the real enemy."

The Germans chuckled.

The Frenchman continued unchallenged through the marine compartment and across a narrow passageway to the armory door. He knocked briefly and before anyone inside could answer, let himself in. The door swung shut behind him.

The racked rifles and submachine guns reflected the overhead light in rows of identical patterns. Falco could remember every one of them.

The ship's armorer, a lean Silesian farmer with big, long hands, looked up from the desk where he was studying an arms manual.

"Yes?" he asked. Hardly anyone ever came to the armory at night and he couldn't imagine what business one of the U-boat men would have here.

Falco flipped the requisition forms to the desk. The

armorer automatically looked down at them, turning his back to Falco. Falco drew a heavy pipe, padded in a glove to deaden the sound, but as he raised it, the German caught the abrupt shadowy reflection in the polished barrel of a gun and wheeled around. The pipe glanced off his temple and the German fell, pulling Falco down with him.

Falco clamped a hand across the German's mouth. They fought silently. The German clawed and kicked himself toward the door. Falco tried to pull him away but one finger reached the knob, then the German's hand. The knob slowly turned. The door opened an inch. Falco lunged for the door. Two hands wrestled for the knob, with the marines on the other side only a few feet away. Falco sank his teeth into the back of the German's neck. He bit hard, tasting blood. The pain forced the German to weaken his hold on the door. Slowly, slowly, Falco forced it closed, with a click that sounded to him like an explosion. He grabbed the gloved pipe again and crashed it down repeatedly on the German's head until the glove was matted with blood and hair and the German stopped moving.

Rapidly, Falco broke down one of the ten submachine guns from which he hadn't removed the firing pins earlier. He put the three parts, barrel, stock and magazine, into slits cut into the lining of his jacket. Falco knew he should take one of the Schmeissers, but instead took a weapon he'd never seen before boarding the *Ludendorff*, a navy Luger. It was actually a long-barreled Luger automatic converted into a submachine gun with a stock and thirty-two-round magazine. Dating back to the First War, it was very rare, almost a legend among weapon experts now, and Falco couldn't resist the prospect of turning it on the Germans.

Falco checked his jacket. The navy Luger bulged but hopefully not too much. He waited a few seconds for his breathing from the fight to slow down, then opened the door.

"Danke," he said to the dead German lying near the desk, but loud enough for the marines to hear. "Going to catch some sleep, huh? I don't blame you." Falco laughed agreeably.

He flicked out the armory's lights and closed the door behind him.

Papers in hand again, he started back through the marine compartment. He felt a sharp pain in his mouth and tasted something strange. His own blood. Sinking his teeth hard into the German's neck, he had cracked his front dental bridge. He had to keep his mouth closed tight to prevent the blood from seeping through his lips right there in the middle of the marine compartment.

"Hey, you!"

The sharp call came from a hammock behind him. Falco turned slowly. A marine, bare-chested, in shorts, motioned to him. Falco could feel salty blood pumping from his torn gums. What if the German said something that demanded a reply?

"Match?"

Falco tossed the marine a small box of matches and turned again to go.

"Wait, I'll give them back," the marine said.

Falco waved that the German could keep them but the marine insisted.

"Wait," he called.

The marine, forbidden to smoke in the compartment after lights out, followed Falco into the passageway just outside, taking an agonizing time to peel open a fresh pack of cigarettes. Falco swallowed a mouthful of blood.

The pieces of the machine pistol felt very heavy, very bulky under his jacket.

"After a big battleship, I bet you won't want to get into a U-boat for a long time," the German said.

Swallowing another mouthful of blood, Falco smiled through tight lips, conceding the German's point.

The German struck a match against the box. It broke in half and he reached for another one.

"My brother-in-law was lost on a U-boat," he said. "Not even in action. Training exercises. It's still down there somewhere."

Falco shook his head and made a sad "Mmmm" sound. Swallowing the blood was making him nauseous.

"I never liked him much," the German reflected, striking the second match and lighting his cigarette. "But what the hell. My sister was nearly thirty. At least someone took her off our hands."

Falco chuckled politely, but felt himself beginning to gag, the blood forced back up his throat to his tightly shut lips. He held out his hand for the matches.

"Oh . . . *danke*," the marine said, handing the box to Falco.

Falco nodded and turned down the passageway. Swiftly he descended a ladder to the level below.

He had lost precious time.

Under the merciless glare of the overhead lights, Maltin's body lay face up, completely nude on the gleaming white porcelain table, the head propped up on a wooden block. The whining sound of an electric saw cutting through his skull filled the operating room.

Ship's surgeon Preisser, in rubber apron and rubber gloves, worked the small saw around the skull from the back to the front in a neat, precise line. He'd gotten over his squeamishness about autopsies and cutting into bodies long ago in medical school, but even now he didn't care for the high-pitched whine of steel cutting into bone.

Still, it had to be done. He'd tried his best to save the U-boat man, had treated the head and stomach wounds swiftly and according to prescribed procedures. But the man died. Preisser had lost a patient. Unavoidable, perhaps, but conceivably he could learn something for the future from a post-mortem. *Mortui vivos docent* . . . the dead teach the living.

Preisser inserted a chisel into the skull cut and tapped it with a hammer. The top half of the skull came off, revealing the glistening dura, the membrane covering the brain. He felt a little surge of excitement, of anticipation, which he always experienced upon entering the mysteries of the human body.

Preisser folded the loose scalp over the corpse's face, like a veil of flesh covering the eyes, nose and mouth. Now at last the half-open eyes wouldn't watch him while he worked. Then deftly with a scalpel he removed Maltin's brain, severing it from the spinal cord and placing it on a steel tray. He examined it closely, identifying the subdural hematoma, the brain injury, and the edema, the swelling caused by the injury, but, the closer he examined the brain lying before him on the tray, the more he was surprised. His treatment had evidently been so effective that while the brain injury had caused swelling, that swelling hadn't become so severe as to push the brain stem into the spinal cord, which would've created fatal pressure on the cardiac and respiratory centers.

Indeed, contrary to Preisser's expectations, the brain

injury had *not* been fatal. Therefore, the stomach wound must have been.

To confirm this, Preisser reached for a knife and entered the body, cutting near the base of the neck, straight down the chest and abdomen and ending just above the genitals. Then he cut through the abdominal muscles to expose the abdominal cavity.

He noted that Kleist had been a remarkable specimen, virtually no fatty tissue and maximum muscular development everywhere, chest, arms, back, legs. Not what one might expect in a U-boat man who had to live and work in confined spaces for prolonged periods.

Preisser observed where he had sewn up the bullet hole in the small intestine, and saw a puddle of greenish-yellow pus, indicating peritonitis and blood poisoning.

But again, something odd. There wasn't enough pus, not enough poisoning to cause death, certainly not in a man this big, this strong.

For a long moment, Preisser stood over the naked body, the skull and abdomen gaping open like a carcass, and tried to understand. He had apparently treated both wounds, the head and stomach, properly and successfully, a testimony to his own skills. Yet the patient died. How? Had he overlooked something, some small wound, a sliver of steel that caused death?

If he did, Preisser had no intention of recording it in his autopsy report. It would do the dead man no good now and would only be embarrassing to Preisser. But he had to find out. Preisser checked his watch—11:08 P.M. It was late and he felt tired . . . autopsies always drained him . . . and he considered putting the body back in the icebox and finishing in the morning. But the *Ludendorff* would reach Kiel by then and there'd be too many other duties. No, if he wanted to find out why Kleist died, he'd have to finish tonight.

Reaching for rib cutters, Preisser opened the chest cavity by clipping through the cartilage of the thoracic cage and exposing the heart and lungs. The tiniest piece of shrapnel piercing the heart muscle might've gone unnoticed yet have caused fatal bleeding. He cut the heart free and examined it carefully. It was completely intact. No wounds. The same with the lungs and all the other internal organs.

Preisser couldn't understand it. To the best of his ability, he'd ruled out head, abdominal, heart and lung wounds, or any other trauma to the trunk, as cause of death. Yet here was this corpse, lying there, mocking him. The mingled odors of corpse and disinfectant that hovered over the autopsy table were sickening him. Faced with retracing all his steps to see if he hadn't overlooked something, Preisser decided to end the autopsy now before he lost a night's sleep.

He began to shove the severed organs back into the body before sewing it up, planning on attributing cause of death to the brain and abdominal wounds, which, with complications, undoubtedly contributed to death anyway.

Then he remembered he hadn't performed one other step necessary to include in his autopsy report, and that was examining the structures of the neck. It didn't really matter . . . nobody ever looked at those reports . . . but his Germanic respect for order compelled him at least to go through the motions.

To inspect the structures of the neck, he reached up into the chest cavity and pulled down on the trachea, the windpipe, to get to the larynx. The trachea resisted at first, then came down with a suction-like sound.

What Preisser saw made his heart pound.

The dead man's larynx, vocal cords and base of the tongue were enlarged, swollen with fluid. Edema here could mean only one thing. Death had come from strangulation.

But that was impossible.

Yet there was the physical evidence shining wetly under the lights and Preisser didn't dare dismiss it. Someone aboard the *Ludendorff* had killed Kleist. But who?

Only a few men had had occasion to be in sick bay within the past two days . . . himself, the ship's corpsmen, the U-boat commander Von Brennerman. Von Brennerman. But what motive could Von Brennerman have for murdering one of his own men? Preisser couldn't imagine, didn't even want to think about it. But he had to do something immediately.

His hand still sheathed in a bloodstained rubber glove, Preisser reached for a phone to call Kapitän Ziegler.

Suddenly he felt something hard and cold pressed against the carotid artery in his neck. Startled, he reached up to brush it away but dropped his hand when he touched it and realized what it was. A submachine gun.

"We have some other patients for you, Herr Doktor," Falco said.

CHAPTER 18

"Short arm. Let's go. Short arm," Beatty bellowed.

Commandingly he strode into the dozing marine compartment. "All right, let's go, men. Short arm."

"Wha'?" a marine asked, opening one blurry eye.

"Short arm!" Beatty barked.

"Oh, God, not again," the marine groaned.

"Everybody up," Beatty commanded, moving between the hammocks.

Everything, he knew, now hung on this chancy tactic, calling a surprise V.D. inspection and catching the marines and the entire off-watch crew with their pants down, without a fight. Surprise V.D. checks were as common as crabs in the service, and that's what Beatty was counting on, that no sailor would question one.

"Hit the deck, men. Milking time," he intoned.

Grumbling, sleepy, but accustomed to this routine, the marines began to straggle from their hammocks, muttering curses. A few wondered why it wasn't Chief Master-at-Arms Goosens calling the short arm, but Von

Brennerman was an officer and you don't question an officer. Not in the German Navy.

"Here we go, man," Beatty said, shaking the tattooed shoulder of a still sleeping German.

The marine cut a cheesy fart and tumbled from his hammock.

"If they look at it one more time," he mumbled, "it's going to fall off."

"I've seen it," another said. "It will be no great loss."

Beatty went from hammock to hammock, rousting the marines, getting them to move faster.

"Whip it out if it's stout," he called. "Into the mess."

Several marines looked up at this.

"Why not here?" one yawned.

"Doctor's lazy," Beatty replied. "Have to bring the peckers to him."

"You don't have to look at mine. I'm a married man," one complained self-righteously. "I haven't even used it since I left home."

"Liar," someone shouted.

One big marine, interrupted in the middle of jerking off under his blanket, had to tumble out of his hammock, hoping that his hard-on would go down unnoticed. It didn't. One of the other Germans saw it, jumped back and screamed in mock alarm.

"Knock it off," Beatty ordered. He turned at the door to make sure there were no stragglers. "Let's go. Pecker check."

He led the marines, groggy and dressed only in undershorts and T-shirts, down the passageway toward the mess.

Seconds later, Hammond, Tanner and Walker slipped through the compartment the marines had just left and ducked into the armory. They broke down the submachine guns and tucked the pieces into their jackets. They loaded extra magazines with ammunition from a locker. The dead armorer lying in a corner with eyes wide open watched them.

The marines, Beatty bringing up the rear, padded barefoot into the mess. They saw Dr. Preisser sitting behind a table. Shanks stood off to the side, buttoning his fly as if he'd just been inspected. Falco stood behind a steam table, holding a mug of coffee. There were no guns in evidence. Falco gave Preisser a look.

"Remove shorts, *bitte*," Preisser ordered.

With a weary collective sigh, the twenty-five marines dropped their drawers, exposing twenty-five rear ends and twenty-five cold, shriveled peckers. Falco produced his Luger submachine gun from behind the counter.

"Up!" he snarled.

The marines were so stunned for a moment they just stared at Falco. Then slowly most of them raised their hands. Two of them, sleepily misunderstanding his command, pulled their drawers up, but quickly seeing their mistake dropped them again.

"Move!" Falco waved the gun.

Shanks opened the massive door of a huge refrigerator and Falco herded them inside. He slammed the door behind them, throwing the giant latch into place.

Beatty swung through a second sleeping compartment, this one on the port side forward, occupied by the *Ludendorff* crewmen.

"All right, here we go. Rise and shine. Short arm, short arm," he called.

There was more bitching and moaning as the crewmen,

nearly two dozen of them, stumbled after Beatty, one hand in his jacket pocket gripping a concealed Luger.

Perth approached the radio room one level below.

In the stillness of the passageway, he heard what sounded like a muffled shot from somewhere above, and froze, listening. It was probably a watertight door slamming somewhere. He hoped so. Shooting this early, before the take-over was well under way and key stations captured, would be disastrous.

There was no way for him to find out. Whatever happened elsewhere aboard ship, he had to go through with his part according to set plan.

He reached the door to the radio room. It was closed. As his hand moved for the knob, he gave himself a conscious order: not to think of himself as a German, or whoever was on the other side of the door as a German, just as an enemy. To act as swiftly and ruthlessly as Falco would.

Perth stepped into the radio room and his eyes swiftly took in the banks of *Telefunken* receivers on all four sides. Below the receivers, wireless sending keys. To their left, typewriters. A lone operator sat at one of the silent keys, inspecting a burned-out tube. He looked up. It was one of the young crewmen who'd invited Perth to join in the singing on the quarterdeck, a German with an intelligent, open face.

"Can't sleep?" he asked with a smile.

Perth said nothing.

"What's the matter?" the German asked. "You don't look so good."

Perth drew a knife. The operator stared, his head tilted in a silent question. Perth hesitated a crucial split second and the German leaped up, flinging a typewriter

206

at him. Perth felt the machine hurtle past his shoulder as he lunged. He grabbed the German in a bear hug as the wireless started to chatter with an incoming message. Perth plunged his knife between the German's shoulders.

Blood spurted in jets as the German, wide-eyed, pulled back and staggered around the room in an intricate little jig, staring at Perth. Perth ordered himself to stab the German again, but he was paralyzed with horror. Only the German had the power to move. The ghastly jig spun the operator around, crashing him into a bank of receivers, against a steel table, all the time staring at Perth. Finally, he crumpled dead at Perth's feet.

Through his horror, Perth heard the wireless still chattering, but he couldn't take his eyes off the youth he'd killed. The body's weight pressed against his legs as if trying to hold him there and he couldn't move. His stomach began to heave. Do what Falco would do, his own voice screamed in his head. He kicked the body away and the explosion of energy broke its spell over him.

He rushed to the wireless and took down the message. He ducked into the decoding booth at the far end of the room, a completely enclosed cubicle with a decoding machine that looked like a big teletype with a complex series of wheels.

He decoded the message. REQUEST LUDENDORFF REPORT WEATHER CONDITIONS AND CO-ORDINATES.

It was a standard request from Group Command to warships at sea, but it demanded a prompt reply.

He rushed back into the radio room to a wireless key. His hands were trembling, yet he had to send with professional speed and accuracy. A slow or sloppy radio operator would never be assigned to any warship, least of all a battleship, and a jumbled message could arouse suspicion in headquarters.

But his hand poised above the key kept shaking. No way to make it stop. He had to go ahead anyway. He tapped the key and incredibly, by the time he hit the second dash, his hand was steady, the message was flying.

BAROMETER FALLING, AIR TEMPERATURE 47 DEGREES, WIND SOUTHWEST 2, CLOUDS CUMULOUS, VISIBILITY 12 MILES, COORDINATES 53 DEGREES, 17 MINUTES LATITUDE, 14 DEGREES 32 MINUTES LONGITUDE.

Then he had to send one more message since Group Command was expecting the battleship at Kiel early in the morning.

REQUEST PERMISSION FOR ONE MORE DAY AT SEA TO COMPLETE TRIALS. ZIEGLER.

Walker slipped out of the armory with three parts of a Schmeisser tucked under his jacket, stock, barrel and magazine. He had two spare magazines taped under his pants, one to each leg. Three magazines gave him ninety-six rounds of ammunition.

He headed down a deserted passageway. By now Beatty should have taken out most of the off-duty crew, but the engines still beat, the fans still droned and the ship seemed as alive and menacing as before.

He started up a ladder. His body ached now in every muscle and bone from the beating by Rheinbolt and the weight of the submachine gun didn't help. Coming through a blackout curtain to the upper deck, he stopped in the shadows as a German passed by. It was Chief Master-at-Arms Goosens. Goosens, he knew, carried a gun.

He made it to the boat deck and headed forward, unseen by the machine-gun crew huddled against the cold, their collars up, at the nearest 37-mm gun. Concealed behind a 4.1-inch turret, he felt one of the magazines taped to his legs slipping and secured it tighter. Then he stole over to a ladder out of the Germans' line of vision and two steps at a time climbed to the signal bridge.

He hunched down in the shadows of a chest-high splinter shield. He peered up. High above him, the ship's masts rolled in a slow arc against the sky and the radar scanners swept around ceaselessly and for a moment he had the ludicrous feeling that at any second the radar would detect him here. He studied the bridge, one level above. In the faint glow shed by the bridge's instruments, he could make out the deck officer, the helmsman, a guard, which meant another gun.

Walker removed the Schmeisser parts from under his jacket and assembled them. Slowly, quietly, he pulled back the breech bolt, bringing a bullet into the chamber. His hand felt oily from the freshly greased gun and he wiped his fingers on his jacket sleeve as he stepped back deeper into the shadows, waiting for Beatty's signal. He had expected to feel bowel-churning fear now, but though his heart raced, he wanted to get going, soon, now, even if it meant shooting. He'd heard of condemned men racing up the steps of the gallows, maybe just to get it over with. That's what he wanted most. To get it over with.

Hammond and Jenkins peered down through a partially open hatch at the forward engine room below. They could see the officer of the watch, the chief of the watch and the throttle man at the control board, but knew that there had to be others there on the control level and lower down on the operating and bilge levels. Too many spread out over too large an area. Too much of a risk that some of them could get away when Hammond and Jenkins made their move.

Hammond retreated down the passageway to the electrical distribution panel, where he had killed the German, Borgmann. He selected two wires that crossed at right angles and with a penknife deftly shaved off most of their rubber insulation. He lit his cigarette lighter and placed the flame under the two wires. The remaining insulation started to burn away. Hammond closed the panel door, leaving a crack open for oxygen to feed the flame, then hurried back to Jenkins at the hatch overlooking the forward engine room. They waited.

At the electrical distribution panel, the flame flickered a moment, almost died out. Then flared up again. The insulation smoked. The flame burned clear through the insulation and the two electrical wires touched with a crackle of sparks.

In the engine room, ominous smoke triggered by the minor short circuit seeped from the control board. From above, Hammond and Jenkins watched as the throttle man tried to discover the cause. The chief of the watch hurried over. They shook heads, puzzled. Two more, then several more Germans appeared when the smoke didn't stop. They were rounding themselves up directly below the hatch.

Hammond swung down one hatch, Jenkins down another.

"Against the wall!" Hammond barked.

The Germans instantly obeyed the submachine guns.

Hammond jabbed his gun into the stomach of the officer of the watch.

"Call the others up," he demanded.

The officer, pale face trembling, signaled to the operating level below.

"All you men, come up here," he called.

The men hesitated. It was against regulations for all the men to leave their posts at the same time.

"Immediately!" the scared officer said.

The men from the lower levels climbed into the control room. They stared at the submachine guns and quickly raised their hands. The control room was crowding up.

The chief of the watch, standing near the throttle board, saw that several men stood between him and the English, their bodies partially concealing him. Slowly, his hand reached to uncradle the phone to the bridge.

Hammond saw it from across the control room. There was no time to get to the German. He spun and fired a fast burst. The German crashed back with bullets in the chest.

Suddenly the control room was filled with a high banshee shriek and another German, who hadn't been in the line of fire, fell as if struck by an invisible ray, a hole burned through his body, the surrounding flesh charred and smoking.

Hammond instantly knew what happened. At least one of his bullets had gone wild and smashed through a main steam pipe, liberating invisible superheated steam at 850 degrees Fahrenheit. There was no way to tell where the lethal jet, or jets of steam, shrieking through the pipe were. Blunder in front of one and it'd tear an arm off a shoulder. But he had to reach the valve and shut off the steam before he and everyone else were cooked to death, and he had to pray that the valve itself was not directly under a deadly jet of steam.

He bulled his way through the Germans, who were too terrified to move, and grabbed the steam valve. The control room was already blistering hot. He wrenched the valve with furious strength. The high shriek began to die down.

The bridge phone jangled. Hammond realized they must've noticed a sudden drop in speed from the loss of steam pressure. Hammond had to answer it.

"What's wrong down there?" the deck officer's voice demanded.

"Had to shut off steam, sir," Hammond replied. "There's a small fire in the shaft."

"Get it out fast," the bridge commanded.

"Yes, sir," Hammond said respectfully.

Walker sweated for Beatty's signal in the shadows of the signal bridge. He'd been waiting only a couple of minutes but it felt like half the night. Maybe something had gone wrong. Maybe he should just go ahead and take the bridge without the signal. But if something went wrong, what was the use in just taking the bridge?

He heard footsteps. It was two Germans. They leaned against the splinter shield just a few yards away, looking out over the bow cleaving the sea and talking quietly. In the shadows, Walker pressed himself back against the bulkhead, barely breathing. But the ship rolled in the swelling sea and for a moment the moonlight picked him out.

"Hey!" one of the Germans called. "Who's there?"

"Just me," Walker answered.

"Oh . . . American?"

"Yeah." Walker glanced from the two Germans to

212

the men at the ack-ack mounts on the decks below. Still no signal from Beatty. Still no time to start shooting. But if these Germans saw his submachine gun . . .

"Come on over here," one of them said.

They hadn't seen the Schmeisser, yet. Leaving it propped against the bulkhead in the shadows, hoping the goddamn moon wouldn't hit it or that when the ship rolled it wouldn't tip over and clatter to the deck, Walker stepped forward.

"What are you doing up here?" It was Seidman, the helmsman who'd been on the bridge when Walker cased it earlier.

"Clearing my head," Walker replied.

He could see the helmsman look at him, then exchange a glance with the other one, a dumpy signalman with a double chin.

"I had a headache. That Rheinbolt can hit," Walker added bitterly, stepping closer so they could see his battered face.

"You gave it to him pretty good too," Seidman said.

"Well, I was just defending myself," Walker answered quickly.

"*Ach*, that's all right. He's a bully."

"The Kapitän's jock strap." The signalman spit contemptuously, then feeling guilty, rubbed it off the deck with his shoe.

"Past eleven," Seidman said, looking at his watch. "Well . . . a busy day tomorrow in Kiel."

"Yeah," Walker said.

But Seidman didn't leave. He pointed to his comrade.

"Hey, remember on the bridge? Tell Fichte. You know, about the *schworzen*."

"The what?"

"The *schworzen*, the *schworze* girls in Harlem."

"Oh that," Walker shrugged. What would he do if he got Beatty's signal, right now? "Well look, *Kameraden*. It's kind of late and I got this splitting head. Maybe tomorrow."

"*Nein, nein*," the helmsman insisted. "Just tell him about Lenox Street."

"Lenox Avenue," Walker said.

"*Ya*. Tell. *Bitte*," Fichte, the signalman insisted, intrigued.

Walker had to get rid of them. He had to make it short.

"Well, you see . . . this chick, she was a cocktail waitress, but on the side she specialized in discipline, if you know what I mean." Walker flicked his hand as if he held a whip. "She was wild for discipline."

"Of course," Fichte said with Germanic approval. "Every country must have discipline."

"Shhh," the helmsman said. "That's not what he's talking about. You Bavarians are morons. Continue, Herr Walker."

They were both facing him and he was facing the bulkhead. The ship rolled again and for an awful moment he heard the concealed submachine gun slipping. The Germans didn't seem to hear anything and then it stopped. But a second later he saw the barrel glinting in the moonlight.

"All kinds of guys came to her, guys you wouldn't believe," he said quickly, to rivet their attention until the gun disappeared in the shadows again. "One guy, this psychiatrist, he was very big for being tied down on a bed and lapping like a dog, if you know what I mean."

"*Mein Gott*," Seidman exclaimed.

"Hell, that's nothing," Walker had to go on. "An-

214

other guy, a senator who ran for vice-president . . ."

"Vice-president?" Fichte was shocked.

"Don't ask. The higher up you go, especially in the government, the worse they get. He'd come in this beautiful suit and Homburg, see, and then he'd strip down and underneath he'd be wearing a pair of diapers. Just diapers. With safety pins. And then he'd pay twenty-five bucks for the girl to take the diapers off and spank his behind."

"*Mein Gott,*" Seidman said again.

"If America gets in, she's going to lose the war," Fichte predicted solemnly.

"Yeah, I guess so," Walker agreed. "Well . . ."

"Herr Walker!"

Walker wheeled. It was Drau, accompanied by a guard. The guard was armed with a rifle.

"Get below," Drau ordered the other two Germans.

Intimidated by the steel in his voice, they saluted and swiftly left.

Drau spun back to Walker.

"We've been searching for you for a quarter of an hour. Where've you been?"

"Here," Walker said.

"Come!" Drau grabbed his arm and propelled him toward a ladder.

"What's up?" Walker asked.

"It's all over," Drau snapped, tightening his grip.

He and the guard hustled Walker from the signal bridge and away from the Schmeisser concealed in the shadows.

CHAPTER 19

"How stupid can you be, Herr Walker?"

Ziegler's voice was filled with cold contempt.

Walker shrugged.

He was finished, he thought. Finished. Beatty and the others were already captured. For a moment he felt sorry for them, but then felt more sorry for himself. Drau stood at the door of Ziegler's sea cabin, watching him closely.

"Why did you get involved in something like this?" Ziegler demanded from his desk.

Though he never liked copping pleas, Walker considered telling how he didn't want to get involved, how he was forced to, but he knew it wouldn't do any good, not with Ziegler.

"What's the difference," he said. "I got sucked in."

"Sucked in. That's all you have to say?"

"That's it."

"That's not what Baroness von Ruser says." Ziegler shook his head.

Walker looked up, puzzled. His survival instincts,

sharpened by a lifetime of tight scrapes, warned him to find out as much as he could and say as little as possible. Maybe the dice hadn't stopped rolling yet.

"Baroness von . . . d'you say Ruser?" Walker pretended to search his memory.

Ziegler directed Walker to sit across the massive rosewood desk.

"Come, come. You *know* Baroness von Ruser from Lubeck. Don't you?"

"Only if she says I do," Walker answered carefully.

"Yes, she does say. She also says you sold her a questionable Renoir."

"Oh," Walker muttered. This was the little business transaction worth fifteen years in jail that he'd been worrying about, and here it was. It had caught up with him faster than he thought. "How did you . . . ?"

"Standard procedure," Ziegler said. "We radioed the names of the rescued men to Naval Group East. They in turn processed *your* name with police authorities in Berlin. As you may know, we have a very efficient national police force, and not surprisingly they know of you."

Ziegler produced a radiogram and handed it to Walker, who reached over for it, leaning his elbow on the desk. Walker didn't even have to read the whole thing. The relevant words leaped out at him: BERLIN . . . RUSER . . . WALKER . . . POLEZEI.

"Ohh," Walker nodded, impressed.

"Yes." Ziegler smiled coldly. "You see, no man's life will bear a close investigation."

Walker kept his mouth shut.

"Until we reach Kiel, you will spend the rest of this voyage where you belong. In a cell." Ziegler nodded to Drau, who stepped forward and prodded Walker to his feet.

Walker had reached the door when Ziegler snapped, "Wait! What is this?"

Walker looked back. Ziegler was studying something on his desk, where the American had rested an arm. The gleaming finish was marred by a dull greasy patch. Ziegler carefully wiped off the spot with his hand and automatically rubbed it through his fingers. A frown crossed his face. He raised his hand and smelled it.

"Gun grease . . ." Ziegler's eyes swung to the American.

He came from behind the desk and studied Walker up and down. The American's sleeve had an oily stain.

"What's that on your jacket?" Ziegler demanded.

"I dunno . . . I must've brushed against one of the turrets," Walker shrugged.

"This is *light* oil," Ziegler said. "Used only on small arms! What were you doing in the armory?"

"Armory? I wasn't in the armory."

Ziegler turned to Drau. "Where did you find this man?"

"We couldn't find him in his compartment," Drau answered uneasily. "We had to look, sir, and found him on the signal deck."

"The signal deck," Ziegler exploded. "He was Commander von Brennerman's responsibility. Get Von Brennerman immediately."

"When we couldn't find the American, sir, we tried to locate Von Brennerman but . . ." Drau trailed off, scared now.

In the silence that hung in the cabin, Ziegler's mind raced.

"Lock him up," Ziegler ordered, jabbing a finger at

Walker. He opened a cabinet and handed Drau a Luger, taking one for himself. "Check the armory. Find Von Brennerman!"

Beatty led a dozen half-naked crewmen down a passageway toward the mess. They passed a compartment with about ten more sleeping Germans. He'd return for them in a minute. They would be the last batch from the compartments. It was almost time to signal Walker to take the bridge.

The Schmeisser's muzzle never left Walker's spinal cord as the guard escorted him across the upper deck. He saw Drau on the boat deck above, gesturing to the machine gunners at the 37-mm mount just beneath "B" turret. The Germans raced down ladders, heading below decks to find Beatty. Within minutes the British scattered all over the ship would be butchered.

The guard motioned for Walker to head down a vertical ladder. Slowly Walker started down face forward, the guard right behind him, the muzzle cold on his neck. In one motion, Walker twisted his head away from the muzzle and grabbed the guard's ankle and pulled. The guard plunged over Walker's shoulder and landed at the bottom head-first, cracking his skull. Walker jumped down, grabbed the guard's submachine gun. There was no time to hunt for Beatty and warn him. But if Beatty heard firing, he'd know. Walker considered firing a burst right there, but the Germans would hear it too, and he didn't want to risk being trapped in the narrow passageway.

He bolted up the ladder, figuring the shooting would start soon enough. He was right. Just as he reached the upper deck, another German coming around a turret saw Walker but in the dark didn't spot the submachine gun and charged at him.

Walker whipped up the gun and fired. The Schmeisser bucked, muzzle flashes stabbed the dark, the guard, too near to miss, staggered to the deck, his chest stitched with bullets.

Silence again. Walker felt a surge of fear. He'd done it. Killed a German. He was in the soup now. No turning back, no bargaining, no talking his way out of this. Every Kraut on the battleship would be out to kill him now.

Walker raced for a ladder leading to the boat deck, hoping to make it to the bridge unseen. From somewhere . . . it was chief Master-at-Arms Goosens . . . a gun cracked and Walker heard a bullet drone past his head. He felt the same cold terror as when the British plane strafed the deck, only more because this time he knew the firing was directed at him. Without looking, he fired back into the darkness and afraid of being caught midway up the ladder, a clear target, he dove for cover behind a ventilator shaft. He imagined Germans closing in on him from all sides. He dropped to one knee, not breathing. He suddenly felt weak. Maybe it was those hours in the sea catching up with him, or Rheinbolt's fists, or the sound of the bullet inches from his face, or all three. But he could barely keep a grip on the gun clutched in his hands, and he didn't dare move. He was scared shitless.

The rattle of Walker's fire reached Beatty and the dozen Germans approaching the mess. Startled, they turned to him, as an officer, for orders.

"Get in there," Beatty barked, drawing his Luger.

The Germans were rounded up inside the mess by

Shanks. But three at the end of the line in the crowded passageway made a break. Beatty's gun roared like a cannon shot in the confined space. One German fell as if tripped. The two others vanished around a sharp angle turn. Beatty and Falco raced after them down several passageways.

The two Germans made it to the armory and grabbed the nearest weapons. They spun around to face Beatty and Falco. They fired. The guns clicked harmlessly. Falco blasted them with his Luger submachine gun. He and Beatty raced away, leaving the armory door unlocked, an open invitation to any other Germans looking for weapons.

Tanner, Lester and Pinkney, emerging topside to round up the machine-gun crews, immediately ran into small arms fire and sprinted for cover behind "A" turret. Their eyes strained in the dark, but they couldn't tell how many Germans fired at them or where the Germans were. There were only two, Drau and Goosens, armed with pistols. While Drau's fire kept the British behind the turret, Goosens reached the vertical ladder on the other side. He bounded to the turret roof and bellied across unseen. He reached the edge and fired straight down at the English. Pinkney dropped with a 9-mm slug that pierced the top of his skull.

Tanner and Lester retreated aft for the shelter of a smaller starboard turret.

More Germans, from the last compartment Beatty didn't have time to corral, poured on deck with guns snatched from the armory. They came up behind Tanner and Lester. The English whirled and opened fire, dropping most of them as they frantically clicked away with their useless Schmeissers. The others scattered for cover. One of them scooped up the gun dropped by Pinkney.

The rattle of submachine guns from the upper deck reached Schnaubel below. Fully dressed, he sat alone in a deserted head. He heard the noise but didn't know exactly what it was and didn't care. He was brain-reeling drunk.

Schnaubel hadn't been rounded up with the others in his compartment. After the humiliation in the shower room, he couldn't sleep and left the compartment shortly after ten to find a bottle of brandy which he kept hidden in one of his supply rooms. Then he went to an isolated head to be alone with his bottle. The place reeked heavily of human waste but after a few swigs he didn't care.

The brandy fired Schnaubel's imagination and his glands, and he thought about the beautiful young boy from the U-boat. Such a boy needed someone like himself, sensitive and kind, and he wanted to go right now to find him. Yes, that's what he would do. He rose dizzily, then sat down again. He was too afraid of the boy's lover, too afraid of more cruelty and violence. If that was the kind of lover the boy wanted, insensitive and filthy, that's all the boy deserved and he, Schnaubel, was too good for him. But too good for him or not, Schnaubel could still see the boy's lean thighs which knit together at the firm, tight buttocks, and felt a tormented hunger.

He drained the rest of the bottle and heard the strange noise again. At first he thought it was the ringing in his own head, but then it sounded like someone hammering. What could be going on topside so late at night? Curious, he lurched to his feet and headed for the upper deck. He couldn't remember where the nearest ladder was, but finally found one.

He stumbled to the upper deck and gasped. Darting figures, gunfire, stabs of flame crisscrossed the deck. It was impossible. Men on the ship were firing at other men on the ship. Schnaubel couldn't tell why, but he had to get away or he'd be hit himself. He turned to hide in a door when a sustained burst lit up the deck like a flash of sheet lightning and outlined the forms of several shipmates. They were firing at a figure concealed near him, behind a turret. It was the big U-boat man who had hurt him in the shower room. And the big man was firing back.

Schnaubel's numbed brain couldn't imagine why this was happening. Only that his shipmates were firing at the object of his own hatred.

With an enraged cry, Schnaubel charged Lester from behind. Lester heard him and spun, but too late to fire. Schnaubel flung himself straight at him. The German's 260 pounds knocked Lester off balance and carried both of them clear of the turret. Across the deck, the Germans saw two dark figures and opened fire.

The night lit up again in staccato flashes.

"*Nein,*" Schnaubel screamed, throwing up his arms. A bullet ripping into his mouth ended the scream.

Lester tried to scramble back behind the turret. A burst caught him in the back. As he lay, his legs jerking as if still wanting to run, Drau rushed up and smashed his skull with his pistol butt. A second German seized Lester's submachine gun.

Below decks, more Germans were getting more guns.

Over thirty crewmen, from below and topside, hadn't been rounded up into the refrigerator before the shooting started. Seeing what happened when they tried to fire weapons from the armory, several of them scrambled further below to the ship's ordnance storeroom, tore open a crate and snatched up untampered submachine guns.

Now these men were fanning out all over the *Ludendorff.*

On the upper deck, crouched behind the ventilator shaft, Walker heard the crack of guns, saw in the darkness muzzle flashes that revealed for a split second, like the frame of a film, a running figure, a crumpled body, an arm signaling. Then darkness again, though the stark images remained in his eyes a second longer. No telling how many Germans had guns now, but it was too many. Still, nobody had fired at him since the first time. Was it thirty seconds ago, a minute, five minutes? Maybe they didn't know where he was. Maybe they were just waiting for him to show himself.

Ten, fifteen yards off he saw a ladder to the boat deck, which was the only way to the bridge. There was also no firing, no dying, on the boat deck. Another good reason to get his ass up there. He rose slowly. His legs shook. Clutching the submachine gun, he took a deep breath and in a low crouch dashed for the ladder, afraid that at any second a bullet would slam into his back. He took the ladder two steps at a time and threw himself belly first on the boat deck, breathing hard. He shot a look down. It was too dark to see very much but apparently nobody on the upper deck had seen him.

Suddenly, as he rose, a gun blasted at him from behind. He wheeled, saw a 20-mm machine gun firing at him across the deck, the flaming muzzle aimed almost straight at him. There was no place to hide. The machine gun couldn't miss at such close range. But the tracers screamed over his head and he remembered what Beatty had told him. Machine guns were regulated, couldn't fire at anything on the ship itself. The German, probably not part of the machine-gun crew, either didn't know it, or seeing Walker with a weapon had just panicked. Walker stood up and with machine-gun bullets tearing over his head, raised his Schmeisser, took slow, deliberate aim and killed the German behind the 20-mm.

He ran for the vertical ladder leading to the third level. But suddenly more firing bullets slamming on all sides, drove him behind a cluster of lifeboats. He huddled below one of the boats. Two Germans, seeing the 20-mm blasting at Walker, had fired up at him themselves. Now they charged up to the boat deck to get him.

Walker squeezed off a short burst that caught the first German at the top of the ladder. But he forgot to keep the Schmeisser low and his next burst went over the second German's head. The German retreated aft. Walker fired a long burst, heard a click, realized he was out of ammunition as the German made it up a ladder to the signal bridge above. Protected by the splinter shield, the German fired down at him.

Huddled below the lifeboat, Walker tore off a fresh magazine taped to his leg and swiftly reloaded his Schmeisser. The German above knew where he was, so Walker began crawling for another boat when a second submachine gun fired at him from above. He couldn't move. To shoot back, he'd have to raise his head into two lines of fire.

Bullets chewed through the fragile hull all around him, showering splinters, chunks of wood. He was afraid the firing would tear the boat apart, disintegrate it, leave him completely exposed. He was helpless to do anything about it except crouch there and wait for the bullets ripping through the lifeboat to rip through him.

Shanks on the forecastle saw Walker on the starboard deck above, trapped behind the riddled lifeboat. Clutching his submachine gun, Shanks started running. In a split second he'd already calculated what he had to do to save Walker, and since Walker was essential to the mission Shanks did it.

He swung around to the opposite, the port side, of the ship and sprinted for a ladder at the base of the superstructure. Across fifty yards of exposed deck it looked a mile away. Zigzagging when he heard bullets whining past his head, he hit the ladder at top speed taking it three steps at a time. Near the top he felt his hamstring muscle tighten. The old man knew what was going to happen but didn't stop. He reached the boat deck, lungs straining, when the back of his left leg exploded with crippling pain. He shot a look across the boat deck. Walker was still pinned down by murderous fire from above.

Shanks half-ran, half-hobbled for a vertical ladder leading to the signal bridge and the Germans shooting down at Walker. He drew fire from somewhere below, couldn't chance it on that ladder, limped low to the other one and hauled himself up, one rung at a time. His heart pounded, his left leg hung in agony, his eyes began to blur. He pushed himself higher, staggered to the signal bridge and coming up behind the Germans cut loose with his submachine gun, emptying the whole magazine into them.

On the level below, the bullets banging through the lifeboat suddenly stopped. Walker peered over the gunwale. The Germans above him were gone. He cautiously inched away from the boat, ready to duck back if he drew fire again. He didn't. Hugging the bulkhead, he made it to a ladder. There was no cover on a ladder. He mounted it as fast as he could. He saw Shanks on the signal bridge, sagging, exhausted, against a searchlight, two dead Germans lying nearby at crazy angles.

Walker looked up. Above him loomed the bridge.

Beatty and Falco exchanged fire below decks with two Germans in a narrow, unprotected passageway. Backing up, the Germans disappeared around a corner. When Beatty and Falco reached it, the passageway was empty. The Germans were gone. Beatty studied the nearest doors. One of them was closed. Staying out of the line of fire, he tried it. The heavy steel door was locked. Above it a small sign read Auxiliary Transmitting Room.

"Stay here," he ordered Falco. He raced down the passageway.

In the auxiliary transmitting room, the two Germans desperately tried to get a transmitter working. Gunners mates, they had no experience, no idea what they were doing. They flicked switches, twisted dials. One of the switches suddenly turned on the power. The dials lit up.

"*Macht schnell . . . macht schnell,*" one hissed as the other fumbled to hook up a microphone.

Beatty reached the upper deck, still swept by fire. He grabbed a coil of rope lying near a winch and in a crouch ran to the rail. Nobody had seen him. Lying flat on his stomach, he tied one end of the rope to a cleat, strapped his submachine gun across his back and slipped over the side. Hand under hand he let himself down the glass-smooth side of the battleship, the sea boiling below him. He could feel the *Ludendorff*'s vibrations trembling through the rope and the rushing wind threatening to blow him off. He lowered himself slowly, the leaping spray from the sea stinging his face, making the rope slippery, treacherous. Beatty knew the auxiliary room had a porthole. But the glass could already have been covered by a steel battleport, or the Germans inside could have swung the battleport shut.

The Germans got the microphone connected.

One of them began shouting into it. "This is the *Ludendorff*. This is the *Ludendorff*. We've been boarded. Repeat. Enemy has boarded."

The other twisted the dials, trying to raise up a frequency. All they heard was static, then faint music, then at another position, a voice, words. He turned up the volume. Adolf Hitler's voice, in a furious haranguing speech, filled the transmitting room.

Sweating, swearing, the German twisted the dials again as the one at the microphone kept shouting.

"This is the *Ludendorff*. Enemy has boarded."

High above the sea, Beatty reached a porthole. It was covered with a battleport. No telling whether it was the auxiliary transmitting room or not. Propping his feet against the smooth hull, he swung himself toward a porthole on the right. His boots slipped. He hung, dangling, his feet clawing for purchase again. They finally got it. His arms were beginning to ache. He couldn't hang on the rope much longer.

He reached the other porthole. The battleport was open. He peered through the glass, saw the two Germans huddled over the transmitter. Gripping the rope with one hand, he unslung the submachine gun and squeezed off a burst, shattering the glass.

The Germans inside dove for their guns and fired at the porthole. Beatty twisted away, then as he started to twist back to fire again, the machine gun in his right hand slipped.

He felt the wet barrel slide through his fingers, felt the heavy gun plunge toward the sea. His hand flashed down and somehow hooked into the trigger guard and he had it again.

He got a tighter grip and swung back to the shattered porthole, spraying the compartment with bullets. His final burst smashed the transmitter.

Walker untaped the third and last magazine from his leg and reloaded his Schmeisser as he huddled out of sight on the signal bridge, his eye on the wheelhouse directly above. He heard boots behind him. It was Steeger, the German who'd taught him how to use a submachine gun on the fantail, dashing up from below. Steeger fired, bullets smashing all around Walker, one of them tearing through his sleeve as he threw himself to the deck, rolled and raked Steeger with a short burst. Steeger's head jerked as if yanked by a huge hook in the mouth and his body crashed back down the ladder.

Walker shot a glance back up at the bridge. Only two ladders led there, one port, one starboard, making the bridge extremely dangerous to attack. Which one should he take? He remembered that traffic flow was port ladder down, starboard up. It probably didn't matter, but maybe the Germans out of training were keeping a closer eye on the starboard ladder. Walker headed for the other one.

As he climbed, the fear he felt before vanished. After

all the firing, somehow he was still alive and the adrenalin pumping through his blood had turned the fear into a cold fury, part reckless, part cunning.

At the top of the ladder, keeping his head low, he peered at the bridge. Through the window, in the ghostly glow of the instruments, the wheelhouse seemed deserted. But the ship was on a steady course. The helmsman had to be at the wheel, crouched down out of sight. Whoever else was up there, and there couldn't be many, he hoped, was also staying low. Walker wondered if the huge window was bulletproof.

He fired and as the bullets crashed through the glass he leaped up and barged into the wheelhouse with a sustained burst at everything in sight. Bullets splattered against steel. Glass shattered. Papers on a desk flew. Someone screamed. A pistol barked. A German lunged for him. The Schmeisser bucked. Blood sprayed across the compass platform.

Then silence. After the relentless firing, a frightening silence.

Walker rose from one knee. He didn't even know he had dropped to it. Smoke hung mid-high in the wheelhouse. Slowly . . . it took a few seconds for his eyes to focus again . . . Walker looked around. There were three bodies. The helmsman sat against the wheel, legs outspread, head sagging. Another German lay across a desk, staring up as if in surprise. The third was crumpled at the base of the compass platform. Most of the face was hidden by an arm but Walker could see the plastic shine of Drau's scar.

Walker reached down, dragging the helmsman away from the wheel. Suddenly a shot crashed out behind him. He spun and fired blindly, the bullets ricocheting dangerously, striking angry sparks in the wheelhouse and the navigator's chartroom beyond, where he caught a glimpse of a dark figure. The Schmeisser clicked empty. Walker froze. The figure, a dark silhouette, rose slowly, gun in hand and took a step toward him. Defenseless, Walker backed up. It was Ziegler. Ziegler took another step. Then fell sideways like an axed tree.

Walker approached cautiously. Ziegler was unconscious, a mat of blood above the left ear where he'd been hit by a spent ricocheting bullet.

Now Walker realized the firing on the decks below had stopped. Suppose he'd captured the bridge while the Germans had the rest of the ship?

He ducked out to the wing, and not showing himself, peered down. The upper deck was strewn with bodies but in the dark, he couldn't see who they were. Men with their hands raised were being herded below by someone with a submachine gun but which were British, which German? The man with the gun, to speed up his prisoners, fired a burst straight into the air and in the muzzle flash Walker saw it was Falco.

It was over. He heard someone laughing and realized he was doing it himself. In the abrupt transition from murderous battle to safety, he felt strangely lightheaded. He swung into a little victory jig on the wing, kicking his heels, clapping his hands, laughing to himself, the laughter triggering more laughter because they had *done* it. They had taken the *Ludendorff*. All by themselves. This goddamn mother of a battleship. And on top of that, he was rich now. Rich. He'd soon have more money than he ever had in his life, and the thought brought another wave of triumphant laughter as he spun in a dizzy dance.

Walker stopped himself. He knew it was crazy, carrying on alone like that on the wing of a warship in the middle of the Baltic.

Suddenly the *Ludendorff* lurched erratically and through the window Walker saw the wheel spinning out of control. He rushed into the wheelhouse and gingerly took the helm and steadied it. The deck beneath his feet still pitched but within moments leveled out, the great ship responding to his touch. He could feel the engines throbbing through the deck plates, through the massive wheel and into his hands. He stood there, controlling the greatest warship in the world all by himself.

Walker aimed her into the oncoming swell and watched as the bow knifed through the sea. He spun the wheel left and felt 50 thousand tons surge at his command. He twisted the wheel back and forth now, the *Ludendorff*'s bow plunging into the waves, the sea breaking over the forward gun turrets and hurling spray through the shattered bridge window into his face. The battleship and he were one.

A phone to the left of the wheel shrilled. He knew it had to be one of the British, probably Beatty, calling to find out what was going on up there.

"Admiral Walker here, mother fuckers," he shouted into it. "Admiral Walker here!"

And then the words strangled in his throat.

At first in the moonlight it looked like a buoy or a rock. About a mile to starboard. But then he realized what it was. A raft. A motor-powered raft heading away from the *Ludendorff*.

Swiftly, Walker spun the wheel, pointing the battleship's bow toward the raft. If it was Germans escaping from the *Ludendorff* . . . what else could it be . . . he had to stop them.

As he swung the *Ludendorff* to starboard, he tried to

232

keep his eye on the tiny raft in the dark. He squinted painfully and got it in focus again on the rolling sea.

Then it disappeared on the far side of some waves and it was gone.

CHAPTER 20

Within minutes, davits creaked, lowering one of the *Ludendorff*'s powerful twenty-seven-foot launches into the sea.

Beatty could spare only two men to go after the escaped raft. He nodded to Falco, who'd hunt it with the zeal of a hungry wolf. Most of the other men had some training at repairing machinery and were already down below helping Hammond. To go with Falco, Beatty had to choose Walker.

Clutching submachine guns, Walker and Falco leaped into the launch as it dipped below the upper deck.

"What if we can't find it?" Walker shouted up to Beatty.

"Then we're all in the shit-house without paper," Beatty shouted back.

Falco at the wheel, the launch leaped through the Baltic, in the direction taken by the raft.

Walker switched on the searchlight mounted on the cabin roof and swung it from left to right in a 180-

degree arc ahead. The brilliant beam bounced off the distant waves, picking out steep troughs and crests of foam.

Walker's eyes ached from peering into an endless succession of waves with no sign of a raft.

The sky was turning from deep black to the deep glowing blue of before dawn. In the emerging light, in the distance, they saw off to the left a broad, dark hump rising out of the Baltic. An island.

Walker and Falco had the same thought. Chances were the Germans would've made for the island. Falco spun the wheel.

As the launch arrowed closer, Walker could make out a ribbon of beach several miles long. Behind it, hills. The massed silhouette of trees. Above the trees, a smudge of smoke drifted, indicating the island was inhabited and probably had a wireless, a telephone, to reach the mainland. They couldn't let the Germans get to it.

Walker swung the searchlight beams across the sea that rolled toward the island.

"At one o'clock," Falco shouted.

Now Walker saw it, too. To their right, over a mile off, two men on a raft, its little engine straining for the island. If the Germans reached it first, it'd be hell trying to find them.

Hurtling across the water, the launch swiftly closed on the raft . . . three-quarters of a mile, a thousand yards, half a mile. In the dawn light Walker could distinctly see the two men. One was bare-chested. The other wore a life jacket. Both shot wild glances over their shoulder at the launch.

The raft reached the rollers riding into the surf. Walker leaned across the launch's gunwale and cut loose with his submachine gun. The Schmeisser's range was barely two hundred yards and he saw the bullets splashing short.

The Germans leaped from the raft into knee-high water and raced to the beach. Walker kept his eyes riveted on them. They seemed to hesitate a second, then ran to the left diagonally for the wooded hills that came down to the sand.

The launch hit the surf and Falco, cutting the engine, threw the small anchor overboard before the momentum stopped so that the anchor dug into the sand. The two men, gripping their submachine guns, leaped into the surf. Falco had miscalculated the depth and they plunged almost neck high in water, struggling for footing on the muddy sea floor. Pounded by the breakers, then sucked back by the receding tide, holding the submachine gun over his head, Walker took nearly a precious minute of time struggling to the beach.

Falco was already there. The Germans had disappeared. Falco hand-signaled Walker to stay ten yards apart. They advanced up the hill in a low crouch.

At the top, staying low, they peered over the rim. They were at a high point on the island, the land stretching out before them level for about a mile, then sloping down into shallow valleys and hills leading to the sea on the other side. The island was approximately ten square miles, Falco figured, small actually, but big enough for the Germans, unless they were spotted soon, to hide out here for days. But the *Ludendorff* couldn't spare an hour and still hit the U-boat base at Skagen.

They saw nothing move anywhere on open ground, and with the sun rising behind them, ran for the wall of fir trees to their left, the most likely place for the Germans to hide if they had taken the same route up the hill from the beach.

The carpet of dry needles everywhere crackled loudly under their feet as they made their way through the dense firs. It betrayed their position but there was nothing they could do about it. Clouds of insects darted into their faces. Walker felt one getting trapped in his ear but didn't dare take his hands from his gun to get at it. It buzzed maddeningly in his head.

He became abruptly aware that Falco was no longer near his side. He looked around. Falco was gone! Walker ducked behind a tree, all senses wide open. Through the firs, almost blending with the dull gray of their bark, which was why he hadn't seen it before, stood a grayish wooden structure about thirty-five yards away. Smoke wreathed from an iron chimney on the slanted shingle roof.

Staying behind cover, Walker crept up to it.

It was a one-story structure with two big windows on each side of a single door. It looked like a farmhouse except for two things. A spidery radio antenna jutted from the roof and a spindly German corporal sat on a tree stump just outside the door. A Mauser rifle rested on his lap.

Walker wondered what was going on inside the shack. Were the Germans from the *Ludendorff* in there already? Was a wireless flashing an alarm all over the Baltic?

Christ, where was Falco?

The door opened, then shut behind a lean, blond sergeant whose eyes swept the surrounding woods. Walker was sure the sergeant was looking straight in his direction and his finger closed around the submachine-gun trigger.

The sergeant looked up at the sky a moment, then opened the door again.

"Bluger," he called out, "how about some smoked fish for breakfast?"

"We had it yesterday and the day before," Bluger complained at the window, his thick eyeglasses reflecting the sun.

"Don't be a pain in the ass. Everyone likes it except you," the sergeant insisted.

"I like sausage, not herring every day. God, I hate this island," Bluger growled.

Through the half-open door Walker could see Germans setting a table, others getting dressed.

The two from the *Ludendorff* hadn't found this shack or the place'd be jumping. But that wasn't much comfort. The island evidently had some military importance and the two Krauts were bound to run across Germans somewhere else, even if they didn't come this way.

On his stomach Walker inched away from the shack and with a start nearly backed into Falco, who had already observed the German post and was waiting for him silently behind a tree.

Falco in the lead, they skirted the German clearing and once out of sight headed down the other side of the hill. The *Ludendorff* crewmen, Falco reasoned, knew they were being chased and tired men being chased run downhill if they have the chance.

At the bottom of a gully, the ground flattened out again with a clearer view all around. There were no men in sight. A cow switched flies with its tail, the rusted bell around its neck tolling tinnily. A broken wagon sagged on a cracked wheel near a long narrow shed with no windows. A door at the far side, not firmly closed, creaked on its hinges in the wind.

Falco studied it a long moment. Nothing unusual about a shed door not being locked or even closed. On an island this size, nobody would go around stealing from his neighbor. But the area down here had a distinctive smell, and if the shed was what he thought it was, it was hardly likely that the owner would ever forget to keep that door closed tight.

"No guns," Falco whispered to Walker, gesturing up the hill to the German post, which, though hidden by trees, was easily within hearing range.

Walker, throat tight, nodded.

Keeping out of the line of fire from the partially open door, they dashed for the shed and flattened themselves against the side. Falco kicked the door wide open. He crouched low and ducked inside. Walker waited another second to hear if there'd be any firing . . . no sense in both of them dying in a trap . . . and when there was none ducked in behind Falco.

The first thing that hit Walker was the heat. A dense, heavy heat. Then eye-stinging, lung-choking smoke. Walker thought the shed was on fire. But as his eyes quickly adjusted to the dark he saw strange shapes. They were slabs of brown-glazed fish hanging by their tails, strung from horizontal racks in a network of rows from floor to ceiling. They were in a smokehouse. The fish were spaced so closely together that he couldn't see more than a few feet in any direction. Someone could be standing silently, waiting, on the other side of the next row.

Nothing in the smokehouse stirred. All Walker could hear was the faintly tinkling cowbell outside. The smoke, the smell of brine and the sweetish smell of damp burning maplewood clutched at his lungs. It was getting hard to breathe. He wanted to cough, felt the sharp reflex and choked it down. If the Germans were here, they'd been inside longer and must really be hurting.

He listened for a sound, breathing, anything. A minute crept by. In the 120-degree heat, Walker felt his body pouring sweat. Something burned his neck. A drop of hot fish fat had almost made him hiss with pain.

A stifled gasp came from somewhere. Falco had heard it, too.

Falco ducked into another row, out of sight. Separately, they advanced through the maze of hanging fish in the direction of the sound.

The floors creaked. Now the Germans had to know where they were. Walker wanted to spray the whole place with bullets but remembered Falco's warning. He parted the curtains of fish with the muzzle of his gun.

Suddenly a hanging row ahead of Walker stirred. He swung his Schmeisser at it like a club, but too soon. The gun had finished its arch when the German burst through, charging full force. He hit Walker straight on and carried him backward, the Schmeisser flying out of his hands.

The big, bare-chested German leaped on Walker and grappling together they plunged through the rows of hanging fish, knocking the weighted racks down on all sides. Walker heard fighting on the other side of the shed but couldn't worry about Falco as the German, bigger than he by forty pounds, hurled him to the floor. Walker pulled the German down with him. The floorboards were greasy with fish, and clawing at each other's faces, they spun around, their feet slipping, skidding crazily. Walker struggled for footing, threw a punch, missed and lost his balance, landing hard on his back.

He saw the German dive for the submachine gun.

The weapon was too far away for Walker but he spotted a hook hanging from a beam. He lunged for it and in the same sweep of motion leaped for the German who was pulling back the Schmeisser's breech bolt, raising it to fire. Walker swung the murderous hook. With a thunk it speared through the German's temple.

Breathing hard, hands torn and bloodied, Falco, who'd dispatched the other German, rushed to Walker's side and propelled him toward the door. Before they could reach it, they stopped. Through the door they saw a figure in the distance, coming down the hill. Walker recognized him as Bluger, from the post above. Bluger was heading straight for the smokehouse. Within minutes after he discovered the two dead crewmen, the Navy would call a massive hunt by sea and air for the *Ludendorff*.

Falco and Walker hurried back to the bodies and quickly stripped them of *erkennungsmarken*, papers and anything else that could identify them as coming from the *Ludendorff*. Just as Bluger reached the smokehouse, they slipped out a small rear door.

They ran back to the beach, Walker thinking how the Germans would look, discovering the two dead sailors and trying to figure out where they had come from, how they got here and who killed them.

The two men reached the beach and swam out to the launch.

The American heaved up the anchor and they started paddling the launch in order not to use the engine until they got far enough away from the German island.

Walker, breathing deeply, clapped Falco on the shoulder.

"Man, we're home free," Walker grinned.

Falco said nothing. He knew better.

CHAPTER 21

The *Ludendorff* lay motionless in the water, a crippled, vulnerable giant, when Walker and Falco returned in the launch.

Hammond was urgently trying to replace the high pressure steam pipe shattered by his submachine-gun bullets. But with only a few men to help, even if he succeeded, it was slow, painstaking work. Meanwhile the battleship seemed glued to the middle of the flat, glassy Baltic.

The morning sun to the British was a merciless spotlight focused on only one thing, the *Ludendorff*. Twelve men commanding an enemy battleship that couldn't move, that could barely defend itself if discovered, was more than they'd bargained for and it chilled their blood.

Walker went below to change his clothes, which stank from fish. He heard his name called from a dark recess on a passageway and took a few steps closer. It was Ziegler locked in one of the ship's cells.

"What do you get when this is over?" Ziegler asked through the bars.

"Just helping some pals," Walker shrugged.

"That's very generous of you," Ziegler said dryly. He looked around to make sure none of the British was near. "Perhaps we can talk," he suggested.

"I already have a deal."

"You know the Baltic is full of German warships," Ziegler warned.

"I hope they're in better shape than this one, Admiral," Walker said. "Remember the short arm? Eight of your men have the clap."

Walker climbed back to the bridge, a thought shooting through his mind about what he'd do if they ever got the hell out of here alive and he collected his money.

Eventually, he wanted to go back to the States because for getting rich there was no place like it. But America might soon get involved in the war and Walker already had enough of war. Screw being drafted and sent off to fight again. So until it was all over, he was better off staying in some neutral country and making his money work for him. Maybe some kind of business. Sweden looked like she was going to stay out of the war and manufacture stuff for both sides and get rich. With a $25,000 stake, he might be able to make a couple of smart investments and get rich there, too.

Walker entered the wheelhouse just as Beatty, eyes tensely scanning the surrounding sea, reached for the voice pipe to the forward engine room.

"How're we doing, Hammond?" he asked tersely.

"Fine, sir," Walker heard Hammond's voice reply.

"How much longer?"

"Can let you know in a few minutes, sir," Hammond answered from the bowels of the ship.

"He's a good man," Walker said to Beatty.

"He does his job."

"All your boys did."

"So did you," Beatty said.

"Yeah, well . . . the money was good," Walker shrugged.

He didn't hate Beatty's guts any more, in fact had to give him credit for having giant balls. But Walker was still leery of any kind of praise or show of friendship.

"About our deal," he began. "You owe me . . ."

"Commander, sir," It was Hammond interrupting on the voice pipe. "We'll need another hour. At least."

"Christ, Hammond," Beatty exploded. "We can't afford all day to repair . . ."

"*Replace,* sir, not repair," Hammond corrected, not concealing his feeling of superiority over Beatty when it came to his province, the engine room.

"Just get it done!"

"Unless it's done right, it'll be Guy Fawkes Day, not tomorrow morning before we reach Skagen," Hammond clicked off.

Walker looked up sharply. Nobody had ever mentioned Skagen before, but it sure didn't sound like England.

"What's he talking about?" Walker demanded.

"Look, Walker . . ." Beatty began.

"*What* Skagen? What's going on here?"

Walker grabbed a navigating chart, his eyes scanning it swiftly, nervous fingers walking across the map, across countries, France, Belgium, The Netherlands, the fingers skidding to a stop at the name in small print.

244

Skagen. The small suddenly became very large. He looked up, bewildered.

"Denmark?!"

Beatty said nothing.

"But the Germans have Denmark," Walker said.

Beatty knew he had to level now.

"It's a U-boat base."

"Yeah . . . so?" Walker asked, but as soon as he asked it he knew the answer. "You're gonna attack . . . a U-boat base?"

Beatty nodded, and Walker's shock boiled to anger. He stared at the ship beneath his feet.

"Isn't this enough?" he said. "What are you, some kind of schmuck?"

"Those U-boats . . ."

"What do I give a fuck, U-boats?" Walker jabbed a finger at Beatty. "You bastard. You gave me a snow job."

"I needed you," Beatty said simply. He knew how Walker felt and couldn't blame him.

"You needed," Walker sneered. "You're giving me an I.O.U. Two I.O.U.'s. One to the British Government and one to your old man in case one of them tries to screw me. Then a launch to Sweden."

Beatty shook his head.

"If the Germans spotted you, that'd be the end of everything. You have to stay."

"I've done my share. Shove it." Walker hurled the navigating chart through the gunfire-shattered window.

Beatty saw the rage in Walker's eyes, the fists clenched.

"Ship bearing zero-three-six degrees," Shanks called from the navigator's compartment.

They rushed to the starboard window and saw what

245

the *Ludendorff*'s radar would have detected long before, had there been men to operate it. About eight miles off but closing fast, a German destroyer. Beatty watched grimly as the destroyer cut the distance between them, smoke wreathing from its funnel smudging the sky. Gradually, from its rakish silhouette, he could make out that it was a Von Roeder class, over three hundred men, with five 5-inch guns. A nasty hornet of a ship.

"Now we've had it," Walker said, whispering almost as if the destroyer could hear.

From the deck of the destroyer *Gunther*, Korvettenkapitän Kempf and his deck officer studied the battleship through Zeiss glasses.

"It's the *Ludendorff*, sir," the young deck officer said. "She's dead in the water."

Kempf nodded. He was a short, tough, ambitious officer originally from the peacetime merchant marine who regarded higher-ranking, veteran combat officers with great admiration. Being in a position to help one of them, the commander of a battleship no less, would be an honor and conceivably a boost to his own career.

"Signal my personal compliments to Kapitän Ziegler and offer assistance," Kempf ordered.

On the wing of the *Ludendorff*'s bridge, Perth decoded the blue signal light stabbing across the water.

"Tell them Kapitän Ziegler returns the compliments but no assistance necessary," Beatty said. "Have stopped to work on our sound detection system."

Though it meant less trouble for him, Kempf was somewhat disappointed by the message. He was disap-

pointed at not being needed and even more at not getting a chance to meet the famous Kapitän Ziegler personally. Still, Kempf smiled to himself over one
consolation, that he commanded an agile, relatively simple destroyer instead of a complex monster like the *Ludendorff*.

"Battleships," he shrugged. "Always something
breaking down on those things. Resume course. Make
turns for twenty knots," he ordered.

From the *Ludendorff*'s bridge, Beatty and Walker
could see the destroyer begin to swing away sharply.
Walker's knuckles, gripped white on the rail, relaxed.

Aboard the *Gunther*, Korvettenkapitän Kempf took
one last look at the *Ludendorff* through his glasses,
checked his ship's speed on the engine room telegraph
and its course. They were precisely as he'd ordered. Yet
he was becoming aware of an uneasy feeling, a heavi-
ness at the pit of his stomach. He had no idea why but
from years of experience at sea he knew whenever he
had such a distinctive feeling there had to be a reason.

What was it this time?

The *Ludendorff* came back to mind again. Repairing
its sound detection system. Perfectly reasonable. But the
Ludendorff wasn't entering a combat zone where sound
detection was crucial. She was on some kind of trial
run, as he recalled. On her way back to the safety of
Kiel, in fact. Ziegler, of course, had a reputation as a
perfectionist and might want all equipment to operate
perfectly even if it wasn't essential, but even perfection-
ism had limits.

Kempf's uneasiness went into a higher gear. Could
something other than equipment trouble be wrong
aboard the battleship that lay dead in the water? And if

there was another reason, why would any commander conceal it? Kempf was uncertain about what to do. He didn't want to risk the wrath or ridicule of Kapitän Ziegler, an officer earmarked for admiral's rank, by prying.

Still, if there was something wrong and he didn't do anything, if he just ignored it . . .

"Come to zero-five-zero," he ordered the helmsman. "Make turns for five knots."

Beatty watched the destroyer clawing around and approaching again, suspicious this time. He turned to Tanner, who'd joined him on the bridge.

"You'll have one shot," Beatty said calmly.

"Yes, sir," Tanner replied.

"Miss, or don't hit her right, and they'll have time to radio and we're dead. Clear?"

"Aye, sir. We'll shove one right up their ass."

Meredith, seeing Tanner racing from the bridge, guessed the reason, and also dashed for "A" turret. Meredith thought of removing the muzzle bag protecting the mouth of one of the big guns from sea and weather, but an uncovered muzzle could only arouse fear—or alarm. In an emergency the best thing to do was just shoot straight through the muzzle bag.

Tanner and Meredith, without exchanging a word, set to work in the turret, a huge armored box with massive equipment, shell tubes, shell trays, powder hoists, brass wheels and polished gun breeches that looked like the steel innard of some infernal machine. Tanner checked the port gun breech. They were lucky. It was already loaded. They ducked underneath the gun into the pit below it. They took positions sitting at the face plate of the turret, Meredith at the training controls,

248

which moved the gun right and left, Tanner at the pointer controls, which governed elevation. They rested their heads on the rubber eye cushions of telescopes for visual contact with their target.

The destroyer was out of their line of vision. Under normal combat conditions, the guns would've been swung around to train on the enemy ship. But the Germans were watching and the sight of the *Ludendorff*'s turret swinging in their direction would instantly alarm them. Even God, Tanner thought grimly, would piss His pants if He saw one of the *Ludendorff*'s 15-inch guns swiveling toward Him.

Tanner waited patiently for the destroyer to show itself in his telescope, for its course to intercept the gun's present position as closely as possible, so that any movement by the gun itself would be minimal. He knew that the battleship's great rifles were designed to be controlled not by two men with the naked eye but by rangefinders in the turret, gunnery control officers stationed above the bridge, and complex electronic equipment and computers down in the transmitting station. These computers calculated everything that could affect the ship's aim . . . its own as well as the enemy's speed and course, the roll of the ship, the force and direction of the wind, air temperature, which indirectly influenced muzzle velocity, barometric pressure, which influenced a shell's flight. Tanner knew all this but was too young to be awed or intimidated at having to do the job by himself.

He saw the destroyer *Gunther* coming into sight at the right-hand side of his telescope, first the low-slung bow, then the forward turret with its 5-inch guns. Tanner's eye sweated against the rubber cushion. He estimated her speed at under ten knots. Distance, less than a mile away. By sea combat standards, practically in his lap. He turned the pointer dials on the face plate in front of him. With a whir of machinery the breech above him rose toward the roof of the turret. Outside, the gun muzzle dipped at maximum depression toward the destroyer.

"Let the bugger get a little closer," Tanner told Meredith.

Falco hunched behind a lifeboat on the upper deck, watching the 15-inch gun of "A" turret lowering imperceptibly toward the oncoming warship. He calmly smoked a cigarette. The destroyer was so close now he could see officers on the bridge. The silence aboard the *Ludendorff* was broken only by the waves slapping against the hull.

"Can he take her out with one shot?" whispered Walker, who'd come down from the bridge and crouched at Falco's side.

Falco shrugged.

Walker could see the gun, or was it his imagination, slowly moving to the left, tracking the destroyer.

The great gun crashed. The silken bags of cordite in the breech exploded into a mass of heated gas that thrust against the one-ton armor-piercing shell, forcing it through the rifled barrel at 2,900 feet per second.

Walker saw an angry red flash at the muzzle and a dark blur, like a football, streaking across the water. The blur disappeared against the background of the gray camouflaged destroyer and for a moment Walker thought Tanner had missed.

But the shell, screaming in an almost straight line, ripped through the *Gunther*'s steel skin as if it were paper, penetrated its bowels and exploded near the five-inch magazine. In a chain reaction too swift to calculate, the destroyer's shells, depth charges and torpedoes exploded.

Walker saw a giant ball of flame burst through the destroyer's upper deck, followed by a crash like a thunderclap, as the fiery ball and yellow smoke boiled skyward. He felt the explosion wave, a blast of hot wind rippling back across the water and shock waves hitting the *Ludendorff* below the waterline. A hail of metal rained down, hissing into the sea, and a large chunk, part of a 5-inch barrel, whooshed through the air toward the battleship. Walker threw himself to the deck, but the barrel hit high on the superstructure, carrying away two range finders like a giant scythe before knifing into the sea on the other side of the ship.

Rising to his feet, choking on the brown pall of cordite fumes from the *Ludendorff*'s 15-inch gun, Walker stared at what was once a destroyer.

The bridge was collapsing into the inferno of the blasted deck like a melting wax candle. The hull shuddered with the muffled explosion of a boiler and the destroyer split in half with a horrifying crack that sounded like the sky itself had split open. Barnacle-encrusted bow and stern, both pointed to the sky, drifted apart. The stern plunged below the waves first, then the bow, twisting, sinking very slowly in a sucking whirlpool, as if the destroyer itself didn't want to die.

"A" turret's hatch snapped open and Tanner and Meredith emerged. They saw what they had done and stood motionless, as if reluctant to move any closer.

The sudden appearance of the destroyer and its even swifter annihilation had made Walker forget his fury at Beatty, at being tricked, at learning that capturing the *Ludendorff* was only part of the mission. Now his anger rushed back, fueled by the sight of what could happen to men aboard a warship under fire. He wasn't going to chance that happening to him.

But at the same time he wanted to get something out of this whole thing.

Walker stole a glance around. The English were riveted, watching the destroyer's sinking bow. Walker slipped away from Falco's side and lightly, so that his boots didn't ring on the ladder, rushed below deck.

Ziegler felt a Luger barrel hooked under his jawbone, forcing his head back.

Though he stood on the opposite side of the cell bars from Walker, the German didn't dare move.

"The paymaster's office," Walker said. "The safe. Give me the combination."

Topside, Beatty noticed for the first time that the American was nowhere in sight.

"Where's Walker?" he asked.

"He was here just before," Falco said.

"From now on, we better keep an eye on him all the time," Beatty said sharply.

Falco and Meredith nodded and split up to find the American.

The paymaster's office was locked.

Walker cursed under his breath. He'd have to go down to the mess hall's refrigerator to get the key off the paymaster. If the paymaster was alive. And even if he was, Walker'd have to face more than three hundred Germans in there. With only a Luger. Fuck that. The cashier's window was just to the right of the door and he tried to squeeze his arm through but the bars were too close together for him to get anything more than his hand between them. He couldn't reach the lock.

He remembered seeing lengths of pipe and wood somewhere on the battleship. He ran down the passageway, then down another level where he found the machine shop. He grabbed an eighteen-inch brass rod.

Rushing back to the paymaster's window, Walker poked the brass rod through the bars. He turned the rod to the left at a ninety-degree angle, probing for the lock blindly, trying to catch the knob from underneath and push it up to open the lock. He groped around and hit what must've been the knob . . . it was at approximately the same level as the keyhole on his side . . . but had no idea where he was hitting it. He poked and prodded at various angles. The knob didn't move. His wrist was beginning to cramp up.

Just then he heard from somewhere . . . it seemed to come from another level . . . a faint voice calling, "Walker." They were looking for him already. Christ. He might never have another chance to get down here alone. He had to get at that safe now. He angled the rod up at a forty-five-degree angle and pushed against what he hoped was the underside of the knob. Something moved. He pushed harder. It gave some more. The rod was slipping. He pushed desperately, his fingers unable to hold on at that angle, felt the rod going, felt it leaving his hand, and just before it clattered to the floor thought he heard something else. Like a click.

Almost afraid of jolting the lock, he tried the door. The handle turned. The door eased open. He shot a look up and down the passageway . . . it was deserted. He slipped into the paymaster's office, gently closed and locked the door behind him. In a far corner he saw it, three feet high. A black iron safe.

Over and over to himself, Walker had repeated the combination Ziegler gave him so that he wouldn't forget it. Now, he spun the heavy dial with careful assurance. Three complete turns to the right to 18. One turn left past 18 to 3. Two more right . . .

Suddenly, he heard footsteps in the passageway. Then a voice calling his name. It was Falco.

Walker scuttled from the safe and ducked down behind the pay counter as the footsteps approached. They slowed, then stopped, on the other side of the door. A hand tried the knob. Another couple of footsteps and Walker could sense Falco peering through the barred window directly above him, eyes sweeping the room. He could hear Falco breathing and held his own breath, didn't dare even to blink.

The footsteps passed on. Walker could hear them echoing down the passageway. They'd all be looking for him if he didn't show up in a few minutes.

He hurried back to the safe and not recalling where he'd left off, started to dial the combination from the beginning.

Three complete turns to the right to 18. One turn left past 18 to 3 . . . or was it to 23? His hand stopped. Oh, God. Falco had scrambled the numbers in his brain. Had he forgotten the combination?

He thought of going back to Ziegler to get it again, but Ziegler was clear on the other side of the ship. Too much danger of running into the British. Besides, there wasn't time.

He told himself not to panic. To try to remember. Even if he was off by one number, he'd hit it by trial and error. He began again . . . 18 . . . 23 . . . 16. The safe remained locked. His hands began to sweat. Could Ziegler have said 6 instead of 16?

The more he spun the dial, the more uncertain, the more confused he became, his head a conflicting jumble of numbers. And the safe refused to open. He felt a terrible surge of frustration and slammed the safe with his open hand. His hand hurt like hell.

He tried to think. There must be a record of the right combination somewhere here in the office. He rifled through a ledger book. It was filled with numbers, figures, but none that looked anything like a combination. Nothing in the desk either.

He opened the drawer at the paymaster's window. His heart leaped.

In beautiful, crisp, tightly wrapped stacks, the drawer was filled with money, with Reichmarks. Christ! He'd been wasting time with the goddamn safe when the paymaster, to pay the crew on arrival in Kiel in the morning, had already transferred the money from the safe to the drawer the night before.

Walker figured there must be close to, maybe more than the equivalent of $20,000 in American money. Too much to stash into his pockets. On a shelf he spotted a small canvas bag. He filled the bag with the stacks of Reichmarks. When he was through the bag bulged so much the zipper wouldn't close, so he sadly tossed a couple of wrappers back into the drawer.

Now the bag zippered up just fine.

Concealing it as much as possible under his jacket, Walker headed for the upper deck. He had to hide it someplace where he could put his hands on it immediately.

He peered through an open hatch and saw a handful of the English near the fo'c'sle, Falco talking with Beatty, probably reporting that they hadn't found him yet. Walker turned. The quarterdeck was deserted.

Staying out of sight, Walker headed there. For a moment he considered hiding the canvas bag behind a machine-gun mount or under a tarp covering a lifeboat, but that seemed too easy for someone to run across.

His eyes fell on one of the ventilator shafts rising from the quarterdeck. He looked down inside. The vent was much too wide to wedge the bag in tightly. He reached in and felt around. His hand struck something more than a foot from the top, far down enough to be out of sight. Some kind of metal projection or hook. It might do.

Carefully, he lowered the bag into the vent and hung it by the handle to the projection. When he was satisfied that it hung there firmly, he twisted the bag around twice to make sure it was even more secure. He removed his hand and casually strolled away, just as Falco appeared from around "C" turret.

"Where've you been, *mon ami?*" Falco demanded.

"I went out for dinner. What do you mean, where've I been," Walker asked sarcastically.

"Just answer the man's questions," Beatty said firmly, coming up on the other side.

"I was taking a crap, for Chrissake," Walker complained, easing himself and them away from the vent. "Do I have to raise my hand for permission to take a crap around here?"

"Sir!"

It was Hammond interrupting, streaked with sweat and grime from his labor on the high pressure steam pipe in the engine room.

"We've done our best," he told Beatty wearily. "If she don't hold now, we might as well radio the Krauts 'n ask 'em to tow us in."

"Take us to Skagen, Hammond," Beatty said.

CHAPTER 22

A small red pin flag representing the *Ludendorff* jutted from the map of the Baltic in the Operations Room of Naval Group Command East in Kiel.

That flag, however, wasn't the one which riveted the attention of Kapitän Helmuth Kalmer and made him suspect something, perhaps something terrible, had happened in the Baltic.

Kalmer ran a tense hand over the brush-cut gray hair that grew forward over his forehead, making his face look like a lean old wolf's, and studied another pin flag. This one represented the destroyer *Gunther*, buried by the *Ludendorff*'s guns in thirty-six fathoms of water.

Kalmer, of course, had no suspicion of this. That an enemy force could've entered the Baltic, captured a German battleship and turned its guns on another German warship was inconceivable, beyond the wildest imagining. At least it was beyond his imagining at this moment. But Kalmer, who to his regret didn't command a ship of his own because someone had to direct Operations, had experience in two wars and an intuitive sense of the sea. And now he sensed something about the *Gunther*. It hadn't radioed its position to Group Command in nearly two-and-a-quarter hours. This, despite naval regulations that, if only for their own safety, warships report their positions at precise two-hour intervals. All attempts by Group Command to contact it had met with silence.

"She could be observing radio silence for a reason, sir," Oberleutnant Roope suggested.

"For what reason?" Kalmer asked, turning to the sallow younger officer standing in front of his desk.

"Being hunted by submarines."

"In the Baltic?" Kalmer turned away from Roope impatiently. It always amazed him how certain men won their stripes in the Navy, or rose to responsible positions anywhere, without displaying a shred of intelligence. The map in front of them, glaring like ice under the powerful lights, was enough to shoot down Roope's theory. The Baltic being almost completely landlocked, even if one enemy submarine could slip in, which was highly doubtful, but even if it could, it wouldn't dare tackle German warships because Group Command would immediately seal off the Baltic, trapping the submarine, tracking it down, destroying it like a shark in a pool.

No, Kalmer was certain that the *Gunther*'s radio silence had no connection with enemy submarines. But there could've been a sudden accident, a fire or explosion, and three hundred and twenty-seven men could be dead or in grave danger now.

"Message all available ships in the area," Kalmer ordered Roope. "Give them the *Gunther*'s last reported position. Tell them to commence search. Urgent."

"Yes, sir." Roope looked at the map uncertainly.

"Just one thing, sir. The *Ludendorff*'s out there. Do you include her?"

Kalmer had to think a moment. For once Roope had a point. On a test run with only a trial crew, the *Ludendorff* by all rights should return to base as soon as possible. But she had five Arado seaplanes that'd be invaluable in a search, and much as Kalmer hated to admit it because he'd gone to cadet school with Ziegler and loathed his glacial arrogance, his reputation for small cruelties, no other commander in the Baltic could rival Ziegler in experience or sheer natural skill. If he, Kalmer, were lost somewhere at sea and he could choose one commander, one ship to search for him, they'd be Ziegler and the *Ludendorff*.

"The *Ludendorff*, too," he told Roope. "Order her to join the search."

CHAPTER 23

Not yet aware of Group Command's order, the *Ludendorff* raced for Skagen.

From the upper deck the British buried their dead at sea. The Germans who'd died had already been dumped overboard without ceremony, but the bodies of Lester and Pinkney were carried up on stretchers, sewn into hammocks.

"It was the best I could do, sir," Tanner said.

"You did fine," Beatty said.

He looked around. Some of his men couldn't even be here for this final good-by. One had to man the helm. Others, with Hammond, had to watch the machinery below. There were only Shanks, Falco, Tanner and Perth standing beside the stretchers.

Across the deck, on the far side of the vent shaft concealing the money, Walker leaned against a turret, hands hunched into his jacket.

All together, Beatty had, including himself and the American, twelve men left. More of them, Beatty

260

thought, would probably die at Skagen. Maybe all of them. Beatty had never sorted out his feelings about someday having to die, but now for the first time he could look at it with a certain degree of calm. He had captured the *Ludendorff*. After this, he didn't have to fear facing anything about living or dying again . . . At least not as much as before.

In the strained silence that hovered over the stretchered bodies, broken only by the wind sighing across the decks, Shanks stepped forward, not out of choice but because somebody had to do it and he was the oldest.

"They were good men," he said gruffly, simply. "Lester here, he loved his wife and liked growing cabbage roses. He was having trouble with his son but he'd've worked it out. Pinkney, I didn't know Pinkney . . ." Shanks looked to Beatty for help.

Beatty tried to think of something. Before selecting Pinkney, Beatty had studied every record and form the Navy could supply. He knew Pinkney's birth date, birthplace, physical aptitudes, technical skills, combat experience and performance, decorations. But he knew nothing really. At least nothing that would be fitting now.

"That's all right, Shanks," Beatty said. "Pinkney was a good man, too."

"Thank you, sir," Shanks nodded. "Pinkney was a good man, too."

The afternoon sun was disappearing early behind heavy clouds. The wind tugged at the hammocks.

"They were our friends," Shanks continued. "I got no more to say. May they rest in peace."

Shanks's words, battling against the wind, barely reached Walker across the quarterdeck.

He saw the first stretcher tilted over the gunwale and like a sack of potatoes a body slid down and fell into the sea. Then the second. It was all over in a moment. Beatty and the others still hadn't even looked at him. It was as if he wasn't even there, and for a moment he felt the cold chill of being alone. He shrugged it off. Who wasn't alone? He'd heard guys say they weren't, that they were part of something, with a girl or a family or whatever. But a year later they were fighting or quitting or divorcing, half of them soaking their brains in a bottle, the other half becoming religious and trying to save themselves with mumbo-jumbo, and then you knew all their talk was bullshit from the start. And they knew it too. Of course, there were Beatty and those men. They seemed to have something going for them, something to fight for. But almost anybody, English, German, Japanese, will fight if some government tells them to. It was no big deal. Well, let them fight. Fuck them.

The stretchers lay empty now on the deck.

Walker stiffened as Beatty and the others headed back across the quarterdeck, passing the ventilator shaft hiding the bag of money. Now he had to figure how to get off the battleship, how to save his own ass, before these putzes got themselves all killed.

From overhearing Beatty and Shanks, Walker knew that to reach Skagen, they were taking the *Ludendorff* that night out of the Baltic through the Great Belt, a narrow channel that cut through the Danish islands. Once in the Great Belt, in the dark he could easily grab his money, jump ship in a raft and make it to shore only a couple of miles away. He'd wind up on German-held territory, but by slipping a few bills to some Danish fisherman with a boat there'd be no problem getting to

Sweden. All he had to do now was play it cool, wait till night, and with nobody watching him, split.

"Walker!"

It was Beatty calling him across the quarterdeck.

Obediently, Walker approached, but Perth, white-faced, bolting up a companionway and along the deck reached Beatty first, thrusting a slip of paper at him.

Beatty scanned it swiftly, his fingers tightening on the wind-fluttered page the further he read. It was a radiogram from Naval Group Command East to Ziegler, ordering the *Ludendorff* to search for the missing destroyer. Beatty crumpled the radiogram into a tight ball and threw it over the side. Then he turned back to Perth.

"Tell them message received, that we've set a course to join the search. Then send them false position reports every two hours or whenever requested."

Watching Perth rush back to the wireless room, Beatty knew that radioing false position reports while making for Skagen was a risky ploy. There was no way to predict the odds on the *Ludendorff* reaching its target by dawn before Group Command caught on that the battleship was not participating in the search, was not even in the Baltic any more. Now it was coming down to a race against time.

Beatty turned again to Walker, who, from the look on his face, didn't seem to have much hope of the British winning that race.

"When we get there," Beatty said, "you keep off the opposition."

"What opposition?"

"Whatever," Beatty said. "Use those."

He led the American to one of the 20-mm machine

guns and showed him how to load the canisters and fire it.

"Don't use the sights," Beatty said. "Just stay to the side and follow the tracer patterns."

"Right," Walker nodded.

He stepped behind the big gun. It made a submachine gun feel like a toy. He fired a test burst. The 20-mm bucked like a jackhammer and he saw the tracers arc across the water as he swung the gun right and left, It was a simple weapon and deadly.

"No problem," he told Beatty.

"Okay," Beatty said. He turned to Falco. "Until we hit Skagen don't let Walker out of your sight."

Falco and his assistant Chadwick led Walker below to the shell deck, a claustrophobic, circular steel dungeon lined with gleaming shells beneath "B" turret.

"Now we load," Falco declared.

The three men prepared the 15-inch guns for battle. They winched the one-ton shells to the automatic hoists, which grabbed hold with steel fingers, and then, like a dumbwaiter, raised them into the turret. It was hard, plodding work, sweaty and slow, the automatic hoist rattling and straining under the weight of its deadly burden.

How the hell, Walker wondered, was he going to jump ship before Skagen or, just as bad, before the Germans got wise that the battleship was up to something. He measured Falco and Chadwick with his eyes. He could cold-cock one of them . . . maybe . . . but never two. Besides, Falco still had a Luger jammed into his belt.

"Enough shells," Falco said at last, motioning Walker to follow him.

They descended by ladders deeper into the bowels of the battleship, to the lower powder room, which stored the one-hundred-pound bags of cordite. Walker and Chadwick hefted the silk bags to the powder hoists and Falco pushed a button. The powder hoist raised the cordite bags into the turret through a network of armored, automatically closing doors designed to prevent fires from flashing back into the magazine or flashing up into the turret.

Falco grinned to himself at all the ingenious safety mechanisms built into the *Ludendorff*. With only two men operating each turret they'd have to violate almost every safety procedure in the book anyway. Once things started, there'd be no chance to leave the turret and rush down to the lower powder room for more cordite. So against rules, they had to fill each turret with cordite bags. Falco felt his hands dampen at the thought of entering battle in a turret crammed with all those explosive bags.

Walker glanced at the bulkhead clock . . . 11:57. At this time of year, this far north, he knew that dawn came up very early. He had only a few hours left. Every minute he spent down here brought him closer to German guns. And not just rifles and submachine guns. Big ones this time. Artillery. He had to get to the upper deck, to his money, to a raft.

He waited until Falco and Chadwick were beginning to look pooped.

"Christ, I could use some air," Walker said, straightening up and wiping the sweat from his face. "Whatta you say we take turns a few minutes topside. You go first," he suggested to Chadwick.

"Plenty air down here," Falco grunted, heaving another powder bag.

"I just . . ."

"Plenty air down here," Falco repeated, giving Walker a cold look. "Nobody goes topside until we reach Skagen."

"You're the boss, boss," Walker said.

CHAPTER 24

Kapitän Kalmer at Naval Group Command East felt fear.

For the second time, he studied the radiogram just handed to him, his big shoulders and gray head hunched over the paper in total concentration. It made him forget, for the moment, his concern for the missing destroyer *Gunther*, replacing it with an uneasy foreboding that he now confronted something even more serious out there in the Baltic. Precisely what it was he couldn't say and he stared at the handful of words again, as if the effort would force them to release some hidden secret.

The message had come in at 0438 from the light cruiser *Munich*, one of the warships searching for the *Gunther*. It read: WE ARE AT SAME POSITION AND COURSE TWICE REPORTED BY LUDENDORFF BUT HAVE NO VISUAL OR RADAR CONTACT WITH SAME.

Kalmer looked up from the radiogram to the map of the Baltic. Two red flags, one for the *Munich*, the other the *Ludendorff*, were now so close together, according to their own position reports, that they almost crowded each other off the map. Yet the *Munich* couldn't see the battleship. Kalmer reasoned that two ships on the open sea could be virtually on top of each other at night and miss visual sighting. But not radar contact. That was impossible.

Diamond beads of perspiration formed on his forehead just below the cropped hairline. He tried to think as calmly as possible.

A destroyer suddenly disappears. . . . A search is called. . . . A battleship told to join the search apparently doesn't and sends false position reports.

Why? What happened?

Kalmer ruled out one obvious explanation, a mutiny aboard the *Ludendorff*. Well-fed crews in a Navy headed for victory don't mutiny. Another possibility was that the ship's commander had a nervous breakdown, a crack-up under some kind of pressure. But not Ziegler. Ziegler was a rock.

The only other explanation that Kalmer could think of was almost too frightening to consider. That the *Ludendorff* had somehow, in some incredible way, been captured. The battleship's behavior, Kalmer knew, was consistent with being captured. And if so, there might even be a logical connection between that and the sudden disappearance of the *Gunther*.

Kalmer shielded his eyes from the lights that had beaten down on him all night. In the completely enclosed Operations Room, he was aware that it must be almost dawn outside.

The *Ludendorff* captured. . . . How, he wondered, could it happen? Any British warship large enough to capture the *Ludendorff*, Kalmer reasoned, could never get into the Baltic undetected. Never.

This gave Kalmer little comfort. For it still left him with the mystery of what had actually happened, what *was* happening, to the *Ludendorff*. And though he had no answer, he had to make a decision. He'd wrestled with it long enough.

Rising from his desk, Kalmer scrawled a message and shoved it at a communications officer.

This, he was sure, would flush out the *Ludendorff* by daybreak.

CHAPTER 25

The *Ludendorff* pressed northward on the last lap.

His thick-veined hands on the helm, Shanks's eyes burned with fatigue. He hadn't slept in over twenty-five hours and his hamstring muscle still ached, a nasty reminder of his vulnerability, but he was too busy to dwell on it. It wouldn't do to have come this far and for lack of sharpness run aground on a sand bar.

At his side Beatty peered through the shattered bridge window. The sky was still dark with a sliver of moon, and so was the water. But now a pale silver streaked the edge of the eastern horizon.

Beatty hunched his shoulders deeper into his jacket against the night chill coming off the Great Belt, realizing it wasn't only the sea that laid a cold hand on him.

He turned to Shanks at the wheel.

"How much longer?"

"Soon," Shanks answered.

"How much!" Beatty snapped, his nerves raw.

"Twenty, twenty-five minutes," Shanks replied quickly.

Beatty took a deep breath and got a hold on himself. "Thank you, Shanks."

"Yes, sir," Shanks said, understanding. He was beginning to feel jumpy himself.

The faces of the two men, barely illuminated in the glow of the instruments on the bridge, emerged from dark silhouettes to a bloodless gray as the sky imperceptibly began to lighten. The stars, drained of their brilliance, faded and died. To port, the shore line glided past in black silhouette, and beyond it the low rolling hills of Jutland. Gulls wheeled over the battleship's superstructure. One perched for a moment on the highest tip of the mast. Beatty could smell the air changing, with a stronger tang of salt in it. The *Ludendorff* was nearing the end of the Great Belt and would soon reach the battleground of two untamed channels, the Kattegat and the Skagerrak, which fought each other forever off the tip of Skagen. A rising wind buffeted against the jagged bridge window. The choppy waves dashed themselves against the bow.

"The Rabjerg Mile," Shanks said, pointing to the shore line which they were following on a parallel course.

Beatty saw something moving in the darkness across the beach. At first it looked like a swirling ghost stalking a lonely stretch of shore. Then he realized it was wind-whipped sand, rising to great heights before swooping down and engulfing everything in its path, then hovering low, swirling in a circle before stalking back again.

"Been there for as long as I can remember, back and forth," Shanks said. He nodded through the window. "Skagen's dead ahead."

Beatty strained to see. From a high bridge, especially,

271

judging distances at sea was tricky business, but about six miles up the coast he could make out clusters of low-roofed houses and buildings. In the dim light they all looked a dirty brownish-gray, the same color as the surrounding land, and they seemed to huddle together closely for warmth and safety against the sea.

"Make turns for eight knots," Beatty ordered on the phone to the engine room.

Cutting speed made them an easier target but a huge warship approaching a harbor at higher speeds would arouse alarm.

Beatty turned to another phone to the turrets.

"Send Walker up," he said.

Walker climbed to the upper deck as swiftly as he could. Falco had let him go alone, and if he could make it fast enough, without being intercepted or seen, he could do what had to be done and be long gone before anyone missed him.

But Beatty was waiting for him in the pre-dawn light. Over Beatty's shoulder, Walker could see the humped outline of trees, hills, buildings in the distance.

Beatty pointed to the forward 20- and 37-mm machine-gun mounts.

"Sure thing," Walker nodded. If he could only get rid of this bastard fast enough, before they got any closer.

"If anyone tries boarding, turn the guns on them."

"I thought they can't fire at anything on the ship," Walker recalled.

"They can now."

Beatty shined a flashlight beam at the 20-mm mount. Gaping spaces showed where small wedges of steel had been pried out.

"We removed the profile cams," he said. "Now

they'll fire anywhere. . . . Careful you don't shoot your pecker off."

"Right." Walker smiled. He could still get off the battleship in time if Beatty didn't plan on keeping watch over him. "Uh, when we get there, where you gonna be?" he asked offhandedly.

"Why?" Beatty asked, peering at him.

"In case I need help," Walker shrugged.

Beatty pointed up to the bridge. Its windows looked directly down on the forward machine-gun mounts. If he tried to duck away, Beatty would know it in a second.

"Yeah, good idea," Walker said flatly.

Beatty started to climb back to the bridge . . . there were only a few minutes left . . . but looking at Walker he felt something unexpected. He realized that he almost liked the American. He had dragged him into this messy business and except for some understandable flak from the American, Walker had done damn well, and it wasn't over yet. "Walker," Beatty called.

Walker stopped and turned.

"Yeah?"

"Good luck," Beatty said.

Walker shot Beatty his old charming smile.

"Terrific," he said.

The first weak rays of the sun flashed off the *Ludendorff's* topmost superstructure.

In the cold light that flooded across the sky, the gunnery controls, the masts, the derricks, the turrets all came into clearer focus, like a photograph being slowly developed in a chemical bath.

The battleship emerged from night.

It crunched through the heavy waves and treacherous

tides churned by the Kattegat and Skagerrak channels.

On the bridge, at a signal from Beatty, Shanks spun the wheel and the battleship, answering the helm, swung to port. Its bow pointed straight for Skagen. So did its guns.

Inside the steel box of "B" turret, Falco and Chadwick loaded the 15-inch rifles. Pressing a button near the breech on the loading platform, Falco raised a shell from the rattling hoist to the shell tray. He pushed a lever and the hydraulic rammer slammed the one-ton shell from the tray into the breech and seated it in the gun's chamber. Then he and Chadwick rolled four powder bags to the shell tray and hydraulically rammed them into the breech. They expertly soft-rammed the bags, letting them slide into the breech gently, for a broken bag was a lethal fire hazard. Falco closed the breech with a bang. From his pocket he took a primer, which looked like a 3-inch shell case, put it into the firing lock on the breech and closed the lock. The gun was ready.

In "A" turret, Tanner and Meredith had already loaded their guns. They donned the German anti-flash gear to protect against burns, white gloves and white hoods with holes for eyes and mouth, that made them look like medieval executioners. Then they shook hands and Meredith, leaving Tanner at the starboard gun, disappeared through a crawl hole at the base of the turret and came up on the other side of the thick bulkhead that completely separated the two guns, their hoists and their ammunition supply, so that even if one gun and its crew were totally destroyed, the other might still operate.

Checking everything for the last time, Meredith

shook off his uneasiness at being alone in his side of the turret.

He took his position at the face plate in the pit below his gun. He sat at the training dials, which controlled the gun's movement right and left.

On the other side of the bulkhead, in the second pit, Tanner sat at the pointer dials that controlled elevation and depression.

Every gun aimed and operated independently, but with only two men to operate the entire turret, they disengaged the existing gears and cross-connected them so that both guns were synchronized to operate together.

Tanner placed his eye against the rubber cushion of the telescope. He could make out a dark mound of land and buildings emerging in the bluish dawn light across the water, but they were still too far away, he knew. This was the hardest part, waiting, especially now. A turret usually had anywhere from eighty to one hundred and twenty men crowded, working together. He was by himself. The only sounds were the muffled vibrations of the engines and the drone of the ship's fans. Nervous, edgy, he rose and took a piss in a sand-filled bucket. That was the only thing he didn't like about being a gunner. No heads. Once you went into action, you stayed at your watch no matter how long it took, and if you had to piss, puke or crap, all you had was a sand bucket.

He buttoned his fly and peered through the telescope again. He couldn't make out any submarines yet, but it wouldn't be long now. The turret, like a steel womb, protected him with seven inches of armor, thick enough to deflect all but the largest shells, and everything else in the turret, from the ventilation to the anti-fire systems, was designed so that while almost every man aboard might be killed, even the officers on the exposed bridge, he, the gunner, would remain alive in order to fight. Strange. He was nineteen years old and hadn't known a day of quiet or happiness in his life, but he was the most important man on the *Ludendorff*.

On the bridge, as Shanks followed the pairs of channel buoys into the harbor, Beatty swept it with his glasses, trying to see the U-boat pens. He could make out rows of neat houses, salt and wind-battered, near the shore. Twisting roads. A cluster of piers and warehouses. A beach. The old Skagen church half buried in a sandstorm in 1775, its white tower still defiantly thrusting skyward. From this distance, Skagen appeared to be what it had been before the war, a fishing village and artists' colony. But Beatty knew where the camouflaged U-boat pens were, in the innermost recesses of the harbor, undetectable, like a deadly snake concealed in a garden.

He swung his glasses to the white-hulled fishing boats, their red, green and white running lights still on, that chugged past the *Ludendorff* to catch cod, plaice and herring in the Kattegat. He could make out the glow of a pipe in the mouth of a fisherman in the stern of a boat as he baited his hooks.

Below the bridge, at the starboard 37-mm on the boat deck, Walker studied the shore line. He expected guns on both sides to cut loose at any moment and he wanted to make his play now. He shot a glance to the bridge directly above. Beatty, at the window looking right down at him, would never give him the chance, the time to reach the vent shaft, grab the money, get a life jacket, put it on and jump.

Goddammit, Walker thought. Why didn't the Germans start firing? But he was torn by the thought. When they did start firing, he'd be one of the targets. Maybe he should leave the money and just take off before it was too late. What the hell. He'd be no worse off than when he started and at least he'd be alive. He could hop off the side in a second and Beatty'd never be able to stop him. But the shore still looked at least three miles away and he doubted whether, without a life jacket, he could make it. He was stuck on this goddamn thing.

Then he realized Beatty couldn't keep an eye on him much longer. Not once the Germans opened up. That's when he'd be able to reach the vent. And he did want that money. He'd never worked so hard for anything in his life. He wasn't leaving without it, not if he could help it. He wished the Germans would get wise fast and open up on the *Ludendorff*, because the closer the battleship got, the deadlier the fire on both sides.

"Come on, man," he muttered to the unseen commander of the U-boat base. "Get the rag out."

Skagen's commander, Kapitän Gerhard Dietl, studied the battleship, now barely four miles away, through the wide window of his headquarters overlooking the harbor. Hastily summoned from his shower, his lean, bony chest still wet, one tail of his shirt still hanging from his pants, Dietl wasn't sure he saw correctly the first time.

He squinted with his one good eye . . . the other, issued by navy doctors after he lost the real one in action, was made of glass in a color that didn't match, which gave his face a lopsided, frozen quality. He raised his field glasses.

"The *Ludendorff*," he said. "No doubt of it."

"But we never received a clearance for it, sir," a puzzled lieutenant said.

"You're sure of that?"

"Absolutely, sir."

Dietl's good eye narrowed. In the emergencies of war it wasn't unheard of for a ship to show up seeking harbor without official clearance. But Dietl, a submarine commander before turning prematurely gray and being dry-docked because of wounds and combat fatigue, was fanatical about regulations since their enforcement was now his principal function and only source of satisfaction at Skagen.

Dietl strode outside to the balcony and a signalman at the blinker lights.

On the *Ludendorff*'s signal bridge, Perth watched the distant blue signal light stabbing across the harbor and deciphered for Beatty. RECEIVED NO OFFICIAL CLEARANCE FOR LUDENDORFF TO ENTER THESE WATERS. REQUEST ON WHOSE AUTHORITY.

Beatty thought a moment. He was tempted to open fire now, a range of three miles was damn close, but not when firing with the naked eye in local control. He wanted to ram the *Ludendorff*'s guns down the Germans' throats. There was another factor. The longer he could hold off firing, the less time the Germans would have to get to their own guns.

"Tell them," he ordered Perth, "that we hit a mine. Rudder damaged. Must berth immediately for repairs."

"Oh, Christ," Kapitän Dietl muttered. "Why couldn't they go bother someone else?"

Dietl had his hands full keeping his own U-boats operating and in repair, and didn't know how he was going to spare manpower to repair a battleship.

But Dietl had no choice.

"Very well," he told the signalman. "Give them clearance."

Before the signalman could shutter off the message, the young lieutenant, looking through his glasses again, grabbed his arm.

"Herr Kapitän . . . the *Ludendorff*. There are almost no men aboard. It is practically deserted!"

Dietl grabbed the lieutenant's glasses and swept them across the battleship from bow to stern. Then up the superstructure past the bridge all the way up to the towering radar and down again across the decks. Between the bridge, the boat deck and the upper deck he could make out only two dozen, perhaps three dozen men. He returned the glasses with a superior smile.

"You have not been reading your movement reports, Leutnant. The *Ludendorff* sailed with only a trial crew." Dietl turned to the signalman. "Clearance approved. Tell them we'll send out a pilot and tugs to bring them in."

The two dozen "crewmen," seen by Dietl from a distance and scattered on the *Ludendorff*'s decks, didn't breathe. They moved only when the wind whipped the limp sleeve of a shirt, the cuff of an overall. They were scarecrow sailors, mop handles topped with headless flak helmets.

"They've bought it, sir," Perth said.

Beatty took a deep breath, let it out slowly. He raised his glasses. The camouflaged U-boat pens were becoming visible straight ahead. Huddled at the shore line, they looked like subway tunnels separated by massive concrete walls. In each of the twelve tunnels, still almost invisible in the dawn light, he could see the sharp noses of two submarines. Behind the pens, and protected from bombs by the same roof of reinforced concrete twenty-four-feet thick was, he knew, a whole complex that kept the submarines armed and operational.

Ready to open fire in another two minutes, Beatty remembered Horatio Nelson's warning that no warship could survive a few well-placed shore guns, and thanked his luck that he was catching the Germans off guard.

"Sir," Perth said. He pointed to four squat tugboats and a pilot boat nosing out of the harbor to meet the battleship and bring it in.

"I saw," Beatty said. "Ignore them."

Kapitän Dietl frowned, the expression registering in his good eye while the other remained glassily indifferent. The *Ludendorff*'s commander, he thought, must be extremely anxious about the damage to his ship because it was still approaching too fast to take on a pilot and attach lines with the tugs.

Dietl waited for some sign of reduced speed and for a moment thought he detected it. It was hard to tell at this distance and angle, and with only one eye he had almost no depth perception. But now he could tell from the anxious look on his lieutenant's face that the battleship was still going too fast. When the hell was it going to slow down?

The *Ludendorff* was already overtaking and surging past smaller boats entering the harbor, her giant bow wave hurling them aside like tiny boxes. The smaller craft objected with shrill blasts of their whistles. Within seconds the entire harbor erupted with a howl of angry whistles and horns protesting the intrusion of the battleship.

The *Ludendorff*'s deck officer, Dietl thought, must

be a crazy man. He rushed into the adjoining radio room.

"Reach that ship," Dietl barked.

"This is Kapitän Ziegler," Beatty replied on the ship-to-shore radio.

"Kapitän, I signaled we were sending out tugs and a pilot to bring you in," Dietl shouted, watching the battleship in the distance through the window.

"Yes, I received the signal," Beatty replied. Every second of time he could buy brought his guns closer.

"I request that you reduce speed for our pilot to come aboard."

"A pilot won't be necessary," Beatty said.

"I assure you it is. There are dangerous sand bars. I respectfully request that you reduce speed."

"I've already given the order to my engine rooms."

"They haven't complied. Reverse your engines!"

"I will take responsibility for proper entry. This is my ship."

"This is my harbor. Reduce speed immediately or . . ."

Dietl's lieutenant dashed over.

"Kapitän Dietl, you . . ."

"Later. I'm busy," Dietl snapped.

"Urgent, sir." The lieutenant shoved a radio message into Dietl's hands. "From Kapitän Kalmer, Group Command."

A handful of words jumped at Dietl from the yellow page.

TO ALL SHIPS AND BASES BATTLESHIP LUDENDORFF SENDING FALSE POSITION REPORTS ACTUAL POSITION UNKNOWN REGARD WITH EXTREME CAUTION.

Dietl shot a startled glance at the battleship, banged down the receiver and jabbed a button on the wall.

The clanging bell for general quarters ripped through the vast U-boat base complex, through the underground bunkers, living quarters, messes, machine shops, slips, shore gun emplacements. Quiet and slow moving one moment, the base banged into immediate high gear, leaping to life like some giant, dangerous organism. Boots thundered through the network of underground passageways. The Germans beneath the twenty-four-foot steel and concrete roofs assumed it was another enemy air raid, the kind that had failed so often before.

Through his glasses, Beatty saw Germans, many of them barely half-dressed, pouring out of their bunkers.

A few glanced up as if to spot attacking planes that weren't there, then back over their shoulders at the harbor, at the great battleship. Her superstructure was so close that it dominated the entire harbor, but since she was flying the German Navy ensign, there was no reason for her to strike fear.

Still not comprehending but galvanized by the shrieking alarm bell, they raced for their anti-aircraft and coastal defense guns.

On the *Ludendorff*'s bridge, Shanks turned the helm and the battleship swung several degrees starboard, cutting across the regular harbor channels and, as small craft fled wildly out of the monster's way, bearing straight for the heart of the submarine complex.

Beatty lowered his glasses and signaled down from the bridge to Walker at the 37-mm machine-gun mount to get ready.

Walker signaled back, and stuffing a wad of cotton in each ear, donned a flak helmet. He had no intention of staying at the gun, only of letting Beatty think he would. He had already figured out the fastest route down to the quarterdeck and the hidden bag of money.

Beatty turned from the bridge window to a phone. "Now, Tanner!" he shouted hoarsely.

CHAPTER 26

The twin guns crashed.

The great ship shuddered under the recoil.

The shells, dark blurs above the water, howled across the harbor and tore into the exposed underbelly of a central U-boat pen. Two explosions ripped through it, the first from the *Ludendorff*'s shells, the second from the fourteen torpedoes and over a hundred tons of diesel oil in a sea-ready submarine. An inferno of flame, pressed down by the concrete roof, burst through the open mouth of the pen and shot across the water, engulfing and incinerating a nearby motor launch.

Now Falco's guns roared. The massive roof above the pens shook as if hit by an earthquake as the explosion within hurled shattered concrete and huge pieces of submarine across the bay. At point-blank range, traveling at 1,500 feet a second, the impact of armor-piercing shells with delayed fuses designed to penetrate before exploding was devastating.

Confusion and terror engulfed the harbor.

As soon as the battleship changed course, trawlers

and sailing craft scurried to get out of its path. Now that the *Ludendorff*'s guns opened up, panic swept the small boats.

From the bridge, Shanks and Beatty saw one of the German tugs beating through the water dead ahead. To avoid a collision, Shanks knew he'd have to veer to starboard, then back to port again, a time-consuming maneuver that would throw off the turrets' aim.

Shanks kept the helm perfectly steady.

The fifty-thousand-ton battleship bore down on the tug, its great flared bow towering over it. As the distance closed, Beatty saw the tug disappearing under the *Ludendorff*'s bow and set himself for the crash.

The *Ludendorff* hit the squat, sturdy tug amidships with the power of an express train squashing a toy. With an impact that resounded throughout the harbor, the tug smashed cleanly in half, its bow flying in one direction, stern in the other, the *Ludendorff* knifing between them.

On the bridge, Beatty felt the collision as a mild jolt.

On the boat deck, Walker was barely aware it had happened. He'd been keeping his eye on the bridge window. He could see nobody was watching him from there now. He was about to race down to the quarterdeck to the vent shaft when he saw puffs of white smoke on the shore, followed by the scream of shells. He'd never heard anything like it, a savage, angry scream, getting louder, heading straight for him, and he hunched down behind the machine-gun mount for protection. Geysers of water leaped up behind and on both sides of the oncoming battleship. Barely seconds had elapsed and the German 88-mm anti-aircraft guns that ringed the base were already in action, straddling the *Ludendorff*. Another scream of shells. More geysers erupted off the bow and one shell smashed into the forecastle near the huge painted swastika.

The *Ludendorff*'s heavy armor deflected it like bb shot, but the bursting shell filled the air with the drone and whine of lethal shell splinters. The splinters scythed through four helmet-topped scarecrows at the rail, decapitating them, the mop handles clattering across the deck like brittle bones. A second shell hit just aft of a thirty-two-foot launch hanging at the ship's side from the starboard davit, the launch the British had planned on using to escape from the battleship. Half of the launch disappeared in the explosion, and shell splinters drummed along the upper deck. Walker realized that if he'd been down there at that moment for the life jacket, he'd be dead now. He hunched low behind the machine-gun mount, steel shrieking all around him, afraid to move.

In "A" turret, as soon as the guns recoiled, surging back hydraulically above their heads, Tanner and Meredith rushed from their pits to reload.

Tanner climbed to the loading platform and whipped open the gun's breech, automatically tripping the gas-ejecting air valve. A charge of air screamed up through the rifle, carrying away dangerous smoke, powder residue and sparks out the muzzle. Opening the firing lock, he inserted a new primer. Closed the lock. Pressed the button that raised another shell from the hoist to the shell tray. Pushed the lever and watched the hydraulic rammer ram it into the breech and push it home. Rolled four more powder bags to the shell tray. Soft-rammed them into the breech. Slammed the breech shut. Ready again. It was nothing like training now. The speed, the pressure were so intense, Tanner felt his whole body trembling, his mind unable to think. He was functioning automatically, almost like the guns themselves. Guns, however, couldn't make mistakes. He could. Slow down, he told himself. But he couldn't slow down. He had to move fast, even faster.

He was doing what had never been done before, just he and Meredith, two gunners all alone, operating a battleship's 15-inch turret.

"Ready," he said.

"Ready," came Meredith's voice on the phone.

"Mark."

"Mark."

Falco's guns crashed again two seconds after Tanner's, the echoes of the blast booming back from the shore. The Germans were hastily lowering steel bulkheads to protect the mouths of the U-boat pens, but the fierce shells ripped through them like paper and the submarine crewmen racing through the tunnels for safety died in their tracks. Falco couldn't see or hear how the Germans died . . . it was one of the bad things about fighting at a distance . . . but he could imagine the surprise, then the terror, the panicked running to escape. When a one-ton shell exploded, he wondered what the Germans heard or felt a moment before their bodies were blown into a million shreds of meat.

The hot blasts from the turrets directly below eddied back to the bridge and hit Beatty and Shanks like invisible fists, shattering the windows, squeezing Beatty's breath away.

Keeping his mouth open to prevent the blasts from rupturing his eardrums, Beatty swung his glasses from the 37-mm machine gun on the boat deck, where Walker crouched down out of the path of screaming shell splinters, to the U-boat pens billowing smoke, to a rise of ground above the base. Two huge guns that

dwarfed the 88s, their muzzles thrust upward, were angled against the sky. Beatty suspected they were 38-cm
Siegfrieds. The 88s could kill men. The Siegfrieds were
designed to kill battleships.

Suddenly their silhouettes began to shorten, until
Beatty saw only their black gaping mouths and knew
the Siegfrieds were aimed directly at him.

The muzzles rippled with orange flame and Beatty
suddenly felt a blow on the head as if the entire superstructure had crashed down on him and found himself
lying at the back of the wheelhouse, his flak helmet
dented, his left sleeve warm and sticky with blood, his
arm hanging limp. The Germans had scored a direct hit
just below the bridge on the signal deck. Beatty saw
Shanks, covered with paint chipped away by the blast,
staggering back to the wheel through black smoke that
swirled through the bridge. The blast had singed away
Shanks's eyebrows, giving him what looked like a wild,
crazy stare, but he signaled he was okay. Beatty
propped himself up against the quartermaster's desk, his
shoulder gripped by pain that drained the strength from
every muscle in his body. Through the smoke he
scanned the harbor, the shore line, for something he
feared even more than the German guns.

Huddled below the machine-gun mount, Walker told
himself to move his ass, now, to get to the money and a
life jacket, but it was a long way and he hesitated, the
hail of shell and steel keeping him down. But now he
sensed something and peered over the machine gun. On
shore, the anti-aircraft batteries and the monster guns
had fallen silent. He rose to his feet and saw why.

To the left of the blazing U-boat base, Germans
raced across a pier. For a moment they disappeared as
they split into groups and jumped down out of sight on

the far side of the pier. Moments later, a small boat crept out from behind the pier, then another, then two more, engines growling, accelerating with startling speed. *Schnellbootes* . . . torpedo boats. The German guns had fallen silent to give the *Schnellbootes* a clear field. Low slung, their bows throwing up a luminous foam while their triple Daimler-Benz diesels rose to a menacing whine as they picked up speed, the torpedo boats fanned out to attack.

Now Walker understood why Beatty wanted him at the machine guns. He was supposed to keep off the torpedo boats. But Walker didn't want to fuck with any torpedo boats. He shot another look up at the bridge. It had taken a near-hit. Nobody up there would see him now. He sprinted across the boat deck, as one of the S-boats darted in, unleashing a torpedo and veering off behind its own smoke screen. The torpedo hit below the waterline.

The force rippled through the hull and the decks bucked, hurling Walker off his feet. He hugged the deck so close he could smell the teakwood. He jackknifed up and scrambled down a vertical ladder and raced for the quarterdeck.

Walker reached the vent and thrust his hand down for the bag. His hand clutched at empty air. He thrust down further, desperately sweeping his hand all around the side. He felt the metal projection on which he'd hung the bag, but nothing else. He looked in. Gone. The bag was gone. Could someone've taken it? Impossible. Nobody knew about it.

The *Ludendorff*'s forward turrets roared again, shaking the battleship from bow to stern, nearly jolting Walker off his feet again, and then he knew what had happened to the bag. The battleship's jarring salvoes shook it loose. It had dropped down the shaft to some-where below.

Walker peered into the shaft. Except for a couple of feet near the top, he could see nothing, just an infinite black hole. The shaft seemed wide enough to climb in, but he was torn. After all he'd gone through for the money, why not climb down a shaft for it? But where did it go to? Suppose it dropped him right into a fucking boiler? He peered in quickly again. The shaft wasn't giving off any heat so that ruled out any boiler directly below. But suppose it went straight down to the bottom of the ship, so far that he'd never be able to make it back up? He grabbed a piece of smashed steel from the deck and dropped it into the shaft, listening until he heard a clang as it hit. It wasn't all the way to the bot-tom of the ship. But it was long enough.

Taking a deep breath, Walker climbed into the shaft. He pressed his back and arms against one slippery smooth side, his feet against the opposite side. He let himself down slowly, carefully, first one foot then the other, then sliding his body down.

The vertical steel tunnel became almost immediately pitch black, though he could see a disc of blue sky when he looked up. Below him, nothing, a dark void. The roaring guns reached him, a muted thunder, but the shaft shook and trembled.

Walker felt his legs binding up and had to stop mid-way down the shaft. Catching his breath, he looked up. The blue disc of sky was much smaller now. Smoke of battle swirled across it.

He inched down some more, his legs and arms get-ting weaker, his calf muscles beginning to cramp. He felt himself slipping, braked with his legs, but they held only a few seconds. He was skidding down the shaft, his hands getting friction burns, gathering speed, unable to stop and he knew that he was crazy, he should've split when he had the chance, now it was too late, he was falling out of control and the further he fell the harder he'd crash, he was going to die in a steel tube on top of a bag full of Nazi money, and then came a hard slam and the fall was over. It took some time before all his senses came together again and he could think.

He'd landed at the bottom of a network of horizontal shafts. He could see nothing except the small circle of sky at the top of the shaft. But it was pitch black down here. And a strong smell. Smoke.

There'd been no smoke pouring from the shaft before or he wouldn't've gone down, but there was smoke now from the shells and torpedos. He had to get the hell out of here fast.

He groped wildly in the dark for the bag. Felt nothing. The battleship had lurched when it was hit, and the bag must've slid.

On hands and knees . . . the top of the horizontal shaft was barely a couple of feet high . . . he felt around for the bag to his right. Then to his left. Still no bag. It must've slid further than he thought. He returned to his right, heading slightly downhill because the battleship had begun to list. The smoke was thick now and it was hard to breathe.

Totally blind in the dark, he crawled a few feet, a few feet more, his hand outstretched, feeling ahead like an ant's antennae. It touched something soft.

He clutched the bag. He felt hard stacks of money.

On the bridge, Beatty, propped against the captain's chair, saw two more S-boats, like hounds pursuing a wounded bear, closing in to starboard. Anxiously he waited for tracers from Walker's machine gun to intercept them, but there was nothing. The boats charged in unopposed. Sun glinted off two torpedoes knifing into the water as the S-boats fired and swung away.

Beatty and Shanks watched the torpedo wakes lancing toward them. The first torpedo went wide, flashing past the bow. The second hammered into the stern near the fuel tanks. Oil poured through the gaping wound, spreading out in the water like black blood.

Damn, why doesn't Walker keep them off, Beatty's mind screamed. He shot a look down. The machine-gun mount was empty. Walker could've been killed, but Beatty didn't see a body. The American was hiding somewhere, out of range of firing and shell splinters.

"Find the bastard! Get him back at the guns," he barked.

Shanks dashed for the upper deck.

Eyes stinging, lungs stabbed by smoke, Walker looped his belt through the handle of the bag in order to keep his own hands free, then crawled back along the horizontal shaft to find the vertical one that led to the quarterdeck.

He looked for the small circle of sky again, but the dense smoke must've covered it because he couldn't see it. He felt for it along the top of the shaft. His hands met with cold, solid resistance, an impenetrable roof of steel. In a maze of tunnels branching out across the ship, choking and blinded, he could've wandered from the first and turned into another one. God, he could be lost, trapped down here.

Walker felt a rising tide of terror. The steel walls of the shaft pressing all around him, he scurried on his knees along the shaft one hand on the overhead like a blind man, feeling for an opening. The steel tunnel shuddered beneath him every time a big shell exploded within the *Ludendorff*. The smoke became so thick that Walker, unable to breathe, sank to his belly, gasping and retching. When it cleared some and he could gulp some air, he scuttled on, the bag hanging from his waist, banging against his leg.

Walker forced himself on, but he had to go much slower now, feeling along the shaft both beneath his feet and above his head. Maybe he should've gone the other way, he thought. Too late for that now.

Suddenly, light. Walker saw the sky framed high above his head. He stood up in the shaft. Pressed his back against one side. Jammed his feet against the other. Began to force his way up . . . shoulders and back first as far as they'd go, then his feet.

Getting down had been hard. Weighted down by the bag, going up was torture, inches, fractions of inches at a time. His feet digging in for traction, the higher he got the clearer he could hear the booming of the big guns. He was almost to the top. Another foot to go. He reached up, stretched a hand for the top of the shaft, saw the sunlight strike his fingers.

Shanks, searching for Walker on the boat deck, saw something on the level below . . . an ash-gray figure slowly emerging from a shattered vent shaft.

Walker bellied out of the shaft, and through burning eyes saw how near land was. Close, maybe only a couple of miles. Tightening the bag belted to his waist, he raced to a lifeboat, ripped open the tarp, grabbed a life jacket. A shell thundered overhead and he had to throw himself under the boat as it exploded into the derrick above.

As he crouched low, tugging on the life jacket, he saw something scurrying from a hatch across the deck. Rats. Screeching, panicked rats. So it really happened, he thought, as the rats swarmed over the gunwale and plunged into the bay. The life jacket secure, Walker turned for the rail. He heard sea boots thudding down a ladder. He wheeled. It was Shanks, moving between him and the rail. Shanks, puzzled, saw the bag. Whatever it was, there was no time to talk about it.

"Get back there," Shanks ordered, pointing to the machine guns.

Walker feinted to the left and made an end run around Shanks's right. Shanks moved with astonishing speed and caught him from behind at the rail. Walker smashed an elbow back, catching Shanks in the mouth, but the old man held onto the life jacket. Walker moved with the force of the pull, driving fists into Shanks's hard gut to make him let go. Suddenly, Walker felt Shanks and himself torn apart, hurled across the deck by a blast from a shell that crashed through the armor and exploded below.

Stunned, Walker hit against a twisted davit at the rail. The thick life jacket had cushioned the impact or his spine would've been cracked. He rolled over, checked the money bag, then struggled to his knees, choking from cordite fumes and from fires raging on the decks. He got to his feet and lurched for the rail. From the corner of his eye he saw something. Shanks, lying dazed, trapped under a section of shattered derrick, flames spreading around him. Walker heard the torpedo boats roaring in. He ran to the gunwale and climbed over the rail. He could see Shanks struggling to get out from under the derrick, the fire circling him.

Walker hesitated at the rail. Don't be a putz, he thought. Shanks, the British, they *wanted* to be here. They *asked* for it. So if the old man died, he died. He, Walker, had no stake in it. No stake at all. Don't do anything stupid. Jump!

But in another second, without even knowing why, he vaulted back over the rail. He got a shoulder under the steel beam pinning Shanks and heaved. It didn't budge. He grabbed Shanks under the arms and pulled. The old man was pinned too tightly—Walker braced a foot against the beam and pulled again. Shanks moved. Inch by inch he began to work Shanks out, the edge of the beam tearing at Shanks's shirt, then his bare flesh, leaving a smear of blood.

Shanks gasped but his eyes urged Walker to pull harder.

Walker felt an oven-blast of flame. The circle of fire was burning up the oxygen around them. He could barely breathe. Get Shanks out now or he'd have to leave him. He braced his foot against the derrick again and wrenched desperately. With a scream, Shanks came free, leaving behind a peel of raw skin on the steel beam. They staggered through the fire, choking and spitting white mucous gobs, Shanks's shirt hanging in shreds, his chest streaked black from smoke, red from torn flesh, Walker half deafened from the blasts and explosions, his lungs burning from cordite smoke, his hands seared by the fire.

"Thanks, lad," Shanks gasped.

Walker didn't even hear it. He'd already turned for the rail again and swung one leg over to jump, to free himself at last from the goddamn battleship, when he heard an angry snarl. Straddling the rail, he shot a look around.

The torpedo boats were closing in, their machine guns raking the decks. He heard bullets splattering against the bulkhead behind him. One of those machine guns was firing at him.

With a sinking feeling, he knew he should've jumped when he had the chance. But he'd fucked himself royally, as usual, turning back for Shanks. Jump now and the torpedo boats'd spot him, swing around and machine gun him right in the water. Too late to jump. He was stuck.

Furious with himself, Walker dashed for a ladder. Up the ladder. To the boat deck. If the Germans were trying to sink the *Ludendorff*, and he couldn't get off, he had to stop them as long as he could.

The heavy bag of money hit against his side, getting in his way. He unbuckled the bag and strapped it securely to a 37-mm machine-gun mount.

He leaped behind the twin guns and swung them across the port beam at the torpedo boats coming straight for him.

CHAPTER 27

One behind the other, two S-boats, drawing no fire in their first attack, streaked in closer now, elusive targets with their low-slung hulls flying across the water at forty miles an hour.

Walker pulled the trigger. The machine gun bucked angrily in his hands. The tracers arced across the harbor, kicking up spouts ahead of the lead S-boat. He elevated the gun and the tracers closed in as the boat fired a torpedo. He kept firing. The boat laid a smoke screen and vanished.

The torpedo hit near the *Ludendorff*'s stern and Walker felt the battleship shudder. He swung the 37-mm on the second S-boat. Again the tracers lanced across the water, kicking up splashes ahead of the zigzagging boat. When there were no more splashes, Walker knew he was hitting the boat and kept his finger on the trigger, the machine gun hammering furiously, the spent casings clattering to the deck all around him.

The shells slammed into the torpedo boat's teakwood skin and ripped into the fuel tank. The explosion lifted the S-boat out of the water as if it were going to fly and then it disappeared like a bursting firecracker.

Walker whirled the gun on another torpedo boat. He pulled the trigger but nothing happened. He had emptied the canisters on the twin mount. The 37-mm canisters were too heavy for Walker to reload by himself. He rushed to another machine gun on the boat deck.

In "B" turret, Falco and Chadwick were swinging the synchronized guns a couple of degrees to the left for a direct shot at a repair dock, the machinery whirring softly as they swiveled. Suddenly, before Falco could pull the firing mechanism, the entire gun-booth jerked upward like a berserk elevator, slamming them against the overhead and dropping them down, stunned. A hit had lifted the turret off the roller path of ball bearings on which it rested. They tried to swing the turret again. The machinery ground but the turret didn't move.

" 'B' turret jammed," Falco shouted into the phone to the bridge.

"Can you still fire?" Beatty asked.

"Yes!"

"Then fire!"

Falco fired.

In the other turret, Tanner saw one of the distant Siegfried guns spout flame and knew another shell was thundering his way. Damn good gunners those German bastards, he thought.

The German armor-piercing shell screamed down and drilled straight through the front of the turret on Meredith's side. Meredith was killed instantly. Tanner, separated from Meredith by a thick armor wall, would've survived if they hadn't filled the turret with cordite bags, the only way for two men to operate it swiftly by themselves.

The German shell burst in the midst of the cordite. The bags exploded with shattering force, ripping through the armor wall protecting Tanner and bursting open the whole turret like a lanced boil.

His headquarters rocked by the blasts of the *Ludendorff*'s great guns, Kapitän Dietl studied the smoke and flames raging on the battleship's decks and superstructure, the holes torn through the bulkheads and hull. Taking turns, his guns and torpedo boats could sink any ship, even the *Ludendorff*, given enough time. But there wasn't enough time. The *Ludendorff*, drawing suicidally close, showed no sign of swinging away, even though it was listing heavily to starboard. On its present course, the battleship would ram straight into the U-boat base, destroying it beyond repair.

Dietl felt a nervous pulse beating in the lid covering his glass eye. If it was impossible to *sink* the *Ludendorff* in time, he had to find another way to stop the battleship.

He reached for a phone.

Walker peered uneasily over the barrel of a 20-mm machine gun.

It fired more rounds than a 37-mm and the snail-like canisters were small enough for him to reload by himself. The batteries on shore had suddenly fallen silent again and he expected another wave of attacks from the regrouped torpedo boats. But he didn't expect to see three of them snarling in, all from the port side at once, their machine guns winking, filling the air around him with a hornet-swarm of bullets.

Walker opened up, pouring the full canister into the dancing, roaring torpedo boats, the gun bucking relentlessly in his hands. One of the S-boats fired a torpedo that went wild, then they split up and raced away.

Walker stopped firing. He had chased them off! He was too much for them, the mother-fuckers.

And then he heard it. A deep-throated growl behind him.

He turned. A lone S-boat, using the others as diversion, had slipped up close on the *Ludendorff* from the other side. Walker swung his gun around 180 degrees and opened fire, but too late. The S-boat disappeared below the upper deck and near the stern, out of his line of sight. It didn't reappear. It was following the *Ludendorff*, almost hugging the hull.

But why? He waited, he didn't know for what.

Suddenly, a grappling hook snaked through the air from below. It didn't catch, but the next three did with a clang on the rail and at the side of the ship, about ten yards apart. Now he knew what he was waiting for. He drew back the bolt again and took a deep breath.

The twenty-one crewmen of the S-boat, trained to board and capture warships, began to scale the shell-battered hull of the battleship, automatic rifles and submachine guns strapped to their backs. As soon as one got halfway up each of the three lines, three more began to climb.

Walker held his fire. First one, then two more steel helmets appeared over the side, followed by heads and shoulders. He could see the sun glinting off the wristwatch of a German reaching up to grab the rail and swing himself over. The Germans saw Walker at the 20-mm and stared, more puzzled than frightened. A machine gun, they knew, couldn't hit them once they were on the same ship.

Walker cut loose, sweeping the three Germans off the grappling lines. Already dead, they plunged past the others below them on the lines, knocking one of them off. The Germans in the bow climbed slower now, more cautiously, but they climbed. Still firing to keep the Germans down on the starboard side, Walker sensed something and glanced over his shoulder to port.

Two, three more grappling hooks snaked up and caught at the gunwale. Another S-boat had slipped in on the other side of the *Ludendorff*. Walker tried to blast the hooks off before the Germans could board, but the imbedded hooks, even when hit, stayed, and Walker, afraid of running out of ammunition or overheating his gun, stopped firing and waited.

Almost as if by signal, the Germans came charging over both sides of the quarterdeck, firing at him. Walker heard bullets splattering on the two small gun shields. He raked the deck in a wide arc, cutting down four Germans on the port side, two more dashing for cover behind a barbette. But the fumes from the *Ludendorff*'s guns and black smoke from fires raging all over the ship swirled across the quarterdeck, concealing most of the other Germans who fanned out like dimly seen specters. Walker, afraid they'd trap him, ran for cover. He stumbled on something, a fallen Schmeisser, and picked it up. He hauled himself up a ladder back to the boat deck.

From the bridge, Beatty and Shanks saw Germans running across the upper deck, heading for the superstructure to capture the bridge. Jamming a Luger in his belt and grabbing a Schmeisser, Shanks left Beatty at the helm and raced down to meet them. He waited, concealed above the forward superstructure platform. When the Germans reached it, he opened fire, killing three instantly.

Shanks sped down to help the American but he saw two Germans climbing the ladder leading to the overhang hatch of Falco's turret. He rapid-fired his Luger, knocking one of them off before the automatic clicked empty. The other German had reached the hatch, was opening it, in another second would be able to fire down at Falco and Chadwick inside.

Shanks ran for the turret and up the ladder. He felt his hamstring seizing up again and prayed it would hold. He grabbed the German from behind, forced his hand away from the hatch. The German lunged back and together, they half slid, half fell to the deck. Grabbed in a bear hug, Shanks for the first time in his life felt himself lifted off his feet in a fight. Their faces were only inches apart. Shanks saw the fat pinkish cheeks of a boy, the German saw the lined face of an old man.

Shanks dug the heel of his hand under the German's nose and forced his head back, his fingers clawing to tear out the Kraut's eyes. They crashed down, the German's helmet spinning off. Shanks hammered the German's head against the deck. It sounded like smashing a melon.

He kneeled over the German, trying to catch his breath, his chest heaving. He felt exhausted and sick. Too much smoke, he told himself.

He clutched the fallen rifle and turned. Another German saw him and fired a burst. Shanks spun to fire back but the Mauser felt heavy in his hands, his body slow as if pushing against water.

The goddamn smoke, the old man thought a second before a bullet ripped into his brain.

The German who killed Shanks, joined by a tall sublieutenant, raced below deck to recapture the battleship's control rooms and reverse the engines.

From the deck above, Walker saw them disappear down a hatch. Clutching the submachine gun, he went after them.

From the bridge Beatty saw them, too, and sensed where the Germans were heading. It could mean all their deaths. But wounded and alone at the helm, he couldn't leave the bridge.

It was all Walker now.

Reaching the second deck the two Germans were startled by a voice, calls for help, somewhere down the passageway. A figure behind bars. Rows of stripes on the sleeve.

The sublieutenant rushed to the steel cabinet on a nearby bulkhead. It was locked but one blast from his Mauser blew it open. He grabbed the ring of keys inside and in a second had the prisoner free.

Ziegler grabbed the sublieutenant's Luger and joined by the second sailor dashed down a companionway further below. Ziegler saw the lieutenant's intention to recapture the forward engines and barked, "No." He signaled for them to follow him in another direction.

They'd meet opposition, Ziegler knew, from whoever was manning the forward engine room, and with only three men Ziegler had neither the firepower nor the time for a below-decks gun battle. He had another way to stop the battleship.

* * *

Ziegler led the men to the aft engine room which he'd shut down after trouble with the reduction gears. He knew it couldn't be operating and therefore wouldn't be guarded.

They bolted down a ladder to the deserted control level, then down to the operating level.

The two assault marines hesitated to go any further into the bowels of a ship already taking in water and in danger of sinking, but at a sharp look from Ziegler they descended to the deepest part of the ship, the bilge.

In the cavernous gloom, Ziegler raced through the ankle-deep bilge water that sloshed across the plates to one of the sea valves. He started to turn the valve desperately. The two marines rushed to the other valves and wrestled them. For a moment there was silence in the bilge except for the harsh breathing of the straining men. Then a low groan as the sea came pouring through the huge pipes and headed for the ship's condensers.

The Germans grabbed fire axes from the bulkhead and smashed at the pipes, cracking open the thin-walled tubing in as many places as they could. At first, the water spilled into the bilge with a rushing hiss, but as Ziegler and the others hacked away, it came pouring in geysers under incredible pressure, the hissing turning into a roar as the sea invaded the ship. The ship was slowing down, the water acting as a giant drag. The *Ludendorff* was being scuttled by its own commander.

Ziegler signaled above the roaring cataracts for the two to hurry. The bilge was filling rapidly in the foaming flood of water. If they stayed here much longer, they'd drown.

The sublieutenant, signaling back that he was almost finished, raised his ax to smash one of the sea valves itself when he suddenly sagged over as if exhausted and plunged into the raging water below.

Ziegler looked up. From the operating level just above, someone was firing at them.

It was Walker.

His second submachine-gun burst caught the other German trying to fling himself out of Walker's line of fire. Expecting only two Germans, Walker caught a glimpse of Ziegler scrambling for protection and cursed himself for not spotting all three and killing Ziegler first.

He considered keeping Ziegler trapped below until sea water filled the bilge and drowned the German. But he was afraid that once the bilge filled, the ship'd sink and they'd both drown.

He heard a sound over his shoulder, spun, saw Ziegler, who'd come up behind him, charge. Walker jerked his gun up but Ziegler's body deflected it. The weapon clattered across the plates and dropped into the torrent below.

Knocked to his knees, Walker saw a boot aimed at his face and twisted away. It glanced off his shoulder, and grabbing Ziegler's foot, Walker brought the German down with him.

They rolled toward the rail overlooking the bilge and the rising sea water. Walker got one arm free and hammered at Ziegler's face, but Ziegler's grip tightened. Walker sensed that the rail was directly over his head now, knew they were at the edge, then the rail was past his head and there was nothing under him and together they plunged into the flooding, roaring bilge.

The raging water flung them apart for a second and then Ziegler was on him again. They went under. Ziegler expertly broke Walker's hold, spun him around and

305

whipped a headlock from behind. Keeping his own head above water, Ziegler held Walker under in a powerful grip.

Walker thrashed desperately, trying to pry Ziegler's arm away, but couldn't. He felt his lungs bursting. His thrashing hand blindly touched something underwater. A ladder rung. He grabbed it and pulled himself and Ziegler to it, reaching up for the next rung, then another, hauling himself up against Ziegler's weight. His head broke the surface and he swallowed air.

Ziegler tried to wrench him back into the water. But Walker hooked his left arm around a rung and held tight, smashing at Ziegler with his free elbow, stunning him, grabbing him by the throat, forcing him down and under, holding the struggling German in the rising torrent, feeling him thrash and tear at his hand, then suddenly, like a windup toy, stop and go limp.

Walker let go and Ziegler's body floated away from him face up in a ghastly grimace, a foam of bubbles rising from his mouth.

Grasping at pieces of equipment along the bulkheads, Walker pulled himself through the water blasting into the bilge, sinking the battleship and him with it. He had to close the damn sea valves. He felt himself swept up as if by a vicious wave, grabbed onto something again and struggled to the first sea valve.

At the helm, Beatty felt the *Ludendorff* dragging. He knew that the Germans had opened the sea valves, filling the great ship's belly with thousands of tons of water, trying to drown the *Ludendorff* before it could ram the U-boat base and blow it up. Beatty had counted on the confusion of the ramming attack and the destruction to provide the essential diversion they needed to escape.

Without it, when they abandoned ship, the Germans would slaughter them in the water.

The U-boat base, shrouded in smoke, was a thousand yards away now. Diesel oil poured across the water in a flaming swath, turning the harbor into a raging inferno.

The battleship's speed was creeping lower, steadily lower. He could do nothing now except aim the battleship straight at the pens and pray that Walker had stopped the Germans and closed the sea valves in time.

Water thundered into the bilge.

Hit by conflicting torrents, Walker struggled to shut the first sea valve. The huge wheel wouldn't turn. He positioned all his weight behind the valve, gripped the radiating spokes and strained till the wheel gave, gave some more, slowly creaked shut.

He slogged through the rising, rolling water to the next valve and slowly, agonizingly forced it closed. He felt the muscles under his ribs quiver in rebellion under the strain.

Exhausted, he wrestled with the last huge wheel. It resisted as if frozen. He pushed his body against it with his remaining power.

On the bridge Beatty swiftly lashed the wheel to the binnacle with a short length of line, keeping the wheel rigid, steering the battleship dead ahead, straight for the U-boat base.

He still couldn't be sure the sea valves were shut, couldn't be sure the *Ludendorff* wouldn't sink before hitting its target. But they had to abandon ship. They had to do it now.

He barked the order over the phone to "B" turret and the forward engine room. Then Beatty limped and slipped down the bridge by the twisted ladders on the shattered superstructure.

The bilge water rose to Walker's chest.

He still couldn't get the last valve shut. He wanted to leave it, to escape over the side with his money. But in his panic he was afraid that if he tried, the rising water would sink the battleship before he could ever make the upper deck.

His fingers were welded to the valve, his body coiled around it, one knee jammed against a spoke, the side of his head pressing against another spoke and shaking in a palsied strain. His feet struggled under the water for traction.

For a second he thought he felt the valve move.

Every part of his body fought the wheel. A muscle suddenly sprung, tearing away under his ribs with a shooting pain but his body's momentum spun the valve loose.

He twisted it shut.

Hammond and Jenkins scrambled up from the forward engine room whose bulkheads were paint-blistered from the heat in surrounding compartments. They had four decks to climb, and if it was bad in the engine room, it had to be worse higher up.

The armored deck above swirled with smoke so thick that the lights, though burning, looked like distant, dying stars. They stumbled and groped for another ladder.

On the next level fires raged forward and now they had to retreat aft. As they ran, Hammond heard an eerie sound, like marching boots. Jenkins heard it, too. But with flames behind them, they could only head in that direction. The slow, measured sound, deep and hollow, grew louder, echoing down the steel corridor. Could the *Ludendorff*'s crew, imprisoned in the refrigerator compartment, have escaped, Hammond wondered, and be coming after him? The boots were almost on top of them now. Then he saw where the sound came from. An explosion in the bandmen's mess had sprung open the lockers, spilling out cornets, trombones, a tuba and an array of drums. The drums resting on their sides rolled with the ship, banging against the lockers and each other like a ghost band.

They spotted a shaft of light. Hammond reached it first, a jammed but partially open hatch to the upper deck. Hammond squeezed his way through to the upper deck. He reached down to help Jenkins still inside. As their hands gripped, there was a muffled explosion and Jenkins disappeared in a rush of flame that swept through the passageway. Hammond felt Jenkins' hand still clutching his for a moment longer, then it let go.

Rising, Hammond couldn't believe what he saw. Directly ahead, the U-boat base was a flaming tower of smoke reaching to the sky, the smoke boiling out to engulf the battleship itself. Hammond found a rifle and ran.

Walker staggered topside at almost the same moment, but above on the boat deck.

With the British scurrying topside below him and only seconds left to get off the ship, which was under shore fire again, Walker ran to the machine-gun mount where he'd lashed the bag of money. The bag was still there. He grabbed it and headed for a ladder when a shell burst on the deck behind him.

He ran two more yards and then, though he felt nothing, his left leg buckled and he found himself rolling over on his back. He tried to rise and couldn't. Blood glistened through his pants leg. It was torn open and looking closer he saw his knee. It looked like a squashed plum.

He tried to crawl to the ladder. His knee exploded with paralyzing pain that shot through his whole body. He could see Perth below, at the rail on the upper deck. He shouted but Perth couldn't hear him over the bursting shells and the crump of explosions within the ship.

For some reason that Walker couldn't understand, Perth was firing straight down into the water. Hammond joined him.

A machine gun from below returned their fire. One of the Germans left guarding the S-boat was raking the battleship's gunwales, forcing Perth and Hammond to duck back. The other slashed with a knife at the grappling lines to free the boat and get away. Hammond and Perth saw two lines go limp. Only one line left. They needed the S-boat to escape and had to risk the machine gun again by showing themselves over the rail and firing back. They dropped the German rushing to the third rope, but a bullet caught Hammond below the left eye and tore the back of his head off. His body slumped over the rail and tumbled into the sea. A second burst caught Perth. Walker saw it drive Perth back across the deck, a hole high in his chest. Falco and Beatty reached the rail and fired down, silencing the machine gun.

From the shore, the German guns intensified their barrage. Falco climbed over the rail and hand under hand scrambled down the grappling line to the S-boat. Beatty went next, clutching the line with his good hand and sliding down, rope splinters like daggers stabbing into his fingers. Perth limped back to the rail and struggled over, blood spurting from his mouth. He grabbed the rope and started down, but stopped midway.

"Come on," Falco urged.

Too weak, Perth's feet locking the rope let go. He hung for a moment by his hands, not making a sound, then dropped into the water between the battleship and the torpedo boat. Falco desperately tried to grab him, but the two hulls slammed together and Perth disappeared.

Beatty and Falco were the only two left. Falco ducked back to the controls as Beatty hacked at the last grappling line.

On the boat deck, Walker had shouted for help but nobody heard him over the guns. Seeing Falco climbing over the rail, Walker realized he had to get down there, too.

Buckling the money bag to his belt again he steeled himself for the coming pain and started to drag his body over the catapult to the ladder. The pain surged and he groaned like an animal. He stopped moving and some of it washed away and he was tempted just to lie there. Maybe if he didn't move it would leave. But that was crazy. He forced himself another few yards. He felt weak and the heavy bag was slowing him down but he never thought of abandoning it.

He reached the ladder, hoped he could make it down without passing out from pain. He did. Just barely. Lying on the upper deck, gasping, he heard the S-boat's engines. The bastards were leaving without him. He clawed his way to the rail and saw the S-boat just as it pulled away from the battleship. He shouted. It picked up speed. He glanced around. The battleship was going to crash into the base, taking him with it.

311

Falco swung the boat around in a tight arc to get out of the harbor. The fuel gauge indicated one-third full, enough to cross the Kattegat to Sweden. As the boat turned, Beatty saw a figure obscured by black smoke on one knee at the *Ludendorff's* rail, waving desperately. Walker.

"Falco," Beatty shouted, pointing.

Falco looked up and saw him, too.

"Circle around, one more time," Beatty ordered.

Falco glanced at the harbor filled with flying debris and shell splashes.

"We will never get out of here," he shouted.

"One more time!"

"Merde," the Frenchman muttered.

He spun the wheel as hard as he could. The S-boat swung about sharply, nearly pitching Beatty overboard.

Walker saw it coming around again, looked at the water frothing below, shut his eyes and jumped. He hit the water and the weight of the money bag carried him down, the battleship passing over him. There was a roaring in his ears and he realized it was the *Ludendorff's* great propellers. He was afraid he'd be sucked into the blades. The roaring grew louder and he saw a wild, boiling wall of water whipped by the screws coming closer. He felt a force spinning him crazily, turning the sea upside down, beating at him, and saw a flashing blur of blades and tried to get away but the pull was too strong and he couldn't breathe and he was being sucked into the blades and then suddenly the force hurled him somewhere and air rushed into his lungs.

The *Ludendorff* was past him and he thrashed to stay afloat in its wake.

The S-boat swung toward him, a plume from a

screaming shell leaping off its bow. The boat slowed to a crawl and Beatty, near the stern, reached down for Walker. He missed the American's hand, tried again and speared the sleeve of his jacket.

"Go," Beatty shouted to Falco at the wheel.

Falco opened the throttle and the torpedo boat skipped across the water again.

Grasping the jacket, Beatty hauled as Walker tried to grip the stern. A couple of bills spilled out of the bag cut open by one of the propellers. Then, forced out by the rushing water, a few more bills followed by a stream of them, some sinking, others dancing to the surface. The harder Walker struggled to get into the boat, the further the hole in the bag ripped open, the bills seeping, spilling, tumbling out until there was none left in the bag and they formed a long beautiful green tail behind the torpedo boat.

Beatty got Walker's belly over the stern, and they saw the Reichmarks disappearing in the distance. Beatty realized that Walker could've deserted with a bundle but didn't. He turned to say something but knew the American too well by now to try to thank him, so he said nothing.

"Oh, shit," Walker mourned as the last bills sank from sight.

The Daimler-Benz engine whined as the S-boat leaped across the harbor away from the *Ludendorff*. Beatty and Walker turned to watch her final moments.

The *Ludendorff* bore down on the German base, her sides ripped open by seven torpedoes, decks and hull smashed by twenty-three Siegfried shells, shaken by savage internal explosions, fires raging everywhere, smoke pouring through its funnel riddled in a hundred places, superstructure shattered like a tree struck repeatedly by lightning. Her fuel oil, bleeding into the sea, merged with the blazing diesel oil spilling from the U-boat base and burst into flames, the fire surrounding the ship like a pyre in a Götterdämmerung.

The battleship crashed into the base like a monstrous battering ram. Tons of fuel, shells and powder exploded. The great blast crumbled the impregnable U-boat base, the massive roofs lifting, cracking, crashing down, burying everything below under thousands of tons of shattered concrete and steel. Then the *Ludendorff* disappeared in a series of cataclysms across its entire length, blasts that shook the land and rose boiling through the smoke in great balls of flame skyward.

In the streaking torpedo boat, the three men felt the heat hit them and they hunched down as the explosion rained debris, pieces of turret, gun mount, engine, mast across the harbor. A tidal wave from the explosion surged through the water, lifted their boat and shot it forward.

When they looked back again, there was no U-boat base, no *Ludendorff*, only a black pall of smoke that covered the land, the water and the sky.

"God, that was a ship," Beatty said.

"Yeah, terrific," Walker said.

EPILOGUE

Cesar Falco continued to kill Germans throughout the war. After the *Ludendorff* episode, he was repatriated from Sweden, rejoined the Free French forces in England and participated in the Allied invasion at Normandy and in the liberation of Paris.

On May 15, 1945, he was requested to appear before General Charles de Gaulle to receive the Cross of Lorraine for his part in capturing the *Ludendorff*. Waiting for the ceremony would have kept him in Paris an added seven days, however, and he was too anxious to return home and take over the family's brothel from his ailing father. He didn't appear for the medal. De Gaulle was outraged and made certain that Falco never received the medal or any other decoration from the French or British governments.

On November 19, 1962, Falco, who had never been scratched in five years of war, was stabbed in the neck by a customer, a Frenchman, after an argument in his brothel over the price of a bottle of cheap champagne.

Falco was carried upstairs and died twenty minutes later in a whore's bed.

Vyvvyan Beatty was hospitalized for three months for his shoulder wound, the tibia had been shattered, and spent the rest of the war at his desk at S.O.E.

At war's end, he increased the family fortune by astute investments in South America and eventually remarried his former wife, Lady Evelyn Owen-Childs, who bore him a daughter, Hillary. Beatty tried to take up polo again in his middle age, but it aggravated his shoulder, which, it is said, made him irritable and grouchy. He now takes occasional horseback rides through his Buckinghamshire estate, accompanied by his wife and daughter, at a gentle canter.

Over the years, Beatty would sometimes read about the swift decline of battleships after the war, victims of the superior technology of aircraft carriers, supersonic planes and nuclear submarines, until by the 1970s and the end of the Vietnam conflict there were few battleships left anywhere in the world, and he'd experience a twinge of nostalgia and regret. He knew it was foolish at his age, but with the passing of the battleship he felt, with a sad finality, the passing of his youth.

Sometimes, too, he remembered Walker. After personally giving the American a check for $25,000 and then exchanging a few brief letters with him during the war, Beatty never saw or heard from Walker again.

Terrance Walker used Beatty's money to buy a restaurant on Kungsgatan in Stockholm in 1942. He called it "Walker's Hole" and it did well. He and Sweden were making money in the war.

On the night of September 3, 1943, while he was

checking the register before closing, two men finishing their dinners invited him to their table for a drink. They were Americans. One of them, with rimless glasses and delicate, nervous hands, looked like a college professor. The other, with a black patch across one eye and a Burberry raincoat over his shoulders looked, or was trying to look, like a foreign correspondent. After a few casual preliminaries about Sweden and the weather, the professor said, "We wondered if you knew anyone here in Europe, an American perhaps, who would consider helping his country in a certain business matter."

"Someone who knows his way around and can travel here, Zurich, Lisbon, maybe a quick run across the German border," the eye patch added.

"Sorry, I don't," Walker said flatly.

"I see," the professor nodded. "Might we interest you?"

"Sorry, you can't." Walker started to rise.

The eye patch held his arm. "We haven't finished," he said. The Burberry fell open and Walker saw the butt of a 9-mm Browning.

"Listen, I've already done my share," Walker said indignantly. "Long before you guys ever got into it."

"Yes, we know all about that."

"You're fucking-A-right. And nobody had to come and ask me," Walker added with a touch of superiority. "I was a *volunteer*."

"Of course," the professor said. "That is why we are here. Because of your courage and patriotism."

"Bullshit."

The eye patch leaned in. "How would you like to see your restaurant permit lifted by the Swedish authorities?"

"On what grounds?"

317

"No grounds. We'll bribe them," the American said simply.

"Go ahead. I got enough stashed away already," Walker said, though he knew he didn't.

"Whatever you have won't do you much good if you're deported . . . if necessary kidnaped . . . back to the States to stand trial."

"Trial!" Walker exploded. "For what?"

"Draft evasion," the professor said. "A not uncommon sentence, when we take a personal interest in it, is twenty years at hard labor."

The next morning, escorted by the two Americans who assured him that his co-operation was highly appreciated by his country, Walker boarded a plane to Lisbon. For the rest of the war and into the years of the Cold War, he served his country by moving between various capitals on assignments that at times made him wish he was back on the decks of the *Ludendorff*.

His whereabouts today are unknown.

Bestsellers

At your local bookstore or use this handy coupon for ordering:

Dell **DELL BOOKS**
P.O. BOX 1000, PINEBROOK, N.J. 07058

Please send me the books I have checked above. I am enclosing $_____
(please add 35¢ per copy to cover postage and handling). Send check or money
order—no cash or C.O.D.'s. Please allow up to 8 weeks for shipment.

Mr/Mrs/Miss_____

Address_____

City_____State/Zip_____